PRAISE FOR

MW00424539

"Sexy and fun!"

—Susan Andersen, *New York Times* bestselling author of *Playing Dirty*, on *Anything You Want*

"Erin Nicholas always delivers swoonworthy heroes, heroines that you root for, laugh-out-loud moments, a colorful cast of family and friends, and a heartwarming happily ever after."

—Melanie Shawn, *New York Times* bestselling author

"Erin Nicholas always delivers a good time guaranteed! I can't wait to read more."

—Candis Terry, bestselling author of the Sweet, Texas series

"Heroines I love and heroes I still shamelessly want to steal from them. Erin Nicholas romances are fantasy fodder."

—Violet Duke, *New York Times* bestselling author

"A brand-new Erin Nicholas book means I won't be sleeping until I'm finished. Guaranteed."

—Cari Quinn, *USA Today* bestselling author

"Reading an Erin Nicholas book is the next best thing to falling in love."

—Jennifer Bernard, *USA Today* bestselling author

"Nicholas is adept at creating two enthralling characters hampered by their pasts yet driven by passion, and she infuses her romance with electrifying sex that will have readers who enjoy the sexually explicit seeking out more from this author."

—*Library Journal*, starred review of *Hotblooded*

"They say all good things come in threes, so it's safe to say that this is Nicholas's best addition to the Billionaire Bargains series. She has her details of the Big Easy down to a tee, and her latest super-hot novel will have you craving some ice cream and alligator fritters. This is a romance that will be etched in your mind for quite some time. The cuisine and all-too-dirty scenes are enough to satisfy, but the author doesn't stop there. This novel may also give you the inkling to visit the local sex store—incognito of course. It's up to you."

—*Romantic Times Book Reviews* on *All That Matters*, TOP PICK, 4.5 stars

"This smashing debut to the new series dubbed Sapphire Falls is a cozy romance that will have readers believing that they'd stepped into the small Nebraska town and settled in for a while. This well thought out story contains likable characters who grow on you right away, and their tales will make you smile and want to devour the book in one sitting. Four stars."

—*Romantic Times Book Reviews* on *Getting Out of Hand*

"The follow-up to the debut of the hot new series Sapphire Falls will wow readers with its small-town charm and big romance. This story teaches us that everything does happen for a reason and true love can be found even where one least expects it. The characters are strong and animated. It's a complete joy and highly entertaining to watch the plot unfold. Paced perfectly, a few hidden surprises will keep bookworms up past their bedtime finishing this satisfying tale."

—*Romantic Times Book Reviews* on *Getting Worked Up*, 4 stars

"The Sapphire Falls series has quickly become a favorite amongst romance readers because of its small-town charm and big-time chemistry between the lovable characters. This installment is extra steamy and the storyline captures the comedic yet sweet tale of country boy who meets city girl. Travis and Lauren's banter is adorable!"

—*Romantic Times Book Reviews* on *Getting Dirty*

"If you are a contemporary romance fan and haven't tried Erin Nicholas, you are really missing out."

—*Romantic Times Book Reviews* on *Getting It All*

"The fourth installment in the Counting on Love series will sweep readers off their feet. It's the perfect friends-to-lovers story with a little humor and a lot of steam. Cody and Olivia make a fantastic couple, and readers will adore their journey. Get your hands on this one ASAP!"

—*Romantic Times Book Reviews* on *Going for Four*, 4 stars

"Nicholas's tendency to give her fans a break from the hot-and-heavy stuff by making them laugh every now and then is genius!"

—*Romantic Times Book Reviews* on *Best of Three*, 4.5 stars

ALSO BY ERIN NICHOLAS

The Sapphire Falls Series

The Bradfords Series

Turned Up

The Anything & Everything Series

Anything You Want
Everything You've Got

The Counting On Love Series

Just Count on Me (prequel)
She's the One
It Takes Two
Best of Three
Going for Four
Up by Five

The Billionaire Bargains Series

No Matter What
What Matters Most
All That Matters

The Boys of Fall Series

Out of Bounds
Illegal Motion
Full Coverage

The Taking Chances Series

Twisted Up
Tangled Up
Turned Up

Opposites Attract

Completely Yours
Forever Mine
Totally His

Single Title

Hotblooded

Promise Harbor Wedding

Hitched

Turned Up

ERIN NICHOLAS

Montlake Romance

Published by Montlake Romance, Seattle

www.apub.com

Amazon, the Amazon logo, and Montlake Romance are trademarks of Amazon.com, Inc., or its affiliates.

ISBN-13: 9781542047289
ISBN-10: 1542047285

Cover design by Shasti O'Leary Soudant

Printed in the United States of America

To my family, as always.
To Samantha, who pretty much made me write this
book—I mean, *helped* me write this book. ;)
And to everyone who's fallen for Chance.

CHAPTER ONE

Dillon Alexander pulled his truck to the shoulder of the road and threw it into park. At least he assumed he was on the shoulder. There were nine inches of snow making it impossible to know where the shoulder was exactly. Or where the road was, for that matter. The tire tracks from the cars and trucks that had braved the elements cut into the heavy, wet white inches, but they'd just been guessing as well.

This was one of the storms where they told people to flat-out stay off the roads. And yet, here he was. Because people didn't fucking listen. Which was pretty much why doctors had jobs in the first place.

Four vehicles involved. Paramedics on the scene. Police are responding. The police scanner that he insisted on having on whenever he was outside the hospital squawked on the seat beside him.

The paramedics had beaten him to the scene, which was good. They'd have supplies and equipment. But no way was he not going to show up. He got out of the truck and slammed the door, pulling his gloves on as he trudged up the slight incline toward the flashing red-and-blue lights of the police cars and ambulances. He wasn't technically a first responder, but his two years with Doctors Without Borders had taught him that, in the moment, people tended to care less what your official job description was and more that you knew how to stop bleeding and establish an airway.

He knew that everyone in his small hometown was questioning whether Chance could provide him with the challenge and stimulation and excitement he was used to when providing care in other countries and in the busy ER in Houston.

But as Dillon rounded the front of the first of two ambulances, he had his answer.

Challenge, stimulation, and excitement? Check, check, and check. Even with only her ass sticking out the door of the blue sedan, Dillon knew who was kneeling on the back seat of that car. Kit Derby. Dressed in knee-high black leather boots and fitted black pants that molded to the best ass he'd ever ogled. As he did now as he approached the car.

"I'm here. What's going on?" Dillon asked Hank, the EMT standing by the car, and probably also ogling the view.

"Delivery."

Dillon nodded. Then stopped and frowned. "Delivery?"

"Yep."

"A baby?"

"Yep."

Jesus. A pregnant woman in a wrecked car in the middle of a blizzard?

"Mom is stable?" Dillon asked. He took a step closer to the open back door of the car. A delivery in a car wasn't the easiest thing even when everything went well. Add in the cold temps, the whipping wind, the snow that had cut the visibility to almost nothing, and then any possible complications, and this could get dramatic quick.

"She's thirty-nine weeks and pulled over because her water broke," Hank said. "The car behind her didn't see her until it was too late. Hit the brakes, slid, and smashed into her backside. The driver hit his head hard; his wife has a possible tibial fracture. Otherwise, they're okay."

"And the delivery—"

Just then he heard the squall of a newborn. He felt the smile stretch his lips. That was a good sign.

"Everything under control," Hank said. "Kit and Avery came upon the accident and were the ones to call it in. I guess Kit got in the car to calm the woman down, but by the time we got here, Kit already had her in position and pushing."

Dillon nodded at the good report. And then froze. And not because of the negative-ten-degree wind chill.

Kit had just delivered a baby.

Kit Derby. The town *psychiatrist*.

He immediately moved around the car to the other door and yanked it open.

"Hey!" Kit shouted as cold air and snow swirled in.

Fuck. Dillon glowered at her, not showing any chagrin, but he moved in to block the doorway with his body. "What the hell are you doing?" he demanded.

She was cradling a newborn baby against her chest, as a matter of fact. "I'm hoping that you'll get your ass around this car and either take this baby before he freezes or take care of Sarah," she shot back.

He assumed Sarah was the woman lying on the car seat without her pants on. Also probably freezing.

Fuck. He was such an idiot. But only around Kit Derby. Dillon slammed the door shut and strode around the car—or tried to. He swore as he slid, rather than stomping like he wanted to. He braced his hand on the car to keep from going down and arrived at the open door a moment later.

"Baby good?" he asked shortly.

"Apgar is eight," she reported.

"Get him into the ambulance," Dillon told her. The mother would need his attention more than a healthy full-term baby.

Kit moved to get out of the car, the blanket Hank had given her wrapped around the baby and over his head. With her arms full and her fucking high-heeled boots that were in no way practical for snow, Kit scooted back awkwardly, and Dillon reached for her. He put his hands on the hips of the woman he very carefully never touched—well, almost never—and gripped her firmly as she moved to get first one foot, then the other, on the slick ground.

He pulled her up against his body to steady her and to block the wind as she straightened. One of her boots slid on the pavement, and he wrapped an arm around her middle, pulling her even closer and bracing his feet to keep them both upright.

Thankfully, Hank was right there, taking the baby and heading the short distance to the ambulance. Dillon had no time to think about how much he loved having Kit in his arms and up against him. "You good?" he asked quickly, loosening his hold slightly but not letting go until he knew she was solid.

"Yeah." She put an elbow in his gut and pushed him back. "Get to the mom. Her name is Sarah. She's driving through on her way to Illinois."

For just a flash, Dillon was annoyed by the elbow. He'd been *helping her*. But he shrugged it off. It wasn't the first or last time Kit Derby would annoy him. She'd been annoying him since the third grade.

Dillon ducked into the car. "Hi, Sarah. I'm Dr. Alexander." The woman gave him a small smile, but she looked on the verge of tears. She was a long way from Illinois, in a blizzard, and had just given birth on the side of the road. Any of those things would have rattled someone by itself, but she had all three.

He gave Sarah a quick exam and then turned to call for a blood-pressure cuff and other supplies. Before he could make a sound, Kit handed him the cuff, some clean towels, and gauze pads.

"Thanks," he said tersely. And he wasn't even sure why he felt terse. She was helping him. But he and Kit just always rubbed each other the wrong way, no matter what. He swore that she could be giving him one of her own kidneys, and he'd be irritated on some level. And vice versa.

There was a lot to that, but he didn't have time to think about it right now. Or ever. He'd spent hours and hours of his life thinking about Kit Derby and why she made him crazy.

He checked Sarah's blood pressure and other vitals, asked her a few more questions, and got her ready for transport to the hospital. "You'll be okay till we can get you up to the hospital, but we'll have to do some stitches," he told her. "And get you started on an IV for hydration and some antibiotics."

"When can I see my baby?" she asked.

"The second I get you into that ambulance," he told her with a smile. "I'll bet he can't wait to see you, either."

He wanted to get baby and mom skin-to-skin and get a better look at the kid.

Dillon backed out of the car as Hank, who had handed the baby off to his partner, got into the back seat and draped Sarah with a clean blanket, then helped her slide across the seat to the door. Once she was on the edge of the seat, Dillon bent and scooped her up in his arms, carrying her to the ambulance.

Hank and Mike got her situated and hooked up to an IV. Dillon also instructed them to give her some mild pain medication. Then he swung to look at Kit, whom he sensed right behind him.

"What the hell, Kit?" he asked, having to raise his voice over the wind.

She scowled at him. "What the hell what?"

"You *delivered a baby!*"

"Yeah." She planted her hands on her hips. "You're welcome."

"I'm *welcome?*" he asked.

Her long hair was whipping around her face in the wind, the snow-flakes bright white against the ebony color. Her brown eyes were flashing, and dammit, he wanted to kiss her. In spite of the storm, in spite of the patients in the back of the ambulance, in spite of the fact that she was one of the most infuriating people he knew, he wanted to kiss her. Right there and then.

As always.

Fortunately, Bree McDermott joined them just then. She was a cop and Kit's best friend.

"Kit, what are you doing here?" she asked, raising her voice to be heard over the wind as she approached them.

"I was with Avery when she got the call," Kit said. "It's not like she was going to drop me off at home before responding."

"So what's going on?" Bree asked.

"Dr. Derby forgot which end of the body she specializes in," Dillon said. He knew he was frowning, but it was more about the fact that Kit had been driving around in this shitty weather. No one should be out in this except the people who really *needed* to be. She'd been with Avery, who was the town's fire chief and, obviously, a first responder. But Kit didn't need to be here. At an accident scene like this, all the workers were at risk of another car coming by and losing control and plowing into them, or the cars they were working on and in could suddenly slide down the ditch, or hell, they could all end up with frostbite. Unnecessary personnel were simply a liability. She should be at home in front of her fireplace.

And then there was the fact that even standing in the middle of a blizzard, freezing his ass off, he wanted Kit with an intensity that pissed him off. Big-time. And it had been going on for eleven years now. Just not being around her was the only way to avoid the ache she created in him.

So what had he done? He'd moved from Houston—a nice, healthy eight-hundred-some miles away—to Chance three months ago. He now lived four blocks from her.

Stupid fucking idiot that he was.

"Dr. Alexander is just pissed because he didn't get to be the big hero this time," Kit said with the snotty tone that was incredibly familiar to him and always made him grit his teeth. And want to strip her down.

Dillon coughed and concentrated on the fact that she had delivered a baby, in a snowstorm, on the side of the road. Yep, that worked. He was ticked off all over again.

Bree looked around, almost as if she was trying to find a reason she could leave Kit and Dillon alone. Though, in general, their friends knew that leaving them alone was not a great idea.

"What are you talking about?" Bree finally asked.

"How would you feel if I were counseling someone with depression?" Dillon asked Kit.

"Like I was glad that person was talking to someone—and someone who was at least marginally qualified. Unless you skipped your psych rotation or something," Kit said.

"I kicked *ass* on my psych rotation," Dillon said, his irritation warming him in spite of the cold air. And the chill from Kit.

In fact, he'd very carefully stayed objective during his psych rotation and had resisted any urge to self-analyze. Something a lot of his classmates hadn't been able to boast. But everyone had a few demons. It was a fact of life. You just had to handle it. And *not* hang out with know-it-all, never-hold-back-an-opinion shrinks.

"Well, I kicked ass on my OB rotation," Kit said. "I do have a medical degree, and at last count, I've delivered more babies than you have."

Son of a bitch.

It was always a fucking competition between them. He was just as guilty as she was. And they were about fifty-fifty on who was ahead.

This time she won. In spite of his time in Africa and in the busiest ER in Houston, he had delivered only three babies ever.

"Really?" Bree asked. "You've delivered babies?"

"Five. Counting today," Kit confirmed.

Bree's eyes widened. "You delivered a baby *today*?" Bree's eyes went to the ambulance where the new mother and baby were.

"Yes. I was the first medical person on the scene," Kit said.

A gust of wind made her wobble on her boots, but she looked completely composed. She wasn't even shivering. Drove Dillon crazy.

"And your first thought at an accident scene is to get between a woman's legs and check her cervix?" Dillon snapped.

"When her water has already broken and she's screaming that she's in labor?" Kit asked. "Yes."

"You should have waited for the EMTs," Dillon said with a scowl.

"You mean I should have waited for *you*," Kit said.

"I am the *doctor* here."

"You're not the *only* doctor here!"

"You're on my turf, Kit, and you know it." Dillon couldn't keep his voice from rising no matter how hard he tried.

"Right. Between a woman's legs is your turf. How could I forget?" Kit shot back.

Dillon stared at her, torn between amazement—that she'd actually said that in *that* tone of voice in front of someone else—and laughing. Because that was a pretty good comeback. But amazement won. Kit yelled at him. She'd even thrown a beer bottle at his head once. But she never did it in front of other people. As far as anyone knew, Kit was cool and collected. Always. She was snarky and bitchy and snotty from time to time. But her voice never rose, her cheeks never flushed, her teeth never ground together. She was completely unruffled by him.

In private, that was a different situation entirely, though.

"Okay, Dillon," Bree said, pointing to the ambulance. "In there with the patient. Kit," she said to her friend, "Avery's car—go home. And change your shoes."

Kit looked down at her black leather boots. They were covered in all the things expected from delivering a baby by the side of the road—blood, snow, mud, and . . . other stuff. Dillon didn't even try to hide his grin. Even if she could shoot tequila, drink beer, put away half a pizza, and swear like a sailor behind closed doors, she was a lady through and through in public. And even in private most of the time. The tequila and beer were generally the reasons for the pizza binges and swearing.

"I haven't dressed for a delivery in a long time," she finally said.

"Or for the snow, apparently." He couldn't help it. She'd grown up in Chance. This kind of snow happened. A lot. And Kit was the most organized, always prepared person he'd ever met. How had she not dressed to be outside today?

"Ambulance," Bree repeated to him, pointing.

Fine. The EMTs were done with their workup of the baby and mother. That was where he needed to be right now.

God knew he'd have plenty more opportunities to spar with Kit. Thanks to his love for his family and hometown. Thanks to the free clinic they were trying to open and the fact that he and Kit were arguing over every penny and ink pen and cotton ball. And, of course, thanks to his own stupid fucking idiocy.

"Episiotomy is in chapter four."

Kit shrieked and spun toward the door, her hand over her heart.

Dillon was back to his office much earlier than she'd expected. *Dammit.* She slammed the textbook shut and tried to come up with a reason that she'd be in his office that wouldn't make her look like she was worried about the delivery by the side of the road.

"In all my fantasies about you bent over my desk, a textbook open to photos of gynecologic surgeries was never part of them," Dillon said as he came into the room and then headed around to the other side of his desk.

His words hit her hard and hot. The jerk. He always said stuff like that. When they were alone. Never in public or with other people

9

around. He was antagonistic whenever there were other people around. But when they were alone . . . he managed to always remind her that there was major chemistry between them. And always had been.

He had to brush really close to her to get around his desk, and Kit held her breath. Then worked really hard to act like she hadn't just held her breath.

"I was just . . . looking for you," she lied. She'd been praying that she could avoid him completely.

"Bullshit," he said with a small laugh. "You're in here checking to see if you screwed anything up during the delivery."

She hated him.

No, she quickly corrected, she hated that she cared what he thought. And that he knew her. "I wasn't worried I'd screwed up," she said, adding the *much* only to herself. "I was just checking on what you needed to do to fix her up." She'd heard him say stitches and knew that Sarah had torn slightly during the delivery. The baby had easily been eight full-term pounds, so that wasn't a shock.

"Six stitches," he said, settling into his chair. "She's fine."

Kit breathed out in relief. Then she couldn't help but ask, "Would you have done an episiotomy?" That would have required him making a cut to ease the baby's passage and would have prevented tearing. But cutting wasn't ideal, either, and there was controversy over which was better.

"In the back seat of a car? No."

Kit rolled her eyes. "If she'd been here?"

He shrugged. "Probably not."

That also relieved her. She had been the first medical provider on scene, and the woman had been in labor. She'd done what she was supposed to do, and she hadn't hesitated. She wouldn't hesitate next time, either. And it had turned out well. But the truth was, Dillon was the better *physical* doctor of the two of them. She was the mental-health expert.

And the further truth was that they were an amazing team. He handled the physical stuff, she handled the emotional stuff, and any patient who had them both—like the people who had been injured during the huge tornado that had hit Chance in June—benefited immensely from having them both.

Like they would from the free clinic she and Dillon were working to open. Yes, it was a community-wide effort, and they had a lot of support from the hospital and the town. But she and Dillon were the driving factors. It seemed that they were both always driving factors for *something*—neither of them was the type to sit around and enjoy the status quo—and every once in a while, there was a project they both cared about equally. Of course, even within that equally cared-about project, they had to bicker. Dillon wanted their limited funds to go to his ideas, and Kit wanted those dollars for her plans. Which meant they fought, with an audience of board members, on a bimonthly basis. Then again, if it hadn't been that, it would have been something else. It was just how she and Dillon worked.

"How is Sarah?" she asked.

"Fine. Six stitches isn't bad. She's already been up walking a bit. Baby is nursing. He's perfectly fine, too. She's called her husband, and he'll be here tomorrow."

Kit nodded. "Okay, great. But how is she feeling?"

"I'm sure she's a little sore," he said. "I've given her something for the discomfort."

Kit frowned. "How is she doing emotionally? She's got to be scared. I mean, even though it all turned out well, there could be some big stress setting in. And then the hormones and the pressure of having a newborn and being here alone."

Dillon didn't respond immediately, but he gave her a little smile. "She's really good, Kit. Don't worry."

Kit studied his face. He looked confident. As always. And he was an incredibly intelligent guy. Just like she could deliver a baby, if needed, he could handle mental and emotional issues, if needed. She had to trust that.

"Okay. Great."

"I thought Bree told you to go home," he said. His gaze tracked over her.

She'd stopped in the locker room and changed into hospital scrubs. And thrown away her boots. She shuddered slightly thinking about trying to clean those. No. Way. She'd just buy new ones.

"Though now you're dressed like a real doctor," he said.

How did his eyes on her make her hot even when she was in light-green scrubs? That was so annoying. She frowned. "Knock it off."

The whole real-doctor thing had gotten old clear back when she'd first decided to specialize in mental health instead of family medicine, cardiology, emergency medicine—like Dillon—or any of the other specialties.

She didn't believe that Dillon thought what she did was "fake" anything. He'd worked with the Army National Guard and in Africa and in a busy urban emergency room. He, of all specialists, knew about mental health and its connection to physical issues.

But he still had to be an ass sometimes.

"I wanted to check on the patient, and Bree isn't the boss of me," she said.

"You wanted to hold the baby," Dillon replied.

She cleared her throat. So what? *Most* people liked holding babies. "I wanted to make sure he was okay," she said.

Dillon looked like he was almost smiling. Almost. "Janice told me you went straight to the nursery."

"So?"

He shrugged. "So nothing. Just . . . interesting."

Kit put a hand on her hip. "What does that mean?"

"You just don't strike me as the maternal type."

Her mouth dropped open. She was offended by that. Though that didn't make sense. Why did she care if Dillon thought she liked, and wanted, babies or not? "I don't?"

"Maybe it's *domestic* that I can't picture," Dillon said, sitting back in his chair and studying her. "Yeah, I guess that's a better word."

"You can't picture me in an apron, dusting the shelves and baking cookies, and so I'm not maternal?"

He shrugged. "My mom was a homemaker. That's what I think of. Come on, Dr. Shrink, that makes sense, right?"

"You're also thirty years old, highly intelligent, and have traveled the world. Surely your view of motherhood is *a little* wider than cookies and milk after school."

He gave her a slow grin, and Kit suddenly became aware that she was clenching her hands tightly, her neck was tense, and her voice had risen.

She took a deep breath. He got her going. Every time. He knew her buttons. *Damn him.*

Before she could blast him, her phone rang. She shot him a glare but pulled her phone from her pocket. It was her mother. She turned and headed into the hallway without a word to Dillon.

"Hi, Mom."

"Hi, honey. Have you heard from Grandma?"

"No, why?"

Her mother sighed. "They just shut the road out there, and she's not answering her cell. I'm guessing she let the battery run down, but I want to be sure she's okay for a day or so until they can get the road cleared."

Kit frowned. Her grandmother, Grace, was an eighty-five-year-old ball of fire. She still lived out on the family farm, twelve miles outside of Chance. Alone. She handled it for the most part, but she did have an issue—she wasn't very good at sitting still or being bored. Which was exactly what would happen if she was stuck out there and unable to get outside or drive her rickety old truck around her property. If she got cabin fever, she'd do Lord knew what to alleviate her boredom. She might crawl up into the attic or head into the basement or even try to clear her driveway by herself. She was in good health, generally, but she could easily fall and break her neck, or overtax her heart, or try to lift something and throw her back out.

"No one's talked to her today?" Kit asked, pacing to the end of the hallway, then turning to pace back.

Dillon came out of his office, and her steps faltered. He was also in light-green scrubs, had about a day's worth of stubble on his face, and his hair looked like he'd just run his hand through it. How could he look so hot? It was really unfair.

Fortunately, he didn't notice that she'd stumbled slightly at the sight of him. In fact, he didn't even glance at her as he headed in the direction of the OB department. Chance Memorial Hospital was tiny. The OB department actually consisted of only four rooms at the end of the hallway, but they'd remodeled them two years ago into beautiful suites.

Kit frowned. He'd just gotten back from checking on Sarah. Had something come up with her or the baby? Kit started after him as her mother told her that no one had talked to Grace since last night when Nick, her oldest son, had tried to talk her into coming into town because of the forecast.

"So no one can get out there to check on her?" Kit asked, keeping Dillon—and his fine ass—in sight. But she was behind him. It wasn't like she was specifically looking at his ass. Exactly.

"The road is drifted shut about a mile down the road," her mom told her.

"Crap." It wasn't even that Grace wouldn't necessarily want to leave the house in weather like this; it was more that she wouldn't be *able* to. The feeling of being stuck was unpleasant, especially if you were alone. Kit sighed. "Maybe one of the neighbors can get on his snowmobile?"

"We thought of that, too. Just calling to check with everyone."

Most of those who lived in the countryside around Chance owned snowmobiles. They were primarily recreational, but they could serve a true purpose when the roads were shut to car-and-truck traffic.

"Okay, let me know." Kit was only half paying attention to her mother as she disconnected. Because, sure enough, Dillon had turned in to the second suite on the right. The room Sarah was in. Kit glanced around. No one else was coming. There was no rush of health-care providers to the room. So there wasn't a major medical complication.

Still, Kit wanted to say hello to Sarah and make sure she was okay. Dillon was a fantastic physician. Probably the best she knew. But he kind of sucked at the *feeling* part of medicine. He was a trauma physician, an ex–Army National Guardsman, a guy whose experience included underdeveloped countries, areas devastated by natural disasters, an emergency department in a huge city. He wasn't the guy to stop and ask a lot of "feeling" questions or take the time to listen to the answers even if he did.

The shrink part of her that could carefully compartmentalize her professional side from her personal side found Dillon fascinating. No, that wasn't even true—both sides of her found Dillon fascinating. It was the psychiatrist part of her, however, that had figured out that Dillon had gone into medicine because he wanted to help people and was a natural-born hero, but that he'd gone into trauma medicine because he didn't want to become personally attached to people he might lose.

And she knew that came from losing his longtime girlfriend, Abi, in a car accident their senior year of high school.

She'd further made a note—a *professional* note, of course—that it showed some really good growth and acceptance that he'd now decided to move home and practice in Chance, where the risk of treating someone, and possibly losing him or her, was much more personal.

However, even with that growth, Dillon's initial response to a problem was to stride in and fix it.

Kit's initial response to a problem was . . . to talk about it.

15

Sarah might not technically be her patient, but Kit wanted to be sure the woman, a stranger to Chance and a brand-new mom, had support while she was waiting for her husband to get to town.

Kit turned in to the doorway, her hand raised to knock on the door frame, but stopped when she heard Dillon ask, "So how are you feeling?"

"Good," Sarah said. "Tired. But good."

"I mean . . . are you worried about anything?" he asked.

He was sitting on the foot of Sarah's bed. Looking incredibly uncomfortable. But he was there.

Kit ducked back into the hallway and took a deep breath. Yeah, he sucked at the bedside-manner thing. But like she'd been looking up episiotomies in his office, he was here. Trying.

Dammit.

This was the problem. If Dillon was just the cocky, territorial adversary he'd been all her life, she could deal with it. With him. But he wasn't just the guy who beat her half the time—no matter what they did—and who never backed down from a challenge and who gloated whenever he won. He was also the guy who always wanted to get better, no matter how much he hated admitting there were things he wasn't good at. He was also the guy who pushed *her* to do better, to try harder, and, yes, even to admit her weaknesses.

It was really hard not to like him sometimes.

It was also really hard to not remember what an amazing kisser he was. And how amazing he was at . . . other things.

But Dillon Alexander was good at *everything*.

Kit shook herself and headed for the nurses' station. She shouldn't be eavesdropping. Janice, the head nurse, could help her get ahold of someone who lived near her grandma. And there was a 100 percent chance that someone had cookies or something behind the counter.

The plate of brownies was like a big welcome smile. Kit reached for one as Janice rounded the corner. "Hey, Kit, I didn't think you'd be in today," she said, setting down her armload of charts.

Kit chewed and swallowed her first bite of chocolate and shrugged. "I wanted to check on Sarah and the baby."

"Oh." Janice glanced down the hallway. "Why?"

Kit frowned. "I delivered the baby."

Janice's eyes grew wide. "*You* delivered the baby?"

"Yes." Kit lifted a brow. "You just assumed Dillon did, didn't you?"

"Well . . . he came in with them. So . . ."

Yeah. Of course she had. It wasn't her fault. Anyone would have assumed that. "Do you know anyone out by my grandma's place who has a snowmobile?" she asked, changing the subject of how amazing Dillon Alexander was before it even got started.

"Ted Carter and Jeff McDonald probably both do," Janice said. "Why?"

"No one's heard from her since last night, and she's not answering her phone." With Dillon out of sight, Kit let those words really sink in. It was probably nothing. Grace often forgot to charge her phone or turn it off vibrate when she got home, and she didn't carry it around the house with her like she should. Kit was 95 percent sure that her grandmother was fine.

But that 5 percent was suddenly nagging at her.

"Well, why don't you just have Dillon check on her?" Janice said.

Kit's eyes snapped up to Janice's. "Dillon? Why would Dillon check on her?"

"He's taking the snowmobile out to a few other places. Jack Thomas needs a new O2 tank, and he wants to check on Millie Holden's incision."

"And because of the snow, he's turning them into house calls?" Kit asked. Of course he was. Nothing would stop Dillon from being amazing. She barely stopped herself from rolling her eyes.

"He was going to make both of those stops, anyway," Janice said with a smile. "He's just changing the mode of transportation because of the snow."

He was going to make both of those house stops, anyway. Kit wondered if he wore his superhero outfit under his scrubs. Then she realized that a lot of people thought of those scrubs as superhero outfits.

"Grandma doesn't need a medical visit," Kit said. "She needs to be told to stay off ladders, to not try to scoop her own driveway, and that she's too old to go cross-country skiing. She needs to be scolded right into her easy chair and threatened with major repercussions if she does anything but knit while watching Jimmy Stewart movies."

Janice laughed. "Yep, sounds like she needs *you.*"

Kit couldn't argue with that. She was a pro at knowing the best way to communicate with people, and she could change her approach to fit any situation. *Except with Dillon.* She couldn't help that thought flitting through her mind. It seemed that Dillon was the exception to most of her rules. She was generally calm and levelheaded and rational and knew how to get people to listen to her. With Dillon . . . he seemed to override all her good intentions.

But with Grace, Kit knew exactly what she needed. Firm, no-nonsense threats. The last time her grandmother hadn't been able to get out and around like she was used to had been when she'd had shoulder surgery. She'd been told to stay in the house and take it easy for six weeks. No picking apples or feeding the chickens or weeding the garden or going to water aerobics. So what had she done? She'd climbed up and dusted all her overhead light fixtures. And she'd almost gotten away with it. If she hadn't stepped off the short ladder and twisted her ankle, she would have. She'd not only sprained her ankle, but she'd messed up her shoulder again, and after the surgery to repair the repair, the family had made her move in with Kit's mom temporarily so someone could keep an eye on her. Grace was a feisty, stubborn woman who would probably outlive them all—because she kept giving her family heart attacks with her antics.

"I guess I could take a snowmobile out to her place," Kit said to Janice.

Janice raised both eyebrows. "You don't seem like the snowmobile type."

Janice had not only known Kit throughout her practice in Chance, she'd also known Kit growing up. Janice had been a nurse in Chance as long as Kit could remember. So, her guess that Kit didn't know much about snowmobiles was an educated one.

"I know what a snowmobile is," Kit said.

Janice laughed. "Well, I guess that's a start. How are you and Bree such good friends, by the way?"

Kit had to grin at that. Bree McDermott hadn't always been Kit's best friend. The loud, daring tomboy had run in a very different crowd from Kit's in high school. They hadn't disliked each other; they just hadn't really known each other. Kit's head had been in her schoolwork and her million extracurricular projects and, frankly, on Dillon. Beating him out, being better than he was, taking the number one spot from him in anything they both decided to do—which was practically everything—and then, later, around her sophomore year, daydreaming about him. And then trying not to.

"Bree is the yin to my yang," Kit told Janice.

The older woman nodded. "You two are good for each other."

They were. Bree, the daredevil, made Kit have fun and try new things, and Kit, the academic, kept Bree grounded and helped her relax. Kit enjoyed wine and sushi and theater. Bree liked beer and burgers and raunchy movies. Kit's work wardrobe consisted of heels and pencil skirts or pantsuits. Bree wore a police uniform. Kit loved yoga and meditation. Bree jumped out of airplanes for fun.

But Kit loved Bree like a sister. As she did Avery Sparks, Chance's fire chief and the third musketeer. She valued her girlfriend relationships deeply.

So it kind of sucked that they were both now madly in love. Kit was happy for them. Both women were more . . . at peace . . . now that Max and Jake were in their lives. But that didn't help Kit's feelings of being stirred up and restless a bit. She loved feeling at peace. She loved routine. She loved checking off things on her to-do list. And then making a new to-do list. She loved the sense of satisfaction she got when she sat back and looked at her life and her work and her hometown and her relationships. She had everything lined up exactly as she'd wanted it.

And then Dillon had moved back to Chance.

After almost eleven years of being gone. Very gone. Far, far gone.

And things had been good. For years.

Until the third F4 tornado hit their tiny hometown for the third year in a row, while Dillon and his cousins, Jake and Max, had been home for a class reunion. And working beside him for the mental and physical health of their community in the aftermath—the cleanup and rebuilding efforts that had lasted for two weeks—hadn't even been the worst part.

The storeroom at the hospital where she and Dillon had spent the tornado together had been the worst part.

It had been small and dark and he'd been so . . . *there*, filling up the space and making her feel warm and safe. And making her feel so *needy*, so itchy and jittery and scattered. She hated that.

And then he'd kissed her, and she'd forgotten all about the tornado and how much he drove her crazy and how much she hated how great he was at everything. Because he really was great at *everything*. And that included making out in storerooms.

"Kit?"

Kit shook herself and looked up at Janice. *Crap.* She'd been daydreaming about him and that damned kiss. Again. "Yeah?"

"I was just asking if you were going to call Bree to go check on your grandma?"

She could. Bree knew Grace very well and would gladly take out her snowmobile. But Kit would have to go along. "I think I want Bree to bring her back to town to my mom's," Kit said. "Which means that I'll have to go and talk her into it."

Janice nodded. "That's probably the best plan."

Though hog-tying her grandmother and strapping her to the back of Bree's snowmobile didn't sound appealing. Kit sighed. "Yeah, I'll call Bree."

"Call Bree for what?"

Dillon was six foot four and two-hundred-some pounds of solid muscle. How in the hell did he move so stealthily? Kit turned to reply that it was none of his business, but Janice piped up. "Kit needs a ride to her grandmother's place."

"Your grandma lives out on Deerpoint Road, right?" he asked.

Kit nodded.

"All those roads are closed." He reached past Kit and snagged a brownie.

"Yes, I'm aware," she told him, ignoring the fact that he smelled amazing. Like bury-her-face-in-his-neck-and-just-breathe amazing.

"You'll need a snowmobile to get out there."

She blinked at him. Dillon Alexander did not think she was stupid. He thought she was a pain in the ass. But not stupid. So *he* was just trying to be a pain in the ass. Or something. "What's your point?"

He turned and leaned an elbow on the counter. And proceeded to look her up and down. Slowly. "You're not really a snowmobile kind of girl."

Janice snorted at Dillon's words that so closely echoed her own. Kit lifted her chin. It wasn't as if it was an insult to be called not-really-a-snowmobile-kind-of-girl. She was a lot of other kinds of girl—like professional and sophisticated and educated. But it felt like an insult from Dillon.

"Just because I don't own a snowmobile doesn't mean that I'm incapable of riding on one."

"You have real snow boots?"

"Real snow boots?"

"Those things you were wearing outside a little bit ago were *not* snow boots."

Well, that was true. "I didn't know we were going to have to stop in the snow and deliver a baby when I got dressed this morning," she told him.

"Right. But you're a small-town Nebraska girl. You know what winter can be like. You should be prepared for anything this time of year."

Kit pulled a breath in through her nose. She *was* typically prepared for anything. *Over*prepared, in most cases. The fact that she hadn't been this morning—and that Dillon had been there to witness that—rankled. But she was not going to take advice about Nebraska weather from the guy who'd spent almost a decade in Texas and the southern hemisphere. "Thanks for your concern. But I'm fine."

"I'm just saying that I'm not taking you with me unless you dress appropriately."

She frowned. "Taking me with you where?"

"To your grandma's. You have to stop by Jack's place and see Millie with me, though."

Kit crossed her arms and watched him lick chocolate crumbs from his fingertips. God, she hated that he had the best mouth she'd ever had the pleasure of having on her . . .

She cleared her throat and forced herself to concentrate. "You're going to take me to my grandma's?"

"I'm going out anyway, and as much as Bree likes her snowmobile, I'm guessing she's got other stuff to do."

"The accident has to be cleaned up by now," Kit said.

"Other things like Max," Dillon said. "If nothing else."

Right. Bree had Max to do if she wasn't needed outside in the freezing cold and blowing snow. Even if Bree loved snowmobiling, half of her love for any of her crazy activities had been doing them with Max. Now she didn't have to leave the house to do things with Max. Kit was a little jealous of her friend anyway, and now that she was thinking about how nice it would be to snuggle up with a hot guy in front of a fireplace, sharing body heat during the blizzard, she wondered if Dillon could see the green in her face.

"I'm going out anyway," Dillon went on. "No need to get Bree out in the cold."

"You'd take me along?"

That was not a good idea. She could work beside Dillon. They saw each other at the hospital and around town on a fairly regular basis now that he was living and working here. She could argue with Dillon— about the free clinic, about the color of green the diner used on its new awnings, about her choice of winter weather clothing, and just about anything else under the sun. She could even, sometimes, *not* argue with Dillon when they were in the diner or the bar with their friends or when they ran into each other in the hallways at the hospital. But alone time with Dillon was not a good idea. Not that they could get into too much trouble in a snowstorm on a snowmobile, but she hadn't thought they'd get into trouble preparing for their debate competition when they'd been seniors in high school, or studying for finals in medical school, or taking cover during a tornado.

But they had.

Oh, they had.

"Why not?" Dillon asked, pushing away from the counter.

Why not? *Why not?* As if he didn't remember when they'd spent extended periods of time alone together. When other people were around, they competed. But when they were alone . . . their clothes fell off.

"You think that's a good idea?" she asked, meeting his eyes and willing him to acknowledge what she was getting at.

"Sure, no problem," he said with a shrug.

"Be careful out there. Report in at each stop," Janice told them, moving to the copier several feet away.

"Will do," Dillon said, watching her. Then as the machine started spitting out pages, he looked down at Kit. "I think we'll be okay. It's a little cold out there to worry about you taking your clothes off."

Kit felt her mouth fall open, and she didn't recover until he'd started down the hall. "Hey!" she called after him. "*You* were the one—" She broke off just as she was about to say that *he* had been the first to lose his clothes in high school and in medical school. She might have pulled her shirt off first in the storeroom, but it had been hot in there, and . . .

Dillon just chuckled. "I'm leaving in ten minutes, Dr. Derby."

Damn. Him.

CHAPTER TWO

Eight minutes later, Kit was waiting by the back door that led to the parking lot. She could see his truck, and the snowmobile in the back of it, from here. There weren't many cars in the lot on a day like this.

"That's what you're wearing?"

She turned to find Dillon striding toward her, dressed in full snow pants, fleece-lined work coat, heavy boots, stocking cap, scarf, and thick gloves.

"It's what I have," she told him.

"You're going to wear scrubs and tennis shoes out in a blizzard?"

"It. Is. All. I. Have."

He sighed, as if totally put upon by her. Yeah, she knew the feeling.

"You're going to freeze."

"I have three pairs on," she told him, lifting a leg. "And we're not going to be *out* in it. Once we get to each house, I'll go in and warm up."

He shook his head. "Whatever. I am *not* treating you for hypothermia or frostbite."

"Like I'd want you to treat me," she shot back.

But he would treat her. And she would want him to. Dr. Alexander was the best physician she knew, and part of that was the fact that he'd never turn his back on someone who needed him. Even if that someone drove him beyond crazy.

"Get in the truck," he said resignedly. "But I swear, I'd better not hear one word bitching about the cold."

She did as she was told and stubbornly refused to so much as shiver as the arctic air hit the thin material of her pants. She had a coat on—though admittedly, the red wool was more for fashion than true protection against the elements, too.

Dillon got in and cranked the heat without a comment. So she didn't comment, either. Like with a thank-you. Instead, she sat, hating that he could make her act like a twelve-year-old. He reached behind the seat and pulled out another knit cap and a pair of heavy work gloves.

"At least put these on."

She looked at the items, then up at him.

"I know they don't match your outfit, Doc. But I don't want you to lose a finger. I like you having all ten."

She felt her eyes widen. Because when he said stuff like that, her mind flooded with memories. How could it not? Something most people didn't know about Chance's very own superhero, Dr. Dillon, was that he was a dirty talker.

"You should *not* say stuff like that," she admonished, taking the hat and gloves. "If we're going to be living here and working together, we have to put all of that behind us."

Dillon draped an arm over the steering wheel and twisted to face her. "Say stuff like what?"

"That you like my fingers."

His gaze grew mischievous, and Kit worked to control her thundering pulse as the impending sense of *Oh crap* washed over her. Dillon was a big, smart, demanding, badass know-it-all. And *that* got her going—despite her best intentions and all the self-talk she knew and taught patients. But when he got charming and playful, her resolve—and her panties—seemed to just dissolve.

It was very rare that he was anything but serious and bossy and determined. Which was probably why his fun-loving side was so potent.

"Why, Dr. Derby, I have no idea what you're referring to. I meant that as a professional who needs to do a lot of writing and typing, you need all ten fingers to do your very important job for this town. What did you think I meant?"

She huffed out a breath and pulled on the hat and gloves. "Bullshit, Dr. Alexander," she told him. Then decided that there was no reason not to be very direct and *clear* in her communication with him. That was what she would have advised a patient in her position, after all. "You were referring to liking things I've done with my hands . . . with you . . . in the past." She faced him. "Like letting you lick hot fudge off them, and when you wanted me to touch myself, and, of course, the hand jobs."

The air in the cab of the truck heated easily twenty degrees as Dillon sat staring at her. Kit bit back a smile. She felt rattled when she was around him on a regular basis. It was nice to know that she could make the superhero doctor speechless.

Finally, he shook his head, then pulled off his hat and gloves and tossed them onto the seat between them. "Thank you for that. With those memories, I'm not going to need anything else keeping me warm for a while."

He put the truck in drive, and Kit told herself she should feel smug for shocking him.

But, strangely, she felt like he'd turned the tables on her. Again.

Cute was not a word that Dillon would have typically assigned to Kit Derby.

Hot, sexy, snooty, sophisticated, and classy. Those were all spot-on. But right now, sitting on his passenger seat, wearing his stocking hat pulled down over her ears and his gloves, which were huge on her, with her expensive high-fashion coat and scarf, hospital scrubs, and white tennis shoes, she definitely looked cute.

And he wanted to scoop her up into his arms and replay every one of the memories she'd just put into his head.

Damn her. This woman knotted him up like no other. Ever.

It was bad enough that he'd found her in his office looking up information on episiotomy. She was always trying to get better and learn more, and he respected the hell out of that. Because he was the same way. Which was why he'd headed back to Sarah's room to be sure she was doing okay emotionally after the delivery.

Kit got into his head; there was no denying it. For the most part, he thought that was a good thing. At least when it was professional. When it got personal—and it didn't get much more personal than talking about hand jobs—then it was . . . not as good a thing.

He was grateful for the snow-covered roads and poor visibility because they forced him to concentrate on the job of getting his truck out to the highway instead of on Kit Derby. And her fingers.

He maneuvered the truck over the snow and ice that the city hadn't been able to clear yet. With the rate of the snowfall and the wind, they simply couldn't keep up, and they were focused on keeping the roads that more people needed—like the one in front of the hospital and the one leading to the ER entrance—open right now.

The truck bumped over the drifts, and the only sound in the truck cab was the heat blowing through the vents as they headed as far out on the highway as they could get before needing the snowmobile. They finally got to the end of the road. Dillon wasn't sure that he'd be able to get the truck out again, but the closer to the start of the road that led to Jack's place, the better. Even if Kit wasn't dressed in only scrub pants on her lower half. He shook his head as he parked and went to get the snowmobile unloaded. He really didn't want to worry about her, and he knew that she wouldn't welcome his concern. But damn. She was going to freeze. And he couldn't help that the thought led to images of all the ways he'd be happy to warm her up.

He had the snowmobile fired up and the supplies he needed strapped onto the sled he attached to the back before he headed for the passenger door. Snow swirled inside as he pulled it open, but Kit didn't even blink. She slid out onto the snowy ground, ignoring Dillon's offered hand.

Kit wasn't a snowmobile kind of girl, but she climbed on behind him as if she'd done it a million times. She slid her arms around him, and Dillon realized this was the worst idea he'd had in a very long time. It didn't matter that the frigid wind was biting at his cheeks, or that there was absolutely nothing sexual about the way Kit was touching him, or that there were a good four or five layers of clothing between them. This was as close to Kit as he'd been since the June tornado. They'd been stuck in that storeroom together, and it had taken about two minutes for the scent of her body lotion to get him to the "What the hell" stage. The stage he always ended up getting to when he and Kit were together alone for any extended period of time. But that storeroom was a new record. Prior to that, it had taken him two hours, an hour and twenty minutes, fifty-six minutes, and ten minutes consecutively on the four occasions where he'd abandoned all common sense and given in to the desire to touch her. And taste her. And tell her things that he had no business telling her. Ever. Like all the fantasies he had about her.

By the time they pulled up in front of Jack's place, Kit's teeth were chattering, but Dillon knew better than to comment on it or ask something inane like "Are you cold?"

Dillon got Jack hooked up to his new oxygen tank, accepted the offer of coffee that he typically would have turned down—so that Kit would also say yes—and then got Jack talking about his time with the railroad, knowing that it would be at least forty-five minutes before there was a break where they could get going.

As they climbed back on the snowmobile, Kit said, "You've heard that story before."

"How do you know?" he asked, pulling his hat lower on his ears.

"Because everyone's heard that story before," she said.

Dillon braced for her to tell him that she didn't need him looking out for her and that she could take care of herself.

So when she said "Thanks," Dillon took the thump in his chest as relief that he wasn't getting chewed out. Because it shouldn't have anything to do with Kit's softer side or the husky tone of her voice right near his ear.

At Millie's house, they were not only offered coffee but also cookies. They'd each had a brownie at the hospital, but Dillon was pleased when Kit kept her lips zipped about that and picked up a shortbread without hesitation. He also noted that she sat on the end of the couch closest to Millie's blazing fireplace. So he took his time checking the older woman's incision and going over the instructions and setting up another follow-up visit for a few days from then.

Finally, he glanced at Kit, and she gave him a little nod. Ah, so she knew he'd been stalling. And she appreciated it. And she was ready to go.

How he knew all that from one tiny nod, he couldn't say. Except that he knew Kit. Had known her for a long time. And she very rarely nodded affirmatively at him.

They were headed to her grandmother's place next. Dillon felt a stupid stab of disappointment as he started the snowmobile for the third time. At Grace's house, Kit would actually be able to stay for an extended period while Dillon took Grace back into town. She'd be perfectly comfortable. And warm. But their civil time together would be over. Frigid wind in your face on the back of a snowmobile in a blizzard made conversation difficult, but he'd still felt more camaraderie than they usually had between them. In fact, the last time they'd worked closely—and well—together had been the June tornado.

That tornado had produced a lot of trouble and stress. But Dillon simply couldn't look at it as a total catastrophe. Not then and not in hindsight. Not only had the town come together, and both of his cousins, Jake and Max, and he had decided to move home permanently, but . . . Kit. They'd kissed, they'd worked side by side, they'd helped rebuild their town, and they'd tended to the physical and emotional issues of their neighbors, friends, and family in the aftermath.

Maybe this blizzard wasn't all bad, either. And wasn't it just perfect that he and Kit needed disasters to find a way to get along?

They pulled up in front of Grace Derby's house ten minutes later.

Kit led the way to the front door through the knee-high snow. At Jack's and Millie's, there had been some snow on the front walks, but someone had obviously cleared their paths at some point since the snow had started. It looked like every inch was still in front of Grace's house.

Kit tried the front door, found it locked, and turned away. Then turned again. And again.

"What's going on?" Dillon asked.

"I'm looking for the little garden gnome she hides her key under."

Dillon chuckled. The gnome, and everything else in Grace's front yard, was buried. "I'm surprised she locks the place clear out here," he said, moving to the door.

"She didn't until about two years ago," Kit said, stepping into the drift next to the front steps. "And now she only does it for spite." She plunged her hands into the snow, apparently feeling around for the gnome.

Dillon did the same on the other side. "Spite?"

"She locks it when my dad or uncles are going to come out. Then she pretends she forgot they were coming and that she doesn't hear them knocking. She also moves the gnome around the yard. So they have to search for it to find the key to get in. She feels like it's just enough of a pain in the ass to pay them back for their lectures about her being safe out here."

Dillon laughed out loud. He'd always liked Grace. "I'm not sure I'd worry about Grace on her own against an intruder."

Kit looked up with a bright smile that punched Dillon directly in the gut.

"I know, right?" she said, walking on her knees a few feet to the right and digging in the snow again. "If someone came out here to try to steal something, she'd start pointing out all the stuff she wants to get rid of. She'd help load up his car, and then she'd feed him before he left."

Dillon grinned and resisted commenting that he knew exactly where Kit got her spunk. Kit's mother was a quiet woman who had always struck him as stuck-up and, frankly, bitchy. Gretchen Derby didn't smile much, and she was always perfectly put together. Kit's father, Brad, on the other hand, seemed friendly enough. He was one of the top insurance agents in town, and he interacted with the people and took part in community events much more often than Gretchen did. But neither of them showed the fire and ice that Kit did. Except Grace.

"Got it!"

He turned to see Kit holding a garden gnome triumphantly overhead.

"And the key?" he asked.

She looked from him to the gnome, then to the snowy ground. "Crap." She dug back in, searching for the key in the snow. After a moment, she mumbled a curse and pulled off her glove with her teeth, then stuck her bare hand back into the drift.

"Not bare-handed." Dillon scowled as he knelt beside her.

"I can't feel a tiny little key with those big gloves on."

"You're going to get frostbite."

"Not if I find the damned thing and we can get inside."

This was ridiculous. Dillon stomped up to Grace's door and pounded on the frame. "Grace! It's Dillon and Kit! Grace!" he shouted through the wood. The door had a big window in it, but it was covered with a curtain. Still, he could see that there were no lights on in the room right behind the door. "Grace!" he shouted again, banging his fist against the wood. "Grace!"

He glanced behind him. Kit was still digging and now had both gloves off. That was it. Dillon eyed the old door, the knob, and the lock. He was going to have to buy Grace Derby a new door. He backed up, lifted his foot, and kicked in the door.

The wood splintered just as he heard, "I found it!" behind him.

Well, crap.

He turned to find Kit staring at the now-open door, holding up the key. She looked at him, back to the door, then at him again. "Um . . ."

He wasn't the kind of guy to get off on stuff like fighting or fixing engines or . . . kicking down doors. At least, he hadn't thought he was. But he could not deny that there was a lot of testosterone coursing through his bloodstream at the moment. So his actions could be—and later on would be—chalked up to that. He headed straight for Kit, bent, and lifted her over his shoulder like a sack of potatoes. As she gasped, he turned and carried her into the house.

"Dillon! For God's sake!"

He put her on her feet in the short entryway just inside the front door and then closed what was left of the door. "We're inside."

"Yeah, I noticed. What the hell?"

"It's freezing out there, and you're not dressed for it. You're digging in the snow with bare hands. We needed to get inside. Just . . . go check on your grandmother," he said, not really able to answer the "What the hell?" question at the moment. "The walk isn't cleared, her door is locked, and she's not answering her phone or our pounding on the door."

Kit looked like she had a few more words for him, but all that sank in before she could get started telling him how crazy he was acting. As if he didn't know.

"Fine." She turned on her heel and headed down the short hallway and into the house.

And Dillon took a deep breath.

He wasn't completely shocked by the kicking-down-the-door thing. He'd done it once before, and hey, sometimes you had to do these things. But the touching-Kit thing. Yeah, that did shock him. It wasn't that he didn't *want* to. Often. But he didn't do it. For two very good reasons—she wouldn't be okay with it, and because the touching was never innocent. Not even if he was carrying her inside from a snowstorm.

It was the epitome of stupidity that it bothered him that she was cold. She was a grown, very capable, extremely intelligent woman who had been taking care of herself for a long time. Even during Nebraska winters. But it did bother him. Enough to break down a door and carry her inside.

Dillon scrubbed a hand over his face and reluctantly followed her inside. The entryway was closed off from the rest of the house by another door, and Dillon felt a bit better about breaking the outer one. The house would stay warm with the interior door shut. Still, snow was already swirling into the front entry and would likely begin to accumulate soon. What was left of the door would block some of it, but he needed to find some boards or at least a sheet to tack up there until he could get back out here to fix it.

"She's not here."

Dillon stopped in the wide doorway between Grace's kitchen and living room. "What?"

Kit shook her head, looking distressed. "She's not here. I looked all over."

Dillon frowned and glanced around. "So . . . what now?"

"I don't know." Kit's brow was creased in a deep frown, and her eyes were worried when she lifted them to his. "Do you think she tried to get out and is stuck on the road somewhere? Or did she try to go out to the barn for the lambs? Or . . . I don't know."

Kit Derby always knew. She was the one who was cool in a crisis, the one who could, literally, talk people off ledges. Dillon knew from experience that when Kit started acting out of character, he got a little crazy. Like when she was tipsy and got giggly. Or like when she got worked up about a final exam. Or like when she looked up at him with desire in her eyes and said, "God, I want you."

He cleared his throat. Yeah, all those times she'd been acting unlike her usual capable, got-it-all-together self.

He took the few steps that separated them and grasped her upper arms. "It's going to be okay. We'll find her," he told her firmly. Seeing her upset now made every protective instinct he had roar to life. "Where do you think we should start? Would she head to town, or would she go to the barn?"

Kit just stared up at him. Dillon gave her a little shake. "Kit."

"I don't know . . ."

Bullshit. She knew. She was letting her thoughts spin, fueled by emotion. Kit knew people, especially those she was close to. She would know exactly what her grandmother would have done in the storm. She just needed to focus.

"Think, Kit. Think about Grace. Would she head for town when she knew the storm was getting worse?"

Kit worried her bottom lip.

"Come on, babe. Stop thinking about all the things that could go wrong. Stop picturing her stuck in a ditch. Stop picturing her walking out in the snow by herself. I want you to picture her here in the kitchen, listening to the weather report, making a decision. What did she do?"

Kit's breathing was coming faster, and Dillon knew that she was panicking. Fuck. He could recognize the signs of stress, and he could treat her for hyperventilation, but he was, clearly, really sucking at getting her to calm down and focus. Where was a syringe of sedative when he needed it?

"Kit."

She swallowed. "Yeah?"

"Do *not* get pissed at me for this. I'm trying to help."

Her brows drew together. "For what?"

Dillon lowered his head and kissed her.

It wasn't the same thing as *talking* her through the moment, but he was better at this than talking. And it would get her thoughts off her grandmother wandering around in the whiteout conditions outside. He hoped.

But a moment later, satisfaction burst through his chest as she wrapped her arms around his neck and went up on tiptoe to get closer to him. He pulled her into his body, cussing the thick layers of clothing they were wearing. But he focused on her mouth, the only part of her he could really get to. He deepened the kiss, parting his lips slightly and tipping his head to the side. She was the first to open her mouth fully, but Dillon immediately swept his tongue over her bottom lip and then against hers.

Then she slid her hands to his neck. And her fingers were freaking freezing.

He pulled away with a gasp, and she sank onto her flat feet, staring up at him. He grabbed her hands before they fell away from his neck, though, pressing them against the warm skin under the edge of his coat collar. "Hang on. You just surprised me," he told her huskily.

"Sorry. I . . ." She trailed off but took a deep breath as her fingers flexed against his neck. "I forgot my hands were cold for a second there."

He grinned down at her, covering her fingertips with his. "Let's just be sure they're not."

She wet her lips and took a ragged breath. "Why did you kiss me?"

"To clear your mind." Did that sound cocky? Maybe. He didn't care. Because it had worked. "You needed a reboot."

"A reboot?"

"Like when your computer freezes up and needs to be shut down and turned back on." *Turned back on.* He sure as hell was turned on now.

"So I could focus on my grandma," Kit said, pulling her hands from his neck. "Right."

Yes. Because of her grandma. Of course.

He let her go. "Right."

Kit swallowed. "She would go to the barn first," she said.

Well, the kiss had worked to focus her. That was something.

"Okay, I'm heading to the barn, then," he said.

"I'm coming wi—"

"No." Dillon knew his tone was harsher than it needed to be, but this woman didn't listen to anyone. Especially him. "You are staying right here."

"But—"

"Kit, I can find a freaking barn. And *you're not dressed for this weather.* You stay here and start calling around, see if anyone's heard from her since your mom called."

He could tell she wanted to argue further, but she nodded and reached into her coat pocket. Then she frowned and reached into her other coat pocket. Then she patted her pants. But the scrubs didn't have pockets. "You've got to be kidding me," she groaned.

She'd lost her phone. Dillon pointed to the landline mounted on the kitchen wall by the cupboards. "You know how to use one of those?" he asked.

She frowned at him. "Of course."

"Then you'd better start dialing."

"I just don't . . ."

"You don't what?"

"I don't know anyone's phone numbers," she admitted with a sigh.

He couldn't help but chuckle. "Well, you're in luck. I have numbers in my phone." He did so love saving Kit Derby's day, even in tiny ways.

"You don't have my mother's number in your phone. Or my cousins' or my uncles'." She paused and frowned. "Do you?"

"I do, in fact, have your uncle Bill's number," Dillon said, pulling it up. "I also have Cass and Evan's number." Cassidy was one of Kit's cousins on her mother's side.

"How do you have those numbers?" Kit asked.

"Bill is a patient, and I gave him my number in case he needed anything. And Evan is going to build a deck on my house this spring."

It was no surprise at all that Dillon would have people in common with Kit. They had a whole town of people in common. Chance was a small town, and they'd both grown up here. But it still clearly irked her a little. He'd been officially, fully, back in town for only a few months, but Kit was going to have to get used to this. He wasn't going anywhere.

"But I have something even better," he went on.

"Oh?"

"*My* mother's phone number," Dillon said, reaching for the pen and paper on the counter. "And, as you know, she can get any information anyone needs in this town."

Where Kit's mom was cool and detached, Kelli Alexander, Dillon's mom, was involved and connected. Almost to a fault. Kelli was one of the Montgomery triplets, and the Montgomerys were a founding family in Chance. Kelli had spent her whole life in Chance, and she loved the town and its inhabitants dearly. She would have, or would be able to get, any phone number Kit could possibly need.

Kit took the sheet of paper from him with a sigh.

"Make some calls. I'm going to the barn."

He was at the door before he heard her quiet "Dillon."

He turned back. "Yeah?"

"Be careful out there. Don't take too long."

Dillon fought the grin that threatened. "Of course."

He'd go out there for anyone.

It was all about Grace, *not* Kit.

It was actually even more about *Dillon*.

Kit told herself all of the above as Dillon headed back into the storm to check the barn for her grandmother.

No way would Dillon Alexander sit around inside the house if there was even the slightest possibility that Grace had gotten stuck out in the barn in the storm. No way.

But Kit was practically conditioned to react to his hero tendencies.

Dillon had been her nemesis from third grade on. She'd been the best student in the class in third grade. And second grade. And first. When the teacher had asked for people who wanted to participate in the spelling bee, Dillon hadn't even raised his hand. Until Kit had been about to win. Then he'd piped up with, "Mrs. Anderson? I changed my mind. Can I try?" Mrs. Anderson, only one in a long line of females who couldn't resist Dillon's charm, had said yes and brought him up front. Where he'd beaten Kit by spelling *beautiful* after she missed *government*. Dillon had quickly risen to stardom as the first and only person in their grade—or the grade above—to outscore Kit Derby on something. And she'd never, ever, ever spelled *government* wrong again.

They'd competed at everything from then on.

In spite of his charm and humor and good-guy side.

She didn't deny that those existed. She just denied that they had any effect on her.

Until the night of the thunderstorm when Kit had gotten a flat tire and Dillon had stopped to help her. She'd been horrible to him that day at school, but he'd still pulled over in the pounding rain and changed her tire.

And thus had started her crush. Her very, very secret, never-let-him-know crush. Not only because he made her *nuts* but because she liked Abi, and she and Dillon had been so obviously in love, even at such a young age.

Kit drew in a big breath.

Her reaction to Dillon's heroics was a huge problem. Because he was heroic *a lot*. Especially when she was trying desperately not to react to his . . . anything.

Shaking herself out of the thoughts of Dillon as a charming, happy teen who had turned into a driven, save-the-world badass, she reached for her grandmother's rotary phone and dialed Dillon's mom's number. She liked Kelli and knew that she would be able to help. Kit just felt more than a little sheepish about needing the help. Who didn't know her own mother's phone number?

A woman who was constantly on the go, relied on her planner and speed dial far too much, and who didn't call her mother all that often.

Kit sighed as she waited for the rotary dial to come back from the eight. She put her finger in the plastic hole to dial a six when her eyes focused on the calendar hanging on the wall next to the phone and then the sheet of notebook paper pinned up next to that.

A list of all of Grace's important phone numbers. And Gretchen's number was the fifth one down—behind Brad, Kit's dad and Grace's son; Kit herself; Kit's uncle Bill; and, of course, Dr. Dillon Alexander, whose name had been written over the smudged spot where Grace had erased Dr. Wagner when she'd switched her care to Dillon.

Kit rubbed a finger over the center of her forehead. Of course Grace had switched her care to Dillon. As had more than half the women in town. Ugh. Kit wasn't sure she could handle her grandmother wanting to spend time with Dillon because he was good-looking and charming.

Maybe mostly because he wasn't all that charming with *her*.

Kit shook that off. That wasn't fair. Why should Dillon be charming with her? She wasn't all that nice to him, either, if she was being totally honest. And he didn't need or want anything from her.

He sure kissed you like he wanted something from you. Her whole body warmed as she remembered the kiss Dillon had just laid on her. It had been to distract her. Okay, fine. It had worked. But it also hadn't seemed . . . innocent. That kiss had not been just a favor.

Kit made herself focus on the digits of her mother's phone number and dialed quickly.

"Hello?" Gretchen answered a moment later.

"Hey, Mom, I'm out at Grandma's and—"

"We've been worried sick! I called your phone a dozen times with no answer, and then I called the hospital, and they said you'd gone out in the storm with Dillon to check on patients. Are you okay?"

"I'm fine," Kit assured her. "I'm sorry. I lost my phone. But we're at Grandma's now, and she's—"

"She's at Tina's," Gretchen interrupted. "That was the first thing I was calling to tell you."

"She's at Tina's?" Kit repeated. "Since when?"

"She came into town this morning because she heard the weather was going to get bad. She and Tina have been playing rummy all morning and drinking apple cider."

Kit closed her eyes. She knew what that meant. Cards and cider? The cider was spiked, and they were no doubt playing for big stakes. Grace had lost a car to Tina sometime in the nineties, and Tina had owed Grace almost $500 for the past year or so. The women were sisters, and they loved each other dearly—and fought like cats and dogs.

"Will they be okay?" Kit asked. "I could take Grandma to my house."

"They're fine," Gretchen said. "She plans to stay there for the next couple days."

"But . . . what if she ends up losing the farm to Tina?" Kit said drily. That would hardly be the end of the world. For one thing, Tina didn't want it. For another, Grace would have to move into town, then, and maybe behave herself.

"Oh, they promised they're only playing for dishes this time."

Their mother, Kit's great-grandmother, had owned a huge set of antique china. When she'd passed away, her daughters had divided it up . . . and proceeded to bribe, buy, and steal pieces from each other over the past thirty years.

"Are you *sure* she should stay there?" Kit asked, thinking she'd shoot Bree a quick message and maybe have her check on things over at Tina's later on. Kit paced away from the wall and was brought up short by the phone cord. Right. She didn't have her phone. No texting. No *receiving* texts or calls, either. Crap. She had patients who might need her. One in particular whom she was a little worried about—or, rather, the patient's wife. *Dammit.* Where the hell was her phone?

"They're fine. At least she's in town where she'll be warm and fed and with someone," Gretchen told Kit. "Don't worry."

Kit looked around the kitchen. "Okay, well, we're heading back in, then, I guess." As soon as Dillon came in from outside. And he warmed up some. She could extend the same courtesy he'd been giving her all day.

"Well, don't wait too long. It's getting dark, and the temps are supposed to start dropping even further," Gretchen warned.

"Okay. Talk to you soon."

She disconnected and glanced at the clock. It was nearly five. It wasn't just getting dark. In another hour it would seem like midnight outside. How long had Dillon been gone? Did he know her grandmother's place well enough to not get turned around in the whiteout? What if he'd fallen and twisted an ankle? Or hit his head? Or—

The door to the kitchen banged open, and Dillon stomped inside. Kit let out a long breath, realizing she was glad to see him. She didn't know what it was about this storm that was getting her all riled up. She didn't let her thoughts spin, and she didn't get anxious about things. She was the one who kept the calm, who talked people through panic attacks. She was also a Nebraska girl, born and raised. This wasn't her first blizzard and wouldn't be her last. But this storm felt . . . different.

Lately everything in Chance had felt different. Ever since the tornado in June, things felt off-center. Like they hadn't quite gotten a firm foundation back. Like there was an unpredictability in the air now that wouldn't go away. It felt like things were changing. Or had already changed. And she just wasn't adjusted yet. She really hated that feeling—the out-of-control, not-sure-where-I'm-at thing that she felt swirling around her.

Dillon shook the snow off his gloves, brushed off the front of his coat and pants, and then pulled his hat from his head, and it hit her— he was definitely part of the problem.

Things had absolutely changed. Dillon, Jake, and Max were back in town, and nothing would be the same again. Jake and Avery were together. Max and Bree were together. And Dillon and Kit were . . . in each other's way constantly.

"Looks like she fed the lambs and the cats," Dillon reported. "They have enough bedding and food and water to last for a couple days. But she's nowhere. Do you want to get back out on the snowmobile and go looking?"

Kit licked her lips and shook her head, pulling herself together. "She's not here. She made it into town earlier today but didn't tell anyone. She's with her sister and planning to stay through the storm."

"Thank God," Dillon said with a big grin. "She and Tina can keep each other company, and Tina's liquor cabinet should keep them plenty warm."

Dillon knew this town and the people as well as Kit did. She knew that, cognitively, but when he said stuff like that, it hit her in the heart, too.

He'd come back to be closer to his family and friends and because he was ready to settle down. At least, that's what the rumor mill reported he'd said. Kit hadn't really let herself think about the reasons he was back, focusing instead on all the consequences it brought instead. Like her inability to forget about him for days on end the way she had for the past ten years. But she did wonder what his return meant. If he was "settling down," did that include marriage? Kids? Could she live in a town where Dillon Alexander would be out and about with a woman he loved, raising his kids, going to community events as a happy little family? Would she be able to watch him hold hands with, and maybe even kiss, another woman? Would she have to endure Christmas parties at the hospital where Dillon would bring along his gorgeous, accomplished, sweet, and smart wife and kiss her under the mistletoe? Would he—

"Kit?" Dillon snapped his fingers right in front of her nose.

Kit jerked back, her face flushing hot. What the *hell* was wrong with her? She coughed. "What?"

"I asked you about three questions while you were zoning out there. Are you okay?"

Dillon was watching her closely, and Kit knew she had to be careful. He had not only known her for a long time, but he'd studied her—as she had him—cataloging weaknesses to use against her in their competitions. Whether it was running for class president or shooting for a higher ACT score or doing a better cadaver dissection, she'd learned not to blink when Dillon was around. He kept her on her toes and, deep down where she would never, ever admit it to anyone else, she owed him a lot of her success. If he hadn't been there pushing her, she might have slacked off or even given up a time or two. Or ten. But wanting to be better than Dillon, to wipe that smug smile off his face, to see his name *under* hers on a list, was always worth staying up a little later, pushing a little harder, reading a few more pages.

"I'm fine," she told him, lifting her chin. "I was just thinking about my grandma."

"Yeah, and I asked if she'd care if we raided her pantry and where her extra towels are," Dillon said.

Kit blinked at him, taking in his words. All she could come up with in reply was, "Why?"

"We're staying here tonight." He was only about a foot away from her, and when he unzipped his coat and shrugged out of it, snow showered her feet.

But she couldn't worry about the puddles of melted snow on the floor right now. Dillon had just said something *really* disturbing.

"We're staying here tonight?" she repeated. "What do you mean?"

"It's dark, the snowmobile is now under a drift of snow, and it's dropped at least ten degrees. I called the hospital, and everything is covered. They've got three paramedics on, Tom is there, and Dan's on call, so we need to stay here until morning when things die down and it's light again."

Tom and Dan were two of the other physicians in Chance, and Dan lived only two blocks from the hospital. So everything there was fine.

But the hospital wasn't what had her concerned. She was the only mental-health professional in town, so Tom and Dan couldn't really cover for her. She had patients who might need her.

But that also wasn't *really* what had her concerned.

"We can't stay here," she said quickly. "We can make it back. Come on, it's not that far."

"It's fifteen miles," he said, starting to slip his overalls off, folding them down to his waist and showing off the flannel button-down shirt underneath. "And it's freezing and dark. It's safer to stay out here, and there's no reason not to."

She watched as he bent to unlace his boots, toeing them off and tossing them toward the door, then continuing to shed the overalls, revealing blue jeans that were faded and worn.

When he dressed like that, he looked like a Chance boy. Not a world-renowned trauma specialist who had braved other continents to help and heal. Not the Army National Guardsman who worked in horrible conditions to rescue and patch up people caught in Katrina and other catastrophic situations. Not the polished physician who spoke at national conferences about medical management in natural disasters.

And he looked amazing in fatigues and in suits. But it was more than his lean, muscled body that she appreciated in the blue jeans and T-shirts. In denim, Dillon looked like the young, optimistic charmer she'd fallen for in high school.

"We can't stay out here," she blurted. She and Dillon had a . . . dicey . . . history when in close confines with each other for long—or short—periods of time.

He kicked off the overalls. "Why not? Heat's on. That's really the most important thing."

Finally, Kit dug deep into the well of experience and maturity that the years and her training had provided. And she met the issue head-on so it could be dealt with. "It seems to me that whenever we've spent time alone together, things happen that later cause some . . . unwelcome feelings and . . . responses."

Okay, maybe that wasn't exactly head-on. But at least she'd brought it up.

Dillon propped his hands on his hips. "You mean we end up sleeping together."

So he got the head-on points. She sighed. "Yes."

CHAPTER THREE

"Are you feeling like that will be an issue here tonight?" Dillon asked.

"Do you mean, am I feeling like jumping you right now or stripping down?" Kit asked, her own cockiness rising slightly. Finally.

He gave her a half smile. "Yeah."

"No, not really." Well, the jumping-him thing maybe a little. She was attracted to him. Always had been. And he'd been nice to her today. And he'd brought her out here. And had kicked a door down for her.

That should definitely *not* have made her hot. She was no damsel in distress. And she was a woman who appreciated men who used their brains, not their brawn.

Or so she told herself.

In any case, she'd definitely felt warmer when he'd kicked that door in. And when he'd thrown her over his shoulder? She'd lost her mind a little bit and thought about grabbing the fine ass that had been *right there.*

And then he'd kissed her. He'd just . . . kissed her. Grabbed her and kissed her.

She didn't care why he'd done it, and she didn't care that typically the whole grabbing-her thing would have totally pissed her off. *Should have* pissed her off.

The truth was, she responded to Dillon being physical.

If he went out and chopped wood right now, she *would* strip down, and to hell with the consequences.

"So, nothing to worry about," he said. "We can spend the night here together, wait for the storm to pass, dig out tomorrow. And nothing will happen."

Kit narrowed her eyes. Dillon knew her very well. And she knew *him* very well. She knew that tone in his voice. He was baiting her.

She crossed her arms. "You're right. *Nothing* will happen. So there's nothing to worry about."

He nodded, but he pinned her with a look that said he wasn't missing a single detail of her reactions and body language. "I'm sure you're past all of that, right?" he asked.

Kit noticed he didn't say "we" were past all of that. Dammit. The way he admitted to being attracted to her always got to her. Neither of them would go so far as to say that they were friends, but they respected each other, and they had some chemistry, and it was silly to deny either of those things, at least to each other. No one else needed to know. But when he was so matter-of-fact about wanting her, it made her want him more.

She blew out a breath. He was not the more mature of the two of them. He was not more in control of his emotions. And he wasn't the best one at facing and discussing emotions. That was all her.

No matter how much she hated it right now.

"I wouldn't say I'm really past all of that, no," she admitted as the mature, professional, got-her-shit-together woman she was. Most of the time. "But I do know that I can control myself and learn from past mistakes."

And then he was there, right in front of her, nearly on top of her. "The times we've been together were *not* mistakes, Kit," he said, his voice low and firm. "They might have created some issues afterward, but every time we've been together has been incredible and exactly what we both needed at the time. I know you love to hassle me, but don't piss me off by calling them mistakes."

Heat snaked through her, followed quickly by a very strange emotion that seemed almost like wistfulness. He was right—each time had been exactly what she needed at that moment. The moments afterward were an issue, but the moments when they'd come together and all the frustration and hurt and confusion melted away because they could focus on the one thing that they both wanted equally were moments she wished she could relive. No one had ever made her *feel* like Dillon did, no one had ever made her so aware of herself—her thoughts, feelings, and reactions—the way Dillon did, and she was amazed by what that did for the sex.

She finally gave him a nod. "Okay. You're right."

He studied her face for a moment, then he also nodded and stepped back. "Okay."

It also did something to her that he was almost protective of their past.

"I'm going to take a shower," he told her. "You okay with that?"

"Why wouldn't I be okay with that?"

"You won't feel too tempted, knowing I'm just in the other room, completely naked?" he asked.

Like a light switch had been flipped, the air between them filled with a swirling combination of challenge and heat.

"Tempted?" she asked, pretending to not understand.

"Tempted to sneak a peek? Or join me?"

Dillon started to unbutton the flannel shirt, and Kit held her breath, letting it out only after she saw the black T-shirt underneath.

Tempted. Yeah. So much. But he was taunting her, and nothing made her more stubborn than Dillon Alexander issuing a challenge.

She was not going to be the first to make a move here. Not that anyone should be making any moves. But if someone *did*, it was going to be Dillon.

She gave him a shrug. "I'm fine. Shower. That's fine. No big deal."

He laughed at that—because he knew she was full of shit and knew that this had just become a competition. He turned toward the stairs that would lead to the upstairs bathroom. And the bedrooms.

"Well, you know where to find me if you need anything."

She watched him head up the stairs and shook her head. Very few people saw this side of Dillon. He wasn't the easygoing flirt. Not usually, anyway. Only with her. And even that was rare. He pulled that guy out only when he knew it would ruffle her. Like when they were trapped in a house fifteen miles from town together. Alone. Overnight.

Kit forced herself to stop all that. She was a grown woman who knew every trick the guy upstairs could pull. She could handle him. She could resist him. She would win this battle of the wills.

Her thoughts whirled. There were several methods she could employ to resist Dillon's attack on her willpower. But playing defense was only half the game. She needed a strong offensive game as well.

Kit looked down. She was still in the hospital scrubs, which were wet from the knees down and cold. She couldn't recall the last time she'd had scrubs on. Probably anatomy lab in medical school. They weren't fashionable, of course, and all they did was remind her that she was better in a skirt and heels. She felt more in control when she had her power suits on.

At the moment, however, her feet protested the idea of heels, aching as they thawed inside her wet tennis shoes and socks. She also still wore her coat. She had to look half-bedraggled and ridiculous. Not that she cared what Dillon thought of how she looked, but . . . well, of course she did. It did no good to deny it. She was a single woman who was physically attracted to the man stuck in this house with her, and of course she cared about how she looked.

Then again, if she could *keep* him from looking at her in that way he had—where he was a starving man and she was a double-scoop hot-fudge sundae—she might be better off, actually. He didn't shoot her that look often and almost never when other people were around, but she'd caught it a few times when he didn't cover it fast enough. And then there were the occasions when he'd do it behind someone's back to try to fluster her.

That was the biggest problem—she never knew when he was playing around and trying to get the upper hand and when he was showing how he truly felt.

Kit headed into her grandmother's bedroom. Grace was five three to Kit's five seven, and much smaller than Kit through the hips and breasts, but surely she had *something* Kit could put on while her clothes dried. A few minutes later, she'd resigned herself to a pair of pink leggings that were, no doubt, baggy on Grace but that hugged Kit's thighs and hips like workout pants, and a T-shirt that was probably perfect on the tiny eighty-five-year-old but that showed a few inches of skin when Kit stretched her arms overhead. The shirt was also purple. And said OLD AGE IS NO PLACE FOR SISSIES. She pulled on some thick socks and sighed, looking at herself in the mirror. It would have to do. At least the clothes were dry and the house was warm. And it wasn't like the scrubs had been a great look, either.

She padded back into the kitchen, her toes still cold, but the feeling was starting to return. She tried not to notice that the water was still running in the bathroom on the second floor, but she couldn't help the memory of Dillon's big, naked body from flashing through her mind. It had been a while, but a girl didn't forget stuff like that.

Kit realized that her attempts to ignore Dillon and his crazy-long shower were not working. Her eyes landed on the big cooking pot that sat on the back burner on her grandmother's stove, and she had an idea. She needed to distract herself from the water running upstairs—and the man it was running on—and she needed to show Dillon that she'd been otherwise occupied when he came back down.

Besides, she wanted to wow him. And she knew exactly how. There were some things about her that Dillon didn't know, as a matter of fact.

By the time he *finally* came back down the steps—what had taken him so damned long up there anyway?—she was well into the chili preparations.

"What's going on?" he asked from the bottom of the steps.

She glanced up. And dropped the knife she was using to cut the onion.

She lifted her hand and rubbed the center of her forehead, breathing in a healthy dose of onion fumes and feeling her eyes water as she did it. "Clothes, Dillon."

He had simply wrapped a towel around his hips and come padding downstairs like it was nothing. He had his clothing in a wad under his arm. She felt her willpower crumbling already. Crap. "I really think both of us wearing clothes is a good rule to put in place."

"Why?" he asked, coming farther into the kitchen. "It's not like this is any big deal, right?"

But it was a *very* big deal. Not just the fact that he was half-naked, but he was a *big* half-naked. Dillon was tall and wide, with huge hands and feet and . . . yeah, other things. And he filled up space far beyond his body measurements. She'd never quite figured out how he did that, but Dillon was impossible to ignore. *Impossible.* She knew because she'd been trying for twenty-one years.

"You can't walk around the house in just a towel."

"I'm just going to run my clothes through the washer and dryer. You worried I'm going to get cold?"

"I'm not *worried* about anything."

Worried wasn't exactly the word to describe how she was feeling. She stomped around the counter and through the living room to the master bedroom. The only bedroom on the main floor. The one *she* was going to sleep in while Dillon was far away upstairs overnight. She yanked her grandmother's bathrobe from the hook on the back of the bedroom door and then stomped back into the kitchen. She thrust the pale-blue terry cloth at Dillon. "Here."

"Wonderful." He moved in closer, taking the robe from her. "Wouldn't want you . . . *worried.*"

Why did he have to emphasize that word, as if they were talking about another word altogether? Or was she making that up in her own imagination?

Kit huffed out a frustrated breath—something she did around Dillon a lot—and crossed the room to put the countertop firmly between them again. But she felt his eyes on her the entire time.

"I'll admit, this idea about being dressed isn't so bad," he said. "That outfit is a vast improvement over the scrubs."

She looked down and actually gave a soft laugh. "My grandma's pants and shirt are an improvement? Wow, you really hate the look of scrubs."

"Just on you. Scrubs don't show off your ass like those do. Though I'm going to have trouble if I ever see your grandma wearing those in town."

Kit would have laughed, maybe, but just then he shrugged into the robe. And should have looked ridiculous wearing a robe that hit above the knees with the arms coming barely past his elbows. But then he dropped the towel from underneath it, and *ridiculous* was not a word Kit would have possibly applied. She couldn't see anything. Not really. But she didn't have to see . . . *it* . . . to picture it.

She concentrated on the onions in front of her.

"So what are we doing here?" Dillon asked, completely unconcerned about wearing the bathrobe.

"I'm making dinner. Go put your clothes in the machine." Kit gritted her teeth at how domestic and stupidly intimate that sounded. It was laundry. There was nothing sexy about laundry.

But Dillon didn't move. He was frowning at the ingredients she had spread out on the countertop between them. "What are you making?"

"Chili."

"You're making chili?" he asked.

There was a note of disbelief in his voice, and she looked up. "Yes. I'm making chili."

He'd pointed out earlier that she didn't seem domestic. And he was mostly right. But, like anything, if she put her mind to it, she could do domestic. She'd grown up in this kitchen, and she'd managed to master three things—chili, snickerdoodles, and sweet-potato fries—somehow. She never made any of the above outside of this kitchen, though. She lived alone, and it just seemed that chili and cookies were something you made for other people. Kit frowned at that and wondered why she thought that.

Dillon interrupted her pondering, though, when he said, "I don't eat anyone's chili but my own. Mine's the best. Ever."

Kit narrowed her eyes. If he made chili, it probably was amazing. But it wasn't better than hers.

"You only think that because you've never tasted mine."

He chuckled. "Uh, no. I think that because it's true. And you don't believe me only because *you've* never had *mine.*"

For a moment the horny, thrilled-to-be-cooped-up-in-a-blizzard-with-Dillon part of Kit's brain thought about the things of his she'd definitely *had* in the past. And how great they'd been. But thankfully, that corner of her brain was small compared to the rational we-hate-him-and-his-effect-on-us part of her brain, and she shut it up quick. "I think it because it's true." He scoffed, and she put her hands on her hips. "I've won *awards* for my chili, Dillon. Several times."

"In contests where *I* wasn't entered. But it looks like you haven't gotten too far here. I can still take over."

Oh, hell no. "You come one step closer to my tomatoes and onions and I'm not responsible for where this chili powder ends up." She purposefully looked him up and down. "There's a lot of . . . places . . . showing there, Alexander."

He grinned and took a step around the end of the counter in spite of her threat. "You really think you can get your chili powder anywhere I don't want it to be?"

How the hell did he make *chili powder* sound sexual—and not at all like he was talking about actual chili powder?

"If you think you're so hot in the chili department, get your own pot," she said, falling back on the one thing she could always count on being consistent with Dillon: he could never resist a contest with her.

In the midst of an attempted seduction, or whatever the hell he'd been doing with that sort-of-predatory gleam in his eye, and only a thin layer of baby-blue terry cloth between her eyes and all his glory, Dillon's mood abruptly shifted.

"You're on," he said almost gleefully. He seemed to be taking an inventory of ingredients again. "Where are the pots and utensils and stuff?" he asked, turning to survey the kitchen.

Challenge him to a cook-off whenever she needed to distract him. Noted. And good to know.

Kit shook her head. "No way. You're on your own. You think you're such a chili magician? You're going to have to do it *all* without any help from me."

He nodded. "Okay, fine. Be that way. But when my chili makes you moan, you owe me an apology."

Like *that* would ever happen. "You bet. Absolutely," she said drily, getting back to her chopping.

"And my corn bread will make you *cry*," he promised.

She turned to retort, but he'd crouched in front of one of the low cupboards, and the robe had fallen open over his spread knees. He was facing away from her, so she didn't actually *see* anything good, but again, the memory of the times she *had* seen it hit her. Not to mention when she'd touched it and . . .

He stretched to his feet again, and she quickly spun back to face the cutting board. *Crap, crap, crap.* "You don't eat corn bread with chili," she finally answered, her stupid voice sounding scratchy. "It's cinnamon rolls."

He quickly turned toward her. "Are you making me cinnamon rolls?" he asked.

Her grandmother made cinnamon rolls from scratch and froze them. Kit already had a dozen thawing on the counter. "I'm awesome at chili," she said. "Not cinnamon rolls. But my grandmother is great at everything." She pointed at the rolls.

Dillon's eyes lit up. "Frosting?"

"That I'll have to do. But I think I can swing it."

"I'll make you an orgasmic omelet in the morning if you make the frosting with cream cheese."

The word *orgasmic* made her mouth go dry. And the reminder that they'd be here overnight. Together. And the idea of having breakfast with him. That was one thing they'd never done in the times they'd done . . . the other stuff. Kit cleared her throat. "Oh, really?"

He gave her a slow, lazy smile. "Well, if anyone knows what you consider orgasmic, I think it's me."

She stared at him. He'd really just said that.

Dillon Alexander was in many elite clubs—one of the most highly acclaimed doctors with Doctors Without Borders, one of the golden boys from Chance, one of the recipients of the prestigious Presidential

Medal of Freedom . . . and the only man to give Kit Derby multiple orgasms. But he didn't know that. She was pretty sure.

"You think you know better than I do?" she asked.

He studied her for a little too long and a little too seriously. "Actually, yeah, I think I do."

Kit felt her mouth drop open. "You think *you* know more about how to get me going than *I* do?" she asked. "Seriously?"

He lifted a shoulder. "I think I've given it more thought than you have."

Kit turned to fully face him. "You've given more thought to my sexuality and what I like and need to have an orgasm than *I* have?"

"Absolutely," he said with a nod. "No question in my mind."

"Are you kidding me right now?" she asked him.

"Kit," he said, his tone placating—which only ticked her off more—"you are not the type of woman to spend a lot of time thinking about yourself. You're all about making *other people* better and happier. Do I think you do fine with your vibrator or fingers when you need to? Sure. But knowing where to put it and what speed setting you like isn't the same thing as knowing all of the ways to get you hot and wet and ready so that the orgasm is explosive and truly amazing."

Kit stood staring at Dillon, a million things tumbling in her head. Had he just complimented her while also talking about her being hot and *wet*? Which had actually made her a little hot and . . . yeah, okay, wet.

Damn him.

She should just turn back to dinner prep. She should just focus on making her chili and let this go. He was just picking a fight. Or something. It didn't feel like a fight, but it felt very intentional. And she hated reacting in any way to Dillon's intentional efforts to make her react.

But she just couldn't. There were several words in his declaration that got her attention—to say the least. But there was one that she simply couldn't ignore.

"So you're saying that you think you know *all* of the ways to do that to me?" she asked.

"I really do," he said. He opened the freezer and pulled out a package of ground beef. As if chili was the more momentous thing going on in this kitchen.

"We've been together four times, Dillon. And once was in high school before you really knew what you were doing."

He turned from starting the microwave to defrost the frozen pound of meat. "Before I really knew what I was doing?" he asked. "Well, damn, thanks, Kit."

He didn't look offended or insulted. "You got better," she said, as if it were no big deal. The second time they'd been together? Oh yeah.

That got a grin from him, though. "Yeah, I did," he agreed. "But you were plenty pleased with my first effort."

She hadn't let herself think back to that first time in a *really* long time. Because it was almost embarrassing. She'd been *so* into it that she wasn't sure it was anything in particular Dillon did, actually. She'd been a very horny teenager who had discovered erotic romance novels about three months before that night, and she'd been having some pretty hot dreams. She'd also been mildly in lust with Dillon for about a year by then. She'd been so ready to lose her virginity and had built the whole thing up so big in her imagination that she was pretty sure any guy could have done what Dillon did that night. She'd told him exactly what she'd wanted him to do and when he'd put his fingers and other things where she told him to, it had worked beautifully.

And, like everything else, she just couldn't let that go.

"I seem to remember kind of running the show that first time," she said. She had been embarrassed about it at times when she thought back, but now she was a mature, sexually confident woman who'd had plenty of great sex since then, and she could own what had gone on that night.

Dillon grinned. "You were downright bossy and demanding," he said. "I think that set me up for having a huge thing for women who know what they want and are very vocal about it ever since."

Again he'd surprised her. Because that also sounded kind of like a compliment. He thought his first time with her had somehow influenced his preferences after that?

"Don't look so shocked, Doc," Dillon said. "You know that you've made a lasting impression on me."

"Yeah, like permanent annoyance because you have to share your limelight with me."

Suddenly he looked serious. Very serious. "No. Not annoyance. You . . . push me. For sure. You get under my skin. You're always in the back of my mind. But I don't think I've ever considered that a bad thing."

She snorted. Because her other option was to again just stare at him with her mouth hanging open. "I'm like an itch you can't scratch. Or a toothache you can't get rid of, right?"

"Is that how you feel about me?"

Oh . . . crap. He really was a pain in her ass. Because he made her think about and face things she didn't want to.

The honest-to-God, I'm-a-self-aware-professional-psychiatrist truth was that the only thing Dillon had ever *really* done to upset her was not love her the way she had him. In high school. A long time ago.

She took a deep breath. "I tell myself that's how I feel about you," she said, proud of her ability to be honest and insightful into her own psyche. "But no. You push me, too, and I've accomplished a lot because you were there making me try harder."

He looked almost relieved at her words. The microwave beeped, and Dillon turned away to retrieve the defrosted meat without saying anything else.

"Then prepare to make the best chili of your life," he said, carrying the beef to the skillet on the stove. "Because I'm right here. And I'm not going to let you get away with calling yours the best without some hardcore proof."

Kit looked around the kitchen. Had she been drinking while cooking? Had she slipped and bumped her head? Was she asleep and dreaming? Were she and Dillon stuck together with no one else around, no hope of much distance between them, no ability to leave until morning, and actually getting along?

It seemed that way.

Even more so as the cooking went on. They chopped and browned and mixed side by side. The aroma of onions and meat filled the air, with the scent of cinnamon and sugar right on its heels. The familiar smells in the familiar kitchen slowly took some of the tightness out of Kit's shoulders, but she couldn't completely shake the feeling that she was waiting for something to happen. What, she had no idea. They'd gone from bickering to talking about sex—and the idea that Dillon knew her needs better than she did—and now they were making chili as if they'd done it a hundred times.

They moved around each other in the kitchen easily, as if they could anticipate each other's movements. She was increasingly aware of his body as he stood next to her and reached past her, but the usual tension she felt when Dillon was right *there* and watching her do something had a softer edge. As if she was . . . comfortable. Kind of. The fact that he was wearing only a bathrobe, and one several sizes too small for him, didn't allow her to completely relax. Nor did the kiss he'd given her earlier or, really, the fact that there was an underlying current of desire whenever they were together. But this was more comfortable than she'd been around him in a very long time. Maybe it was that they were in her grandmother's kitchen, a place that Kit had always felt contented and happy. Or maybe it was that while they were competing to see whose chili was best, this wasn't a go-hard-or-go-home contest between them. There were no high stakes here. So yeah, maybe it was that this was a low-key, who-really-cares challenge. Or maybe it was that he was being really nice today. For instance, he'd complimented her more in the past hour than he had in the past year.

But that wasn't true, either. Dillon had always easily acknowledged her intelligence and talents. He didn't like her stepping on his toes in his territory, but he'd never made her feel stupid.

As she simmered her chili, Kit forced herself to think about what she'd admitted to him. She'd told herself that he was like a pebble in her shoe—irritating, something she'd love to get rid of, something that affected how she walked her walk. But the only thing really true about that was that he affected her. How she did things, how she conducted herself, how she approached her work were affected by Dillon. Just like those things had been affected in high school and medical school.

But was it a bad thing?

He definitely got under her skin.

And he made her better.

Fuuuck.

She stirred the chili and tried not to let on that she'd just admitted that to herself.

So, Dillon was not only the best sex she'd ever had. He also made her better at everything else. That wasn't a big deal.

"You okay?"

She whirled to find him right behind her. "Yes, why?"

"Because you're beating that chili like it called your favorite pair of shoes ugly."

Kit looked into the pot of very well-blended chili. Yeah, she was taking it out on the tomatoes and beans for sure. "Yeah, I was just . . . thinking."

"About the time you threw raw eggs at me?"

Kit glanced at him. "Um . . . no." But the memory came flooding back. They'd been taking the Food I class together, and he'd been in her group while his girlfriend, Abi, had been in another. The assignment had been to triple the recipe, and they'd both been doing the math, trying to get it done before the other. Somehow the entire session had turned into a race, and by the time they were done, not only had they beaten everyone else in the class, but theirs was the best fettuccine Alfredo their teacher had ever tasted.

"But you remember that?" he asked.

Kit nodded. "I do."

"Cooking like this reminded me of that. We were a great team that day."

She nodded again.

"We were a good team when we debated Saint Mary's and won the state debate contest. We were a good team when we worked together on the mock trial our junior year. We were a great team when we ran that fund-raiser for the new playground at the park."

Kit swallowed. "What's your point?"

He shrugged. "I guess maybe that we should be making this chili together."

She frowned. This wasn't about chili. The chili was, though, a perfect metaphor. "You're scared?" she asked.

"Scared?"

"That my chili really is going to be better than yours?"

He didn't reply right away, but he finally gave her a smile. "Do you remember what I said right before you threw the eggs at me?"

She arched a brow. "The teacher said our Alfredo sauce was the best she'd ever tasted, and you leaned over and said, 'You're welcome.'"

His smile grew. "Yep. Because it was my idea to add extra butter."

"But I added the extra cheese," she reminded him. "That's what made it better."

"More butter makes everything better," he returned. "And you wouldn't have added the extra cheese if I hadn't added the butter."

"Without talking to me about it first," she added.

"Because you would have said no. But since I just went ahead and did it, you had to come up with something to balance it. And it ended up being amazing."

And then he'd slipped his arm around Abi, who had been watching them go back and forth with a frown, and pulled her up against his side. Where she fit like she was made to be there.

Kit propped a hand on her hip. "What's your point?"

"That I push you," Dillon said. "And that you match me every step of the way. And that everything turns out even better than it would have otherwise because of it."

She didn't reply immediately, which was unusual. Normally she was right on top of whatever he'd said, retorting almost before he was done, primed to argue, no matter what. But this time she thought about what he was saying. And more important, why he was saying it.

"So," she said slowly, "I think I get where you're going here."

Dillon put his spoon down and turned to face her. Kit's heart jumped at the serious look in his eyes. "Do you?"

Be cool. Be calm. You've got this. Kit swallowed and nodded. "Yeah, I do."

She trusted him. Dillon Alexander was a lot of things, but he was, without a doubt, someone she trusted implicitly. He was always totally honest with her.

And she knew that she did *not* want him to be totally honest about whatever was on his mind at the moment.

"You realize that every idea I've had about the free clinic is amazing, and you want to somehow combine efforts so that you can take partial credit."

He blinked at her, and it seemed to take an inordinate amount of time for him to process what she'd said. Or maybe he was formulating his response to push what he'd really been talking about. Finally, he replied simply, "I wasn't talking about the clinic."

She knew that. But *she* was going to talk about the clinic because it was something they would argue about, and that would keep her from taking her clothes off.

"Well, maybe we should," she said. "I mean, that would be a productive use of our time together. We have a meeting in a couple days, and then we have the big board presentation in four weeks. There are several things to iron out."

Dillon nodded slowly. "That would definitely be *one* way to spend the time."

She pretended not to hear the emphasis on *one* as she turned back to stir her chili. "So I think we need to go in there united about how important it is to have some after-hours services. A lot of the patients we want to serve are working shift jobs or more than one job."

Again he nodded. She knew that she could keep his attention on the subject. This clinic meant as much to him as it did to her. It was just that they felt that different things needed the initial focus and were first priorities. Because of course they did. They were both experts in their fields, and their fields were complementary, but they both had good reasons for feeling that their specialty was the most important.

"Of course the problem is *staffing* it after normal clinic hours," Dillon said.

It was. And that was exactly what they'd talked about the last time she'd brought it up. "I think we need to talk with the staff and remind them that what we do doesn't really have 'normal' hours," Kit told him.

"They know that," Dillon said. "They work in a hospital, they do overnight shifts, they work on holidays."

"But the concern is their adding *more* hours to what they already work," Kit said. The hospital was understaffed, as most were, in many areas—but especially nursing—and the hospital board had been clear that all staffing hours would have to be pro bono work.

"Right. Especially in nursing. But lab and radiology will also have to volunteer."

She nodded. "You and I both work well beyond forty hours a week, and we'll be the primary medical personnel *volunteering* in the clinic." The other doctors had agreed to help here and there, but the bulk of the hours were going to be coming from Kit and Dillon.

They wouldn't have it any other way.

"And we're paid for our work hours."

Kit turned, putting her hip against the counter and regarding him for a moment with her full focus. "You don't do it because you get paid well for it. And you'd be volunteering anyway."

He met her eyes directly. "Same for you."

"Exactly."

"But not everyone in the world feels that way."

In the moment that stretched between them, Kit felt the thing that tied them together, that common thread that had *always* tied them together, pulling tight and drawing them closer. They were both passionate about what they did, they wanted to fix the world, they wanted to make their hometown better, and they wanted to serve the people in that town. They both did the things they did because they loved it and knew it was important. They didn't need much compensation beyond that.

"We need to help them feel that way," she finally said.

He gave her a half smile. "You're good," he said. "But even you can't *make* people feel a certain way, Doc."

"But I can help them understand how they already feel. I think that our people truly want to do work that matters, that helps others, and that is important. I think we have plenty of people on staff who will want to help out at the clinic. We just have to help them realize that."

"So we need to have counseling sessions with everyone who works at the hospital? Get them in touch with their inner humanitarian?" Dillon asked. "This will motivate them to volunteer their time in the clinic?"

Kit lifted her chin. "Essentially, yes. We hold team meetings. We bring in lunch and talk to them about why the clinic is important. We tell them all about the programs we want to offer, the reason we think the town needs this, why it's important to *us* personally." She looked him directly in the eye. "You and I are very successful in winning people over, motivating them, influencing them. Think of what we could do if we do it together."

Dillon moved in closer. "Yeah, I'll give you that. When we come together for something, amazing things really do happen."

That was undeniable. In every way. She swallowed, stepped back, and returned to her pot. "Great. So I'll handle the talk, and you're in charge of the lunch. I like chicken salad."

CHAPTER FOUR

Okay, she wasn't ready to go there yet. Dillon realized he should have expected that. One thing Kit Derby would never do was give in to him easily. Fine. He was nothing if not patient . . .

He almost snorted at that. Patience was not one of his foremost virtues. Kit could definitely outwait him. The woman was stubborn, he'd give her that.

But that would make her giving in all the sweeter.

The timer buzzed on the oven, signaling the cinnamon rolls were done. Kit moved to retrieve them, and Dillon stirred his chili.

He didn't want to talk about the clinic. They argued over that fucking project every other week at the meetings and occasionally in the hallways and even twice in her office. He loved the clinic idea. He loved the idea of bringing those services to town. He loved the idea of doing it with Kit. And he loved arguing with her about the things about it that they disagreed on. It gave him a high he couldn't get anywhere else. But he knew she was throwing the project out there right now because she felt the tension and desire, and she was trying to defuse it.

They didn't need to talk about the clinic right now, and he didn't want the sexual tension defused.

He wasn't worried about the clinic. It was going to be amazing, no matter where they ended up with the staffing or even the funding. He and Kit didn't agree on every detail, or even on every service, but the clinic was going to be great because everything was always better when he and Kit did them together.

High school and medical school had both proved it over and over. But then . . . things happened. He'd left the state—hell, he'd left the continent for a while—and Kit had come home, and it had all become just a part of their past.

Then the tornado had hit.

That tornado. It had changed so much. There were still scars around town. A couple of buildings still bore signs of the storm. A couple of people did, too. But in at least a few ways, the tornado had been a good thing. The town had pulled together and rebuilt. And a bunch of people had fallen in love.

He'd at least gotten to kiss Kit. And then work beside her. He wasn't sure which of those things he'd enjoyed the most.

Now he was back, and the last six months had showed him that he and Kit were every bit the amazing team they'd always been. And today . . . this was a snowstorm, not a twister, but Dillon felt like things inside him were swirling around and piling up just like the snow was outside. His emotions, his realizations, the things he hadn't said or done. He was going to have to find a way through all of that. Because, unlike the snow, he didn't think any of it was going to go away on its own over time.

"I was thinking—" he started, but just then his phone vibrated on the Formica countertop. He wiped his hands on Grace's bathrobe and reached for it. The number on the display was the hospital.

"Alexander," he answered.

"Dillon, it's Janice."

"Hey, Jan. You still at work?"

"Lydia can't make it in, so I'm here for the night shift," she confirmed.

"Well, have a coffee or two on me," he told her. There was free coffee for the entire staff 24-7, but Dillon made a mental note to take her some of her favorite from the diner and to include a muffin or two the next time she worked.

"You bet," she said with a laugh. "But I'm calling about Sarah."

Dillon frowned. If there was a medical issue, Tom or Dan would be handling it. Unless Janice was calling to give him bad news about something they had handled. "What's going on?"

"She's . . . freaking out."

Dillon processed that. "What do you mean? How are her vitals?"

Janice sighed and rattled off the numbers. "Medically she's fine, at least until she starts getting worked up and her BP goes up. But when her BP goes up, she starts not feeling well. She's just dealing with a lot, and I think part of it is that she's lonely—too much time to think."

Dillon's mind turned. Okay, his patient was doing pretty well but wasn't happy. Typically new moms had their support system around. Their partners or families. Sarah was far from home, with no one she knew or cared about.

Kit moved into his line of sight, giving him a concerned look. "Everything okay?" she asked.

He shook his head. And realized he had exactly what Sarah needed right here. "Sarah's having a hard time. Anxious, and I believe the technical term Jan used was 'freaking out.' Is that right, Jan?" he asked into the phone, feeling downright smug. Because Sarah was going to be fine. Kit was here.

"You're hilarious, Dr. A," Janice said drily.

"Yes, that's Jan's official diagnosis," Dillon informed Kit with a grin.

Kit didn't smile back. She was frowning. But it wasn't at him; it was about the situation. Dillon definitely knew the difference between a Kit frown directed at him and one that wasn't.

"Has she talked to her husband?" Kit asked.

Dillon asked Jan.

"Yep. But that's part of the trouble. He's not going to be able to make it tonight." Dillon glanced toward the window. It was dark now, but the yard light at the side of Grace's house showed snow continuing to swirl.

Kit nodded. "Baby is okay?"

Again, Dillon asked Jan. "Yep. Nursing, sleeping well, vitals are good."

"So her anxiety isn't really about him or her own condition," Kit said.

"Just that she's alone in a strange place," Dillon said.

"Well, there's nothing 'just' about that," Kit told him. "That's huge. This is one of the most important days of her life, and she's spending it alone."

"Jan's there," Dillon said. But he, of course, knew what Kit meant and knew she was right. He wasn't a touchy-feely doctor. But that didn't mean he didn't understand that there was a time and place for that. Just not from him. He didn't process emotions the way a typical person did. He didn't know why. It was just how he was wired. He knew *about* emotions. But he didn't relate to most. He felt the main things like happy and sad and frustrated and pissed off. But he didn't do doubt. He didn't have time to doubt himself, and once he'd made a decision, he just had to make it work. He didn't do regret. Regret didn't do anyone any good. He had to do what he could do, the best he could do it, every time, and then deal with the result, whatever it was. He didn't do guilt. Everything he did, he did with the best information he had and the best intentions, so he couldn't feel bad about how things turned out. And he especially didn't do grief.

"You need to call her," Kit said.

Now Dillon was the one frowning. "What?"

"You need to call her."

"Call Sarah?"

"Yes."

"Why?" Why did *he* have to call her? He wasn't that good at this stuff in person, but the phone was downright terrible. Besides, he'd done the how-are-you-feeling, is-there-anything-I-can-do-for-you bit with Sarah earlier. Evidently it hadn't been very effective.

"Because you're her doctor," Kit said impatiently, moving around the counter.

For a moment, as unprofessional as it probably was to completely forget that he was on a call about a patient, lust hit him low and hard. Those fucking pink stretch pants. They were a horrendous color and didn't fit her at all. Except that they actually fit her very well. They were like a second skin, and Dillon's palms itched to run over the material to see if it was as soft as it looked.

Sure, it was the material that had him itching.

And that T-shirt. If Kit had reached up overhead into a cupboard one more time, pulling the purple cotton up on her smooth, tight belly, he would have been scratching an itch or two. So to speak.

Seeing her this way—dressed ridiculously and cooking in her grandmother's old-fashioned farm kitchen—did something to him. Something that hit him deep and hard and made everything between them even more complicated.

Unless she went along with it.

If she agreed that there was something here that was worth pursuing, something that had been a part of them both for a very long time and now was, finally, possible, well, then, everything would suddenly be very simple.

"*Dillon.*"

He realized that she was standing in front of him, arms crossed, looking at him with a mixture of wariness and annoyance.

"Yeah."

"You need to talk to Sarah. Ask Jan if she can call you back from Sarah's room."

Sarah. Jan. Work. Right.

"I can't talk to her," he said. "What do I say? I already stopped in and asked how she was feeling and if she's worried about anything, and she said no."

"And that was a couple hours ago," Kit said. "Emotions change. Especially when the excitement and adrenaline calm down, and you're on the other side of the crazy situation and have time to think."

Dillon didn't know if she was specifically referring to their time stuck together in the hospital storage room during the tornado, but that was exactly where his thoughts went with her words.

Yeah, his feelings had changed after the excitement had died down. They'd been less chaotic and confusing and a lot more concrete. But he wasn't sure about Kit's.

He didn't know how she felt about something more between them. He sometimes wished that his first instinct wasn't always to rile her up. But he also looked forward to seeing her, making her cheeks flush and her eyes spark and just hearing the funny, snarky, bitchy, and intelligent things that came out of her mouth when he got her going.

Was that something they could make a real relationship out of?

He didn't know. But he also couldn't imagine either of them in a relationship with someone else. He wasn't convinced any other woman could measure up to Kit in his mind. And he'd have to kill any man he knew was sleeping with Kit.

He would never forget seeing Matthew Fleming flirt with Kit in English class. It wasn't Matthew's flirting that made him want to punch the other guy in the face. It was the way Kit had watched Matthew leave afterward. The soft, dreamy smile on her face when Matthew wasn't looking. That was what had made Dillon ask Mrs. Shawnessy to put Dillon and Kit together for their final project. And why he'd kissed her that night.

Their relationship had never been soft and dreamy. He knew that kind. That's what he'd had with Abigail. Soft and dreamy was nice. Very nice. And sweet. Nothing about him and Kit together had ever been sweet or nice. It was spicy and exciting and difficult.

And he loved it. That was his kind of thing. He liked a challenge, he liked working hard for something, he liked having competition and coming out on top.

He and Kit together worked for him, dammit.

"You know I suck at this stuff," he said to Kit, referring to the emotional side of his care for Sarah.

"I do know," Kit agreed matter-of-factly. "But you have to stop sucking at it."

"I do?"

"You're a physician in a small town now, Dillon. You're not out in the jungle, and you're not knee-deep in mud, putting people back together with duct tape and chewing gum. You have to get better at this."

He couldn't help his grin. Duct tape and chewing gum? That wasn't *that* far from the truth, as a matter of fact. "Why don't you talk to her?" he asked. "This is your thing."

"I delivered her baby," Kit said, meeting his gaze directly. "Do I really have to do *everything*?"

God, he loved her sass. "I'm going to fuck it up if I talk to her."

"No, you won't, because I'll tell you what to say," Kit told him.

He lifted a brow. "You're going to coach me?"

"Yes."

He thought about that. It would work. It would be like making Alfredo sauce. And they'd rocked that. "Okay."

She looked mildly surprised for a moment, but then she nodded. "Have Janice call us back from Sarah's room."

Us. He liked that. And he wanted to tell her that. He wanted to tell her that he loved having her have his back and that he didn't want to do anything without her there ever. He wanted to brush his teeth with her, for fuck's sake. And he was at risk of becoming a sap. Because of Kit Derby. Who would have thought?

"Jan, call us back from Sarah's room. Kit and I have this."

"Will do."

He watched Kit as they waited for the phone to ring. She didn't watch him back. She turned the heat down low under both chili pots and took the ingredients for the cinnamon-roll icing out of the fridge and cupboards—and he was grateful that the powdered sugar was on a high shelf that required her to stretch and her shirt to pull up, exposing the smooth skin of her lower back. Where he wanted to lick her.

He felt like he should say something but was afraid it would be something like, *Let's do this forever.* And then she would probably ask, *What do you mean by* this? and he wouldn't know how to answer.

Make chili. Walk around the kitchen with almost nothing on. Or with nothing on. Help our patients together. Save the world. All of the above.

The phone rang, interrupting his thoughts. Maybe it was the scent of cinnamon and cumin getting to him.

"Hey," he answered.

"I have Sarah here," Jan said.

"Great, put her on."

A soft voice said, "Hello?" a second later.

"Hey, Sarah, it's Dillon Alexander."

"Hi, Dr. Alexander."

"So, how are you feeling now that some of the excitement has died down?" he asked, shooting Kit a look. She certainly hadn't hesitated to tell him how *she* felt after the adrenaline had worn off after the tornado. And the kissing.

Kit had moved closer again and was watching him now.

"The pain is a little better," Sarah told him.

Dillon nodded. "Glad to hear it."

"More," Kit mouthed to him.

Right. This call wasn't really about Sarah's physical pain. *"I'm getting there,"* he mouthed back.

Kit rolled her eyes.

"How far did your husband get before he had to stop for the night?" Dillon asked, easing into the conversation about Sarah's loneliness. At least, that's what he meant to do. But he heard a sniff on the other end of the line and knew he was not too far from the floodgates opening.

"He's in Des Moines."

Okay, yeah, that was still pretty far away. "Tomorrow will be better. The winds are supposed to die down, and they'll be able to get the roads open," Dillon said. That was what his weather app had said, anyway.

He watched as Kit bent and rummaged in a lower cupboard. And stupidly, he wished that he had a better angle to check out her stretchy pink pants in that position.

"I know," Sarah said in his ear, pulling him back to the conversation. Jesus, he was typically a pro at focus and concentration. Even with Kit around. Sure, it was easier when she *wasn't* around, but he'd learned early on that letting her distract him was a surefire way to lose. Usually to *her*.

Kit had pulled notebook and marker from that bottom cupboard and was writing furiously.

"What's your husband's name?" Dillon asked, hoping that wasn't a mistake somehow.

"Tim," she said, sniffing again.

"What's Tim do?"

"He's a high school principal in one of the suburbs outside of Chicago," Sarah told him.

"You're a long way from home. What are you doing in the middle of Nebraska?" Dillon asked as Kit held up the notebook.

But he'd barely read the words *She's going to feel guilty* when he heard an even louder sniff and then the distinct sound of a sob.

Shit.

"She's crying," he mouthed to Kit.

She shrugged as if she'd expected that. He widened his eyes and put out his hand, silently asking for more.

"It's okay for her to cry," Kit whispered.

He'd actually wanted Kit to come up with a way to *stop* the crying, but okay.

But he wasn't going to do this on his own. He hit the speakerphone button and set the phone on the counter between them.

Sarah spoke again. "I was in North Platt for my parents' wedding anniversary party. Tim asked me not to come home tonight. Actually, he asked me not to even go to the party. But I was supposed to have three weeks left."

She was crying harder now, and Dillon opened his mouth, but he felt a pinch on his arm. Kit was scowling at him and shook her head.

"What?" he mouthed.

Kit whispered, "Do *not* agree that she shouldn't have gone to the party."

Dillon rolled his eyes. How had she known he was about to say, "You can never count on babies doing what they're supposed to at this stage"?

Kit tore off the top page on the notepad and wrote, *Tell her no one blames her for what happened today.*

But Dillon kind of did. Sarah never should have gone on that trip by herself this far into her pregnancy. He knew he shouldn't say that and was glad that the phone kept Sarah from reading it on his face, but he frowned and shook his head at Kit.

Kit sighed and wrote again, *Then tell her that she can't focus on the things she should have done differently, only what she can do now.*

Dillon read the words off to Sarah. "Right now you just need to think about getting a lot of rest and relaxing and bonding with Caleb," he told her.

"Okay," Sarah said. "I just feel like I ruined it all."

He frowned. "You didn't ruin anything. Caleb is fine; you're fine."

"But my husband didn't get to be there for Caleb's birth," Sarah said. "I can never give that back to him."

"There are so many moments ahead, though. Lots of important times that he will be there for. This is just one," Dillon said.

Kit quickly scribbled something else and held it up. Dillon squinted at the page. *She needs to mourn what she lost.* She set the notebook down and wrote something else. *But you're right. That's good to focus on, too.*

Well, great, he'd gotten something right. But what had Sarah lost? He pointed to the words and shook his head to show he didn't understand.

Kit wrote again. *The birth experience that she'd been planning on. Ask her what it was supposed to be like.*

Dillon sighed. "Sarah, I know that today didn't turn out the way you expected," he said, keeping his eyes on Kit. She was watching the phone. "But things still turned out well, right? You're a new mom. Your son is here. Just think of all the wonderful things you get to look forward to."

Kit motioned with her hand to say, *Get on with it.*

Sarah sniffed. "Yeah, I guess they did."

"Tell me what you thought today would be like, how you pictured it," Dillon said.

Kit gave him a nod.

"I guess I pictured Tim and me driving to the hospital together and checking into a room and going through all the breathing and focusing exercises we'd learned. I had a book where I journaled about my pregnancy, and in there it had us do a birth plan."

Dillon could hear the thickness in her voice that said the tears weren't over. "What did you have on your birth plan?" He knew what a birth plan was, but he'd never used one with a patient. That was the ob-gyn's territory. If Dillon were delivering a baby, it was guaranteed that nothing was going according to anyone's plan.

"We were going to use our breathing techniques, but I was open to an epidural," she said. She went on to describe the clothes she'd planned to bring for the baby to go home in, the music CD they'd had packed in the bag, her favorite pillow, and the other things that would have helped her relax and feel more comfortable.

And all of that was sitting in a bag by the door in a house hundreds of miles from where she was now.

Dillon got it. Yes, she and the baby were fine, and that was good—of course she felt that way, too—but the fact that all of this was foreign and that she had nothing with her that would work to comfort her made a difference. Especially when she had fully expected to have those things. And her husband.

"I'm really sorry that it worked out this way," Dillon said.

He glanced at Kit and found her looking surprised but pleased. She gave him an encouraging smile. He felt a warmth in his chest and realized a second later that he was feeling satisfaction. For God's sake. He had medals and commendations and titles behind his name, but Kit Derby could *smile* at him and make him feel proud.

"Now what?" he mouthed to Kit.

"Keep talking," she said softly, moving around him to the phone on the wall.

"So tell me about deciding on Caleb's name," Dillon said to Sarah. But he was fully tuned in to Kit.

She dialed the phone, and a moment later he realized she was talking to someone at the hospital. "Rebecca, it's Dr. Derby. Can you go to my office and get my iPad out of my desk? I need you to hook it up to Skype and see if you can get Sarah's husband on it wherever he is. If we can get that all pulled up, then you can give Caleb a bath and weigh him and do a feeding all with Tim there. Also, pull up the songs on the latest Keith Urban album and then find them on YouTube. Oh, and see if Margie can find some of that vanilla-lavender lotion they had in the gift shop for a while."

Sarah was talking about her great-grandfather. That's all Dillon knew. He was far too distracted by Kit to hear anything more than that from the woman on the phone. Kit was . . . amazing.

The Keith Urban album was the CD Sarah had planned to bring to the hospital because Tim had proposed at a Keith concert. Skyping with Tim wasn't perfect, but it would include the new father in some of the firsts that were happening for Sarah and Caleb and was better than his missing it entirely. And the vanilla-lavender lotion would be soothing and might help Sarah sleep better once she wound down. Dillon would have given her a sleeping pill. Which, of course, he might still do. It would help, too. But still, Kit was trying to make Sarah's experience as close to what she'd imagined as they could. They couldn't do everything, but even the effort would touch Sarah.

At least, it was touching him.

"He's so upset."

Dillon realized that Sarah had moved on to talking about her husband.

"He's on the phone with the hospital every ten minutes; he's calling my mother every hour to give her an update. He's just so . . . upset," she said again.

"Sarah," Dillon said sincerely, "I'm going to tell you something about your husband. I don't know him, but guys like to take care of things. Until he's there and able to actually *do* stuff for you, he's going to try to do other things. Calling people and asking questions and giving reports makes him feel like he's making stuff happen."

Dillon noticed that Kit had stopped talking, and her eyes were now focused on him.

Sarah sniffed. "You think so?"

"I do," Dillon told her. "He wants to be your hero, the guy taking care of things, and being so far away and stuck has to be making him crazy. So when he gets there, he might really go over the top. Be patient with him. And don't worry about the staff—they'll be okay."

"Okay," Sarah said. "And you're right. He is that guy—the one who wants to take care of me. Us."

Dillon couldn't take his eyes off Kit. "I can relate," he told Sarah, feeling something strange in his chest. It felt like . . . *rightness*. It was the weirdest thing.

"Hey, Rebecca?" Kit said into the phone. "On second thought, would you call Sarah's husband and ask him what *he* wants to do? Make sure he knows Skype and everything else are options, but I'm sure he has some ideas about how to make this better for his wife. And for him. Just let him know that we're willing to do whatever we can to help."

"Next time you talk to him," Dillon said to Sarah, "tell him that he needs to talk to a girl named Rebecca. She can get anything done that Tim needs."

"Anything like what?"

"Whatever will make him feel like he's taking care of things for you and being involved."

"Oh, okay," Sarah said, her voice brighter now. "That will be nice. Maybe I'll mention to him that I'm craving ice cream. And then he can ask Rebecca to get me some?"

"That's perfect," Dillon agreed. "And hey, when he does get there, let him do some things for you, okay? Just for a little bit. Even if it's something you can do yourself or someone else has already done, let him do it. Let him bring you coffee or get you another pillow or grill the nurses or buy you balloons."

"Okay."

Dillon could swear he could hear Sarah smiling. "I'll be in to see you sometime tomorrow."

"Thanks, Dr. Alexander."

They disconnected at the same time Kit hung up with Rebecca.

They just stood looking at each other for several long seconds. Dillon crossed his arms and leaned against the counter behind him, waiting for her to speak.

But she was completely silent. Almost . . . speechless.

Dillon felt the corner of his mouth curl. Apparently, there was a first time for everything.

Finally, he asked, "What?"

"I just . . ."

He tipped his head. "What?"

"That was . . . great."

Yeah, it had been. There'd been something about that whole thing that had felt really . . . great.

"Was it?" he asked nonchalantly. But really wanting her to say it again.

"It really was."

"I just said what you told me to say."

"Not the whole time. That stuff about men needing to do things—that was really insightful."

Dillon chuckled softly. "I'm a man, Kit. I know a few things about how we think, at least."

"Is that how you feel? You want to take care of everyone and everything? You need things to *do*?"

"Of course."

She nodded. "And she's feeling helpless, too. But you gave her something to do for him, a way to feel like she was meeting *his* needs, something else to focus on than what *she* needs . . ."

Dillon wasn't sure he was totally following that, but he realized she was complimenting him.

Kit took a breath. "That was all really . . ."

"Great?" he offered with a grin.

"Yeah." She shrugged. "Really great."

Dillon wasn't used to Kit being anything less than eloquent, and long-winded, when she was talking about his virtues—or the lack thereof. But frankly, he'd take a *great* from her.

"You know that without you I would have just told her that she was doing *great*," he said, loving that Kit smiled at that, too. "And that would have been the end of that."

"Maybe. But sometimes it's not the words, it's the tone and who is saying it."

"And I did okay."

"You really did. You have a great voice. On the phone, you're very soothing and calming and—"

She stopped, and Dillon *had* to know what she'd been about to say. "Kit." He said her name low and slow, and he watched her take a deep, maybe a little shaky, breath.

"Sexy."

He felt his eyes widen. "Sexy?"

"Your voice is very sexy."

"And you think that mattered to Sarah?"

"I don't know. But it's deep and husky when you're being sweet, and that was probably very reassuring to her."

"It's deep and husky when I'm being sweet?" He smiled widely. Yeah, he really liked this conversation.

She sighed, the note of exasperation clear. "Yes. And other times."

With that, he reached for her. He couldn't have stopped himself for anything. He took the hem of her shirt between his thumb and forefinger and tugged. She took a step forward. "Come here and tell me all about the other times."

She didn't fight him. She took another step closer. "We were a really good team just now."

"We were."

"That was . . . nice."

Ah, *great* and *nice*. Kit was clearly out of her element at the moment. He liked that idea more than he should.

"It always is." He said it with complete sincerity.

"And you doing that—talking her through that even though you didn't really want to, that was . . ."

"Say it, Kit," he urged, purposefully making his voice even lower.

She sighed, clearly annoyed with what she was about to admit. "Great. And sexy."

"I'm suddenly even more motivated to work on my bedside manner."

She rolled her eyes, but she didn't try to move back. "You don't care what I think."

Dillon knew his expression was completely serious when he said, "Oh, honey, that's not true at all."

She swallowed hard. "You shouldn't care what I think."

"I've been caring for far too long to stop now."

Again, Kit just stood looking at him without saying anything. And Dillon became *acutely* aware of the lack of clothing between them. In fact, he was about five seconds away from her being very aware of that as well. He didn't mind her knowing that she affected him. She knew. Very well. It was partly that damned body spray and lotion she wore. It was like catnip to a cat. He wanted to inhale it and roll around in it and just go crazy when he got a whiff.

"Kit—"

But he didn't have a chance to finish that thought—whatever it was—because Kit rose on tiptoe and put her lips to his.

CHAPTER FIVE

There was absolutely nothing in the world that could override Dillon's instincts once he and Kit were mouth to mouth. The desire to possess her superseded everything else. Like common sense. Like every other time.

He put both hands on her ass and pulled her up against him. Not that there was a long way to go. She had already wrapped her arms around his neck and was arching into him, trying to get closer.

Dillon made a note to work diligently on his bedside manner. It was good for his patients, of course, but *damn*, it was more than good to have Kit up against him again.

And then he stopped making notes about anything but the way to get Kit to arch and moan and tighten her grip and open her mouth. She did all those things as he licked along her bottom lip and then sucked the tender flesh into his mouth. Her moan fired every nerve ending in his body. And they all had one message—*take her*.

Dillon turned her and backed her into the counter. The firm surface behind her butt made it so much easier to press right where he needed to be. Kit's body had always seemed made for his. She was the perfect height to fit against his frame. Her curves filled his palms perfectly. She responded to every touch of his hands and lips like he had the only key to her locks. And he fucking loved it. He loved her taste, her smell, the sounds she made, the desperate way she gripped his shoulders, the way she ground against him as if she *needed* him. That's what he loved most. Kit needing him.

And he was more than fine with her needing his help with a post-delivery mom and baby by the side of a snowy road, with her needing him to take her on his snowmobile to her grandmother's house, with her needing him to tromp out to the barn or kick down a door. But at this moment, he was *driven* by her needing him to press and lick and stroke her body until she came apart.

Kit was always wound a little tight, but there were times when she was practically vibrating with everything she tried to do and take on. And, in his very informed medical opinion, there was nothing better for tension like that than a good, hard orgasm. Or three.

He lifted her to the countertop and stepped between her knees. He loved these thin cotton pants. As he stroked his hands from her hips to her knees and back up, sliding under the hem of the shirt to the silky skin of her back, he felt the heat pouring off her, surrounding him and sucking him in.

"Damn, you feel amazing," he told her gruffly, his lips against her neck.

"Keep going," was her only response.

Dillon knew that she was caught up in the maelstrom of the chemistry that combusted whenever they touched, and he was more than willing to ride it to the end. He ran his hands up and down her back. On the third pass, he unhooked her bra and slid his hands under the straps and around to the front to cup her bare breasts.

She sucked in a quick breath, then arched closer. He thumbed her nipples, knowing from experience that he could get her very close to the edge just hanging out right there. Her high-strung tendencies seemed to carry over into sex. Kit went from zero to wound-up-turned-on-let's-go in minutes. He had never been with a woman who could climax as quickly as Kit did. She knew her body, she knew what she liked, and she was an overachiever. That meant hard, fast, amazing orgasms that made a man feel like a king.

Of course, Dillon liked to think that he was the only one she was quite as *successful* with, but he also had no doubt that, like everything else in her life, Kit got exactly what she wanted out of her sexual relationships.

As if to prove his point, she reached down and pulled her shirt up. He leaned back to let her whip it off over her head, tossing her bra along with it a second later. Then she lifted his hands back to her breasts.

Dillon loved to argue with Kit, but there was no way he was going to balk at this suggestion. With the bright kitchen lights above, Dillon teased and tugged until she was panting, then he bent his knees and put his mouth to a nipple.

"Yes," she encouraged simply.

Always a guy to respond well to praise, Dillon licked and sucked, perfectly content to stay right there for the next hour or so. But Kit was soon squirming on the counter. He lifted his head and saw that she was working her pants down.

She looked up at him. He lifted an eyebrow. "Don't stop on my account."

"Wanna give me a couple inches?" she asked, pushing him back with a foot so she could slide her pants down.

"Oh baby, I've got more than a couple for you," he said, unable to resist the juvenile quip.

She rolled her eyes but snorted. "I certainly hope so."

"Like you don't remember."

"It's been a while."

She kicked the pants to the floor, and Dillon assumed either she'd taken her panties down at the same time or hadn't been wearing any. But he couldn't look away from her to take clothing inventory. Because she was now naked on the counter. He wasn't sure he'd look away from a naked Kit Derby for *anything*.

"It hasn't been that long." He certainly hadn't forgotten one damned thing about being with her. The way she looked, and moved, and drove him absolutely fucking wild by refusing to say anything dirty until he'd teased her to the point of begging. He reached for her, fully ready to start the get-her-begging process right that instant.

"Take this dumb thing off," she told him as he stepped closer, and she tugged on the sleeve of his robe.

He shrugged out of the robe, letting it fall to the floor.

Kit's eyes raked over him, her breathing getting faster and her throat flushing. Kit was cool and composed almost all the time. And she pulled off *seeming* cool and composed even when she wasn't. But her body betrayed her when Dillon was around.

"Come here," she said softly.

He stepped closer, and she ran her hands up over his chest to his shoulders.

"You knew this was going to happen," he said.

Kit always tried to rush right to the main event and hated when he made her talk when they had sex. Which he found incredibly ironic. She was the talker. Talking about personal thoughts and feelings was what people paid her for. Hell, she got on his case about not talking enough with patients. And she'd been incredibly bossy the first time they'd had sex. She'd known exactly what she wanted and how to get it. But the times they'd been together since then, she tried to distract him, and she kept her mouth busy doing other things. As much as he'd loved all of that, he'd been very interested in the fact that she wasn't as verbal. He'd wanted more of that, he wanted to tell her everything that was turning him on, wanted to hear every one of the dirty fantasies she had, how she was feeling, what she wanted him to do and how she wanted him to do it. In detail. And that was when she wanted to stick with the action only. But he never let her get away with keeping quiet. And it pissed her off.

Which made the sex even better.

He knew he shouldn't think that. Or like it. But damn, he did. Because it was about 60 percent bullshit. Just like the other stuff they fought about and over.

Dillon cared how Kit felt about him, and she cared how he felt about her, so . . . they fought. It was just easier than labeling those intense emotions any other way.

He lifted a hand to her breast, rubbing his thumb over the tip, not quite giving her exactly what she liked. "You knew, didn't you, Kit?" he asked.

"Why do you always have to run your mouth when we do this?" She dropped her hands to his cock, wrapping her fingers around his length and stroking.

Dillon's eyes nearly crossed, and she succeeded in derailing every thought from his mind but *thrust, hard, now* for the moment. He pressed into her grip and didn't even mind the smug smile that flitted across her sweet lips. But that smile combined with the intense pleasure coming from her fingers around his cock made him squeeze her nipple harder, and she moaned.

This was what he missed with other women. The crazy-sweet-kinda-stupid-super-hot back and forth with him and Kit. The way they jostled for the upper hand—sometimes literally. The way they gave as good as they got, and then some. Kit didn't just meet him partway on things. She had to outdo him. And that made for some freaking amazing sex.

He pinched her nipple and got a delicious squeeze around his cock.

"Damn, Dillon," she breathed.

Oh yeah, that was a good start with the talking. But not nearly enough.

"Tell me you knew this was how it was going to end up," he said, pinching, then letting go and dropping his hand to stroke her hip softly.

She tightened her grip on his cock, and Dillon locked his knees so he wouldn't go down. "Let's just fuck," she said. "We don't need to discuss every little detail."

Ah, she'd said his favorite word. She knew he loved it when she said *fuck*. She was playing dirty.

Just the way he liked it.

He leaned over and sucked her nipple into his mouth. Then let go just as she started to squirm. He blew on the tip, and she moaned. He put his mouth to her ear. "You might know all of my buttons, but remember, Katherine Marie Derby, I know yours, too." He ran a hand up her thigh, brushing over her clit very lightly. Too lightly. Way too lightly. "And I might be the only person who likes to win as much as you do."

And the battle was on.

Kit turned her head and captured his lips as she stroked up and down his shaft, squeezing perfectly, using exactly the amount of pressure to make lightning streak up his spine.

Oh yeah, she knew his buttons, all right.

But Kit was going to be the one begging *him* tonight. Over and over.

"Dillon," Kit gasped. "I need you."

She also knew how much he loved when she seemed to turn everything over to him. But he wasn't buying it. Yet. Her surrender was always sweet, but it was hard-earned.

"Oh, honey, you know better than to rush me," he chided, running his hand up her inner thigh.

The faster and harder she wanted it, the more he drew things out. Which made her lose her mind. In the best possible way.

◆ ◆ ◆

"Come on, Dillon," Kit groaned. "Let's just do this."

"We're going to *do* this," he told her gruffly. "But this is the first time we haven't had a deadline, the risk of people walking in on us, or a reason to get to bed—to sleep—early. Don't you think for one second that I'm not going to take advantage of all that."

Kit sighed. It was amazing to her that she could be so exasperated with a guy while holding his cock in her hands.

But she was. Because it was Dillon.

The man loved to play with her. And it definitely got physical sometimes. The sex had happened only a few times. But there had been an obstacle course in sixth grade that had scarred her—literally. She had a thin moon-shaped scar on her left knee from where she'd fallen on the gravel. There had been the decorating committee for Homecoming their freshman year that had scarred Dillon. Also, literally. The scar on his left elbow was wider and longer than hers, but she didn't think he counted that as a win. That thing had bled like crazy after he'd fallen off the ladder and caught it on a screw on his way down.

But yeah, whether it was streamers or neuroanatomy or sex, Dillon loved to mess with her, to get her to the edge of her control, and then soak it in when she lost it.

Of course, deep down, when it came to losing it during sex, she didn't exactly *mind*.

In fact, it wasn't even that deep down.

But she hated that he knew that he was the best she'd ever had.

And it made her all the more determined to be the best *he'd* ever had.

Dillon loved to be in charge. But even more, he liked *winning*. If he won control, wore someone down, made it so she had no choice but to submit, *that* was his lose-it point. Especially when it was her.

Dillon was a lot of things, but hard to figure out was not one of them.

"So you're not taking your time here because it's gotten more difficult to go hard and fast?" she asked, stroking up and down the silky, hot column of steel that she was afraid she might start drooling over if she wasn't careful. God, the guy was built. It was so unfair.

He paused, as she'd known he would. She liked that she could mess with him a little, too, but he'd also stopped playing with her nipple, which was a very unfortunate side effect.

"And why would it be more difficult?" he asked.

"I heard about the back injury. The crazy guy in the ER in Houston about nine months ago? Thought you were his dead brother come back to life to torture him for sleeping with his brother's wife. Your wife, I guess."

The guy had been, apparently, about three hundred pounds, several inches over six feet, on drugs, and super pissed off. He'd picked up Dillon and thrown him across the room. Kit remembered being horrified and worried sick when she'd heard about it. But, in true Dillon Alexander style, he'd ended up with a concussion and a five-day paid vacation from work.

And his back was fine.

"I'm fine," Dillon said, one eyebrow arched.

Yeah, he was. She'd seen him lifting and bending and throwing things around during the town cleanup after the tornado. She'd seen him restrain someone who outweighed him by at least forty pounds in the Chance ER about a month ago. And he'd played softball all fall with the other guys in the town league. Plus, he'd had absolutely no trouble getting and sustaining an erection. No worry about nerve damage or anything there.

Then, as if to prove his point, he scooped her up and turned, taking the five steps to the kitchen table. And Kit couldn't help that it made her totally hot. Like kicking-down-a-door-and-throwing-her-over-his-shoulder hot.

"Does this feel like I'm having a difficult time?" he asked, thrusting into her grip as he set her down.

It felt like exactly what she wanted him doing to her, right now. She ran her hand down his length again, and then lower still.

Dillon let out a long hiss. "You're trying to distract me."

"Uh . . . duh."

Dillon stopped again, meeting her gaze, his mouth curling in a way that—though she'd never admit it, of course—made her melt a little.

"Dr. Katherine Derby, did you just say 'duh' to me?"

"Yeah, so?"

"And now we're to 'Yeah, so?'"

She stroked him again. "Yeah. So?"

"So maybe, just for that, I'm going to give you something you want sooner versus later."

"Oh?" That was intriguing. She had a list of wants, as a matter of fact. "Maybe I—"

But suddenly she found herself on her back on the tabletop. Dillon had hooked his big hands under her thighs and flipped her backward.

"What are you—"

But that was a dumb question. That he answered without saying a word a second later. Her thighs still in his hands, he opened her legs wide and set about making her *just about* cry uncle.

Dillon's good-at-everything absolutely included the things he was doing with his lips and tongue and fingers between her legs.

Kit gripped the edge of the table with her fingers, certain her knuckles were white as she held on. Her neck arched, her eyes closed, and without thinking, she said, "What did I do to deserve this?"

Of course to answer, he had to put his tongue back in his mouth for a bit. Another one of those unfortunate side effects. But it also proved her point that there were better things he could be doing with his mouth than *talking* when they had sex.

Because when Dillon talked—in that low, husky voice that made her want to climb him like a tree—it made her never want to have clothes on or leave his bed ever again in her life.

He was sweet and sexy and dirty, complimentary and teasing, exasperating and funny, all at the same time. And when he was talking during sex, Kit had a hard time remembering that falling for him was a really bad idea.

"You were cute," he told her.

Kit thought about those three words far longer than she should have needed to. She finally lifted her head. "What?"

"That whole 'duh' thing was cute," he said with a shrug.

"Cute?"

He nodded. "I know. I was as surprised as you are. But damn, Kit, when you're cute, I can't resist you."

Oh, crap. That seemed way too similar to the thoughts she'd just been having. Not resisting each other was not a good idea.

"Dillon—"

"Stop thinking so hard," he told her. "There's nothing to be concerned about here. You're not cute very often."

"Oh." That was true. *Cute* was definitely not a usual state for her. She swallowed. "But you're going to keep going down there, right?" she asked.

He gave her a grin that made her regret everything.

And then he lowered his head, and she went right back to thinking he was pretty damned amazing.

And if that didn't sum up her relationship with Dillon, she didn't know what did.

It didn't take long before she was gasping his name, on the verge of a delicious, long-overdue orgasm. She pulled against the edge of the table, pressing more firmly against his mouth. "*Yes. Please*, Dillon."

He gripped her butt tighter with one hand, while the other helped out his tongue, and less than a minute later, she shot over the top of the orgasm rainbow—colors and light and glitter, she could have sworn it, floated around her, and everything was happiness and sunshine.

Damn, the guy was good.

She felt him shift back and heard the distinct sound of a condom package tearing. She forced her eyes open, instantly mourning the swirling ribbons of color that disappeared in the full light of her grandmother's kitchen.

Where she'd just had sex. On the table. Where they ate brunch every other Sunday.

"Oh my God!"

Kit started to sit up, but there was a big, turned-on, determined doctor between her legs.

"Dammit, you already started your list?" he asked.

She had only gotten as far as propping up on her elbows. He was in the way of her sitting up fully. She was in a very exposed and vulnerable position.

But she didn't feel exposed and vulnerable.

She felt strangely at ease. And . . . horny. Still. On her grandmother's table.

She frowned. "What list?"

"The list of all the reasons this was a terrible idea. You always start that list about five seconds after an orgasm."

She couldn't deny it. "Yeah."

"And *this* is why I don't let you come like that before *I'm* a lot more involved."

"You don't *let* me come?" she asked.

He nodded, as if that were obvious. "It's why I've never given you an orgasm like that before," he said.

"You *gave* me that orgasm?" Kit asked. But yeah, he had. "You sure? You sure I didn't *take* it? That I didn't just use your tongue because it was the closest one that could reach that spot?"

He stood looking at her, a bemused expression on his face. "So I was the closest tongue? Really? That's what you're going with here? That any old tongue would have done?"

Kit squelched the feeling that it sounded ridiculous when he said it like that. "Yes," she said, completely confident. Or faking it like crazy, anyway. "You were here."

"Uh-huh. You do remember the part about me flipping you on your back, spreading your legs, and completely worshipping your pussy, right?"

Okay, *that* should not have caused a rush of heat to rip through her and settle low and deep between her legs.

But it so did.

She cleared her throat, then hated that she'd cleared her throat. "I . . . remember."

"That I started that?" he pressed. "That you didn't ask me to do it. Or trick me into doing it. Or . . ." He narrowed his eyes. "Wait. Did you trick me into doing that?"

Lord, she really loved when he was a smart-ass like this. Because Dillon was often sarcastic, but not necessarily playful, as he was being now. "What are you talking about?"

"Have you harnessed your cuteness?" he asked. "Have you realized how powerful it is and learned to turn it on and off as needed to get what you want?"

She wanted to laugh. No way had she harnessed her "cuteness." There wasn't much there to start with, for one thing. And she didn't emotionally manipulate people. Not even Dillon.

But she lifted her chin instead of grinning. "Yes. I've been in control since you broke down that door and carried me inside." He'd know she was lying, but no way was she going to admit that she had been, quite simply, overcome by him.

"Ah, you got me to knock the door down, too," he said, nodding as if it was all becoming clear now. "That does make more sense. That was pretty unusual for me."

Maybe. But the I'll-take-care-of-everything, nothing-fazes-me thing was not unusual. Her eyes traveled over his naked body. How had she forgotten he was completely buck naked and in the perfect position to make her all kinds of happy? Oh yeah, they were *talking*. And as much as she really did like his body, she liked his mouth more. In a nonsexual, he's-very-funny-and-sweet-sometimes way. Her gaze focused on that mouth again. Well, *mostly* in a nonsexual way.

"Dillon," Kit said, lacing exasperation into her voice, "I cannot believe that I'm lying here, completely naked, and you're standing there, also completely naked, and you're *still talking*."

His eyes tracked over her. Slowly. "Your list isn't so long that you're ready to get dressed, then?" he asked.

She did make a list of reasons not to have sex with him ever again whenever they found themselves naked together. He knew it because she'd recited the list to him as she'd dressed the last two times.

But the main thing on that list was that they didn't like each other. Which was one of the biggest lies she'd ever told. Of course, he knew that. But he never corrected her. It was almost like he was making a bigger point by not even arguing with her about it.

The second thing on the list was that they lived almost a thousand miles apart. And that was no longer an issue.

After that, her reasoning got a little fuzzy.

"My list of reasons why this is a bad idea only has one main thing on it today," Kit told him.

Dillon lifted an eyebrow.

"You take too damned long." She reached for him and pulled him in, wrapping her legs around his waist.

Dillon gripped her hips and thrust into her without another word.

Kit sighed as a combination of heaven and hell rippled through her. She lay back, closed her eyes, and waited for the magic.

But nothing happened.

She cracked one eyelid. "You okay, Dr. Alexander?"

He was, quite clearly, gritting his teeth. But he shook his head. He unlocked his jaw and said, "You know what I want to hear."

Ugh. She really needed to stop having sex with this guy. He wanted her to talk dirty. He always wanted that. *Made* her do it. He loved to hear it. Just like she loved when he got flirtatious, he loved when she got naughty.

Dillon was the only guy she felt comfortable saying dirty things to. She had stubbornly refused to analyze that for several years now.

"You really think that you can just sit there all night waiting?" she asked. She tightened her inner muscles around his cock and felt his groan all the way to her bones.

"I think I can hold out longer than you can," he said, his voice husky.

She actually laughed at that. Which tightened those muscles again and got another groan out of him. "You think that you can stay right there"—she flexed again—"doing nothing until I say all those dirty words you like so much?" Usually he got her talking naughty long before he got inside her.

"Yep."

Then the bastard reached between them and circled one finger around her clit.

Kit bit back her own moan. Yeah, this game of chicken was *on*.

She lifted her hand and circled her own nipple with a finger, her eyes on his face. She saw his eyes darken, and she rolled the nipple between her thumb and finger. He pulled out slightly, then eased back in. She felt the pleasure shoot through her, and her toes actually curled a bit.

But then he stopped again.

She tightened around him and felt his fingers dig into her hips slightly, but that was the only reaction. She narrowed her eyes, then licked her finger before returning to her nipple.

He cleared his throat, his eyes locked on what she was doing, but his hips remained motionless. So she reached down and knocked his hand out of the way, replacing his finger with her own on her clit.

She circled and pressed, moaning from the pleasure but also to drive home the point that *she* was going to be fine here, with or without him.

He had to have felt her muscles pulsing around him as the sensations built.

"Dammit, woman, just say it," he ground out.

"You mean beg you?" she asked in a sweet tone she knew would make him crazy.

"Yes."

She circled faster, squeezing her nipple and wiggling against him. With him filling her up and watching her touch herself, Kit suddenly realized that she really didn't need him to do anything more. She could take control of this situation and make it turn out perfectly. She was going to win this round—

Just like before, his sudden movement surprised her enough that she didn't register what he was doing until he'd done it.

He'd scooped her up and then pivoted to sit in the kitchen chair at the head of the table. Now she sat in his lap, straddling his thighs, and, oh baby, he was as deep as he could go now.

In this position, he could grip her hips and take a nipple in his mouth—which he did, sucking hard and then biting gently.

Kit gasped, completely forgetting about doing anything to herself. She wanted Dillon to do it. All of it. Now.

"If you're not going to ask me to fuck you," he said gruffly against her breast, "how about *you* fuck *me*?"

There was no way he didn't feel how that affected her.

The wave of heat and lust made Kit feel like she was melting into him, and she wanted nothing more than to *move*. She needed friction and pressure, and she quite frankly didn't care at all who had the upper hand here.

Kit could just get the balls of her feet on the floor, but Dillon seemed happy to help move her up and down on his lap. He clasped her hips in his big hands, helping lift and lower her, while grinding against her on each thrust. The deep penetration combined with the way her breasts rubbed against his chest, his hands on her, his hot breath against her neck and, yeah, okay, the gruff "Fuck yeah, Kit" and "That's it, honey" and "God almighty, I love fucking you" definitely worked. Kit felt her climax bearing down, and she picked up the pace. She liked it hard and fast, and she was supposedly in charge here this time. She wasn't going to make this some long, drawn-out, leisurely stroll toward pleasure. She was going at it full tilt.

She wrapped her arms around Dillon's neck, put her mouth to his, and kissed him, their tongues stroking like their bodies were, and within minutes those ribbons of color and glitter started floating around her. She moved against him faster, and the colors intensified, and a moment later her world exploded in glitter and happiness and a soul-deep *Oh yeah*.

Kit sagged against Dillon and delighted in the feel of him taking over completely, thrusting up into her, pressing her down against him as he thundered toward his climax as well. When he shouted out her name, Kit felt the heat and pleasure that had started to die away pulse to life again, and she hugged his neck tightly.

They stayed like that—Dillon's hands splayed over her back, holding her against his chest, while she clung to him, waiting for everything to fade back to normal.

Eventually, she loosened her hold on him. In this position, he was still deep in her, and she couldn't help but shift on his lap just a little as she eased back.

He cocked an eyebrow. "Watch the wiggle. Unless you'd like to find yourself on your back on that table again."

She would love that, in fact. "You're a sore loser, you know that?"

He squeezed her butt. "If this is what losing feels like, I need to rethink my stance against it."

"You didn't get what you wanted, though," she said, making herself move back and get off his lap.

She missed it within three seconds of standing up.

"I got exactly what I wanted, Kit," Dillon said. He also stretched to his feet and headed for the bathroom just off the kitchen.

Uh-huh, of course he wouldn't admit that she'd gotten *her* way. She pulled her clothes back on, her skin still tingling from having Dillon's hands all over her.

Well, at least they'd gotten the sex over with and out of the way. Now she could compile her list of why that shouldn't happen again for a few years, and they could get through the storm and then get the hell out of this close proximity that was too damned tempting and stupid-inducing.

But she only got to number two on her list—if she couldn't get a grip on her emotions, how could she expect to counsel others about getting their own grips, which came right after number one: every time she had sex with Dillon she fell for him a little further—when he came out of the bathroom, cleaned up and with that stupid robe on again. It really did very little to cover up that big, magnificent body that did such magnificent things to *her* body.

"So, let's hear 'em," he said.

"Hear what?"

"Your reasons that you're going to give me for remaining fully clothed for the rest of the night."

She could *not* tell him the two reasons she'd just come up with.

And then the lights went off.

Kit looked up and sighed. The power had just gone out. Saved by the storm? "Because we're going to get *very* cold without clothes on."

He chuckled. "The last thing I feel when you don't have clothes on is cold, Kit."

She was grateful she knew the room so well. She moved toward the stove where the two pots of chili were—had been—simmering. "We should eat before this stuff gets cold," she said, ignoring the naked comment.

Because . . . yeah. That would be one way to keep warm tonight. But there was also a fireplace in the living room, and that was a lot less dangerous.

She rummaged in the drawer just to the right of the stove and found two flashlights. She turned one on and set the other on the counter for Dillon.

"We should take all of this into the living room," she said. "We can get a fire going. And we should put on a few more layers." She shot him a look. "Seriously."

"You're right. Don't want to risk frostbite on anything important."

She reached for bowls. "Isn't everything pretty important when it comes to frostbite?" She dished her chili into a bowl and then Dillon's into another.

The flashlight lit the room enough for her to see him, but she knew she would have felt him moving toward her even without the light.

"You're right. I want to be sure we're keeping everything nice and warm on both of us."

She thrust the bowl of chili and a spoon at him as he got close. She needed some space. She knew who she was—who she wanted to be—but Dillon had a way of breaking down those walls. He shook her composure; he made her question herself. That wasn't always bad. She had a tendency to be a know-it-all, and he kept her ego in check. Even if it hurt sometimes. But he also had a way of making her feel . . . weak. He could get her to do and say things that she never would otherwise. She became a sassy bitch when he needled her. And she became a quivering mass of needy nerve endings that craved his touch like a . . . She didn't even know. She just lost herself a little bit when she was with him.

She understood emotions from a very analytical point of view. She knew what lust and love and infatuation could do to a person, and that a lot of it was a true chemical reaction in the brain. But she also knew she did *not* like having that reaction herself. She liked control, she liked knowing herself, and she did not like the idea of being "crazy" over someone or being uninhibited.

"You should eat," she said, trying to cover the panic that could very possibly be showing in her eyes. She was glad for the dim lighting.

He took the bowl with a knowing look that she hated. After they'd had sex in the past, she'd left. She'd been able to leave. Now she was stuck, and that meant facing the fact that she wanted him again. Already. And she was very afraid that was never going to go away.

"I'm going to put more clothes on." Kit set her bowl down with a clatter on the countertop.

"To stay warm, right?" Dillon asked, taking a bite of his chili, watching her closely. Kind of like a wildcat watched its prey.

Kit shook that off. She was projecting. She felt like prey—trapped with no escape—but that didn't mean Dillon had malicious intentions. But as she moved past him, he caught her upper arm, pulled her around, and kissed her. Deep and hot and sweet.

When he let her go, grinned, and then took a bite of chili as if he hadn't just rocked her world, Kit realized that he had *very* malicious intentions. *Wicked* was, after all, a synonym for *malicious*.

CHAPTER SIX

Dillon watched Kit disappear into the bedroom. To put more clothes on.

Well, that was fine. For now. But she was running. She always ran. In the past, he'd had to deal with it. She wasn't *wrong* when she said a relationship between them was complicated. But those complications were over now. They lived in the same town, they were here working together, and, no matter what she said, they did like each other. A lot.

Having a long-term relationship with Kit wouldn't be easy. *She* wasn't easy. She was demanding and opinionated and proud and strong.

And he wouldn't have her any other way.

And she couldn't run this time. Not very far, at least.

He ate his chili without tasting it. Then he tried hers. It was amazing. Of course. He had yet, in all the years of knowing her and competing against her, to find something Kit Derby wasn't amazing at.

Except admitting her own feelings, of course. Which was ironic, considering her profession was to make people—okay, help people—admit their feelings.

He grabbed a beer from Grace's fridge and finished off the second bowl of chili, too. And realized Kit was stalling. Or planned to stay in that bedroom all night. Which was fine with him. Kit and bedrooms were a fantastic combination. But he would be on the other side of that door if that were the case. Or maybe she'd fallen asleep because he'd worn her out.

Dillon's body pulsed with need as he thought about their physical activity. Damn, that woman did things to him.

And she *was* going to talk dirty for him before this night was over.

Dillon rinsed the bowls by the light of the flashlight, and then his patience was officially used up. He stalked to the bedroom door and turned the knob.

Kit wasn't asleep. But she was in bed, under the covers. And reading a book by flashlight.

And the emotion that slammed into him at the sight of her like that wasn't frustration or desire. It was, *Holy shit I want that.* Not sexual want but deeper, every-night-forever want. He wanted Kit propped up in bed reading a book when he came through the door every single night.

Dillon gripped the doorknob tightly and took a deep breath. "Seriously?" he finally said.

She looked up. "What?"

What? Really? "You didn't eat," he pointed out.

"I realized I wasn't really hungry."

Uh-huh. She'd been hungry when she'd been spread out on the table and riding him in the kitchen chair.

And like that, the lust was back twofold. Dillon shifted. "Thought we were going to get the fireplace going."

"It's pretty warm in here under the blankets."

"Is it now." It wasn't an invitation, but he didn't care. He strolled to the side of the bed and reached for the covers.

"You need more clothes on," she said, lifting an arm and pointing to the closet.

That was when Dillon realized that she was wearing gloves, and her arm was covered in a thick, bulky long sleeve. She had a hoodie zipped up to her chin, a stocking cap on her head, and a scarf around her neck.

It astonished him to realize that when he'd come through the bedroom doorway, those details hadn't registered. It had been the overall picture and the way his mind had transposed the sight onto an image of his own bedroom. She'd been in his bed, propped up against his headboard. And she'd been wearing a skimpy silk nightgown.

He was either drunk from that one beer in Grace's fridge, so overcome with lust for this woman that he couldn't see straight, or he was losing his mind.

Or maybe he just wanted all of that—her in his bed all the time, not just for quickie sex here and there—that his imagination was four steps ahead of reality. Or forty hundred steps.

There was a ways to go before Kit would be up against his headboard for reasons other than him tying her there with silk ties . . .

Dillon reined in *that* part of his imagination, too. Holy hell, he was in trouble if he couldn't even make it through a normal conversation without imagining tying her up for sex. Or marrying her.

He cleared his throat. "More clothes." Maybe that was a good idea. Maybe the sex had, literally, blown his mind. He needed to get a grip. He crossed to the closet. "You think there's stuff for me in here?"

"There's some stuff of my grandpa's on the left side," she said.

Dillon glanced over at her. "Really? He's been gone a long time, hasn't he?"

She laid down her book. "Yeah. Fifteen years."

"Wow."

"She said she's never going to be over him. They moved everything into this house together, including the clothes, and she said if he can't help her move it out, it's not leaving."

Dillon felt a pang in his chest. Wow.

"You think it's okay if I wear some of it?" He didn't really remember Kit's grandpa. He had no idea how big of a man he'd been.

"As long as you don't leave with it on," she said.

He looked over to find her watching him, a soft smile on her lips. He wondered if she even knew she was smiling. He liked it. He liked all of this. Him riffling through the closet for clothes while she watched him. As if they'd done it a million times before. It was so . . . domestic. And weird.

He turned back to the closet. Now that the power had been off for a while, the north wind against the old house with probably less-than-adequate insulation was cooling the house off quickly. "We really should go out into the living room." For one thing, her in this bedroom was messing with more than his libido, and that was concerning him slightly. Not greatly but slightly. And not because he was allergic to the idea of domesticity or settling down and having someone in his bed reading every night before she went to sleep. But because he wanted it to be Kit. That seemed as clear as anything had ever been. And it had taken only a blizzard to make him see it. Okay, a tornado and a blizzard. Thank God he'd figured it out before they had a major flood or something.

But he had a feeling that convincing Kit of that was going to be tough.

"I'm good right here," she said from the bed.

He sighed. Because everything with Kit was tough. It was like she was programmed to give him a hard time. Unless he was touching her bare skin. She'd argue the color of the sky with him. Unless he was kissing her neck.

He studied his selection of male clothing. Apparently George had really liked suits. "Was your grandpa a banker or something?" he asked.

"Insurance."

"Ah." Finally, he pulled a pair of sweatpants and a white dress shirt off their hangers, plus a red sweater from the upper shelf, and grabbed a suit jacket. Hey, it wasn't about fashion. It was about layers. And not freezing to death.

He shrugged out of the robe that was definitely no barrier to the draft in the room as he turned to face Kit.

She didn't say anything, and she certainly didn't avert her eyes.

He started pulling the clothes on. "I'm afraid I'm going to have to insist on you coming out to the living room where the fireplace is."

She lifted an eyebrow. "You're going to have to *insist*?"

"In other words, I'll carry your pretty ass out there if I have to. And hold you down if you try to leave." His body stirred at the idea. "Now that I think about it, please make me carry you out there and hold you down."

Kit opened her mouth to respond, then snapped it shut. She threw the covers back and got out of the bed.

So she did know when not to push him. Interesting.

She came around the end of the bed, and he got a good look at her. She had to have been wearing two pairs of sweatpants, at least. She also clearly had on a few pairs of socks, a sweatshirt under her sweatshirt, and . . . dammit, she looked cute.

"You're doing it again," he told her as he pulled on the suit jacket. Her grandfather had been a little smaller than Dillon but not much, and he was grateful the layers were going to work.

"Doing what?" She stopped and looked up at him.

"The cute thing again."

She looked genuinely puzzled by that. "What'd I do?"

He moved closer. "Why? So you can keep doing it or so you can stop? Because you remember what happened last time." Her cheeks went instantly pink.

"So I can stop," she finally said.

But it seemed that she'd had to think about that. "Hmm," he said. "Well, I'm not sure you can stop doing something you're unintentionally doing in the first place." That was the key, Dillon realized. She was cute because her defenses were down. They'd never spent time together that felt so . . . normal. And she couldn't keep her walls up around him indefinitely. Not when they were stuck together, and she was out of her element—like the hospital or running city committees or just generally kicking ass—she had to let them down, and then she was definitely cute.

"What's cute about this?" she asked, looking down at her crazy outfit.

He reached up and tugged on the edge of the stocking hat. "You're sexy as hell in your skirts and heels. You're kick-ass in jeans and T-shirts and work boots. But in mismatched clothes that belong to your grandmother because you're trying not to freeze to death, you're cute. That's the best I can explain it."

"Earlier, when you said I was cute, I wasn't wearing clothes."

And there was the sass. Never far from the surface. She might relax and let down her guard a bit, but she'd never not be willing to go toe-to-toe with him.

"That's true. I guess maybe it's just you, then." And it was. It wasn't the clothes. Or the lack of clothes. It was just her being real. And that should have worried him more than it did. "A new layer I've discovered." He moved in even closer so she had to tip her head back to keep eye contact. "You know how I love discovering new things about you."

"Yeah, yeah, you've learned how to make me say dirty words."

He grinned. He had done that. "Well, I was actually referring to when I found out that you're addicted to *Parks and Rec*. But yeah, the dirty-words thing was an awesome discovery, too."

She was obviously surprised. "You remember that?"

"That you watched *Parks and Rec* whenever you were on the treadmill at the gym?" he asked. They'd also discovered that they both liked to work out late at night when the gym down the block from the main building of the medical school was mostly deserted. He'd found her there the first night by accident, but the combination of her sweet ass in workout pants and the fact that he didn't like her being there so late alone quickly made his three-days-a-week gym habit into six days. She'd been good for his cardio.

And other things.

"Of course I remember," he told her. "I've always loved your laugh."

He wasn't sure he'd intended to say that, but it was true. She'd watch the show on her phone propped on the reading rack on the treadmill. She always wore earbuds, so he couldn't hear the show, but he could hear her laughing.

That had done crazy things to his libido, too. Or his heart. But he liked to chalk it up to physical attraction versus anything more complicated. At least, he had in the past. Now he was starting to think that complicated was inevitable. And exactly what he wanted.

"I . . ." She seemed downright stunned. "I didn't realize you'd paid attention," she finally said.

"I have, most definitely, paid attention," he told her. "I know that you study with classical music, but you unwind with classic rock, and that you party with country."

Her eyes were almost completely round now. "How . . . how do you . . ."

"I've studied with you, and I've been with you at parties, Kit."

She cleared her throat. "Unwinding and partying are different?"

He shrugged. "Evidently. When you unwind, you prop your feet up and you drink wine, slowly, and you sing along to Bon Jovi and Guns N' Roses. When you're in the mood to party, you dance, you laugh, you drink hard liquor, and you love Garth Brooks and Dierks Bentley." He watched her process that and felt like he'd just won a major competition. He fucking *loved* making Kit Derby speechless.

"I'm right, aren't I?" he asked. Just like making her talk dirty, he did love to make her admit when he'd done something well or had done something that impressed her.

"I just . . ." Finally, she nodded. "Yeah, you're right."

"Some of my favorite words from you."

She rolled her eyes.

"I guess that I've noticed how you unwind and party, because those times are rare," he added. "And you're always beautiful, but you're fucking *gorgeous* when you're having a good time and relaxing."

Again, she was clearly stunned.

"We should make a fire," she finally said.

He became aware that it was indeed getting a little chilly. "I'm all over it," he told her, taking her hand as he headed down the short hallway. And she let him. And it felt natural. All of which was interesting.

Once in the living room, Dillon went to work building the fire. He was certain Kit knew how to build a fire, but he kind of liked doing the manual-labor stuff. It wasn't especially evolved or liberated, probably, but he liked the idea of doing things to help take care of her and this situation. Just like he'd told Sarah on the phone—guys liked to *do* things. And he'd been doing a lot of talking tonight already. Judging by Kit's reactions, he was doing okay, but that wasn't his forte. He should probably reel it in while he was ahead.

Kit gathered blankets from around the house. When she came back into the room the second time, the fire was roaring, and she tossed her armload of blankets and pillows onto the floor. "It's freezing upstairs," she told him. "Since she pretty much lives down here, Grandma shuts the vents and the doors up there to keep from paying to heat the whole house."

"I noticed. But the water was hot." He stretched from his crouch in front of the fire. "Want me to open the vents up there?"

"It's just for one night, and it will take a while to warm things up even if you do," she said. "We should just stay down here."

He looked down the hallway toward the bedroom they'd just come from. "Oh?"

There was only one bed on this floor that he knew of.

"Yeah. The couch is okay with you, right?"

Couch. Right. He should have seen that coming. He nodded. "Sure. Hell, it's warmer out here than it will be back in that bedroom."

She studied the fire. "That's true."

"You can cuddle up with me on the couch," he said generously. "I don't mind sharing body heat with you at all."

Kit ignored that. She went to the couch and pulled it away from the wall. "Maybe I'll take the couch."

Dillon chuckled as he went to the other end of the couch and helped her move it closer to the fireplace. "I'll fight you for it."

Her eyes lifted to his. "Oh, really?"

He nodded. "Winner takes the nice warm couch by the fire. Loser gets the colder bedroom."

"And how are you going to fight me?" she asked, straightening from her end of the couch.

"Well, we could wrestle," he said, eyeing the pile of blankets in front of the couch.

"Or?" she asked.

He laughed and looked around. His gaze fell on the cabinet underneath the television. It had a glass door, and he could see the board games and decks of cards stacked on the two shelves inside. "Strip poker," he said, moving toward the cabinet.

"I suck at poker," she said.

He turned with an eyebrow up. Kit had just admitted to not being good at something? He really was getting her out of her element. "All the more reason I want to play, then," he said, squatting in front of the glass door.

"Something else," she said.

"Strip something else," he tossed back.

"We're going to strip? I thought the main objective here was staying warm."

He pivoted on the balls of his feet to give her a slow smile. "Exactly."

She didn't argue further. "Monopoly."

He groaned. "Monopoly takes forever. And what will you strip for?"

"Every time I have to go to jail?"

"No way. That's not going to happen often enough."

She laughed softly. "You're not even going to try to pretend that this game, whatever it is, isn't all about getting me naked?"

"Nope," Dillon said, studying the selection again. "And you'll be naked *again*."

"Right," she said drily. "Well, why don't we just arm wrestle, you win, and I take my clothes off."

Dillon opened the cabinet and pulled a long rectangular box from the shelf. He pivoted to face her, holding it up. "Because I have a better idea."

She looked from the box to him. "Chutes and Ladders? That's a better idea than me just stripping down?"

He grinned. There was no question that he wanted her naked again, but he liked surprising her. And the fact that he wanted to *talk* to her as well as lick her from head to toe would probably really surprise her. Because it kind of surprised him. Not that she wasn't fun to talk to. She was one of the brightest, sharpest, smartest people he knew. But being offered the chance to just get her naked by pinning her wrists to the floor really did seem like something he'd jump right on.

But apparently this was what happened when he and Kit were given prolonged time alone together. They'd never had that before. And he was proud that he was interested in more than just running his hands—and tongue—over every inch of her.

He shut the cabinet and moved to stand in the middle of the blankets. "Every time I go up a ladder, I get to kiss you—wherever I want—for ten seconds. Every time I go down a slide, you can ask me any question you want, and I have to answer."

She studied him, chewing the inside of her cheek. Then she turned and went into the kitchen.

Dillon frowned but didn't say anything. He just gave it a minute.

She returned with a bottle in hand. It was a jar that said APPLE CIDER on a handwritten label that was Scotch-taped to the side. "Every time I go up a ladder, I get to take a shot," she said.

"Of apple cider?" he asked.

"This is Grace's apple cider," Kit said with a smile.

Ah, spiked. He nodded. "And the slides?"

She met his eyes directly. "You get to ask me any question you want, and I have to answer."

"Let's do this," he agreed readily. He knelt and started spreading out the blankets. Kit helped, arranging the pillows, and soon they had a nest of blankets in front of the fire that would keep them nice and warm and comfortable. And that would be perfect for laying her back and unzipping her hoodie and . . .

Dillon shut that down. They had a game to play. And he did want to play. He had several places he wanted to kiss her, and he definitely had some questions. He was also very curious about her questions for him.

Kit was studying their arrangement, again chewing the inside of her cheek.

"What?" he asked.

She shook her head. "Nothing."

"Hey." When she looked up, he waggled his fingers in the universal sign for *Give it to me*. "Spill. What are you thinking?"

"Just that . . ." She shrugged. "It would be . . . warmer if we made a fort."

He blinked at her. "A fort?"

"A blanket fort," she said, lifting her chin but not quite meeting his eyes.

He looked at their blanket bed.

"If we are more enclosed, it will stay warmer," she said.

She wasn't wrong. And being more enclosed sounded like a hell of an idea. And a blanket fort? When was the last time he'd been inside one of those? When he was ten? It sounded like fun, and most of all, it had been Kit's idea. Yeah, he didn't need her to strip to be completely, over-the-top turned on by her.

This snowstorm was either going to be the time of his life or the biggest mistake he'd ever made.

"Let's do it," he said.

She grinned, and he knew that he'd made the right decision. Even if he was now never going to get over her.

With Kit's instructions, they moved the sofa even closer to the fireplace, then they secured some of the lighter-weight blankets to the mantel by setting a lamp and three bricks from the back porch on top of the edges and using the hooks that were always there for Christmas stockings. Then they draped the blankets down and over the back of the couch. Once those were in place, they added two sheets, one on either side, to make walls. The rest of the blankets and pillows were again arranged on the floor.

Dillon ducked under one side, studying the finished product. It was a perfect, cozy, romantic tent. He might never leave.

Kit crawled in on the other side and grabbed a pillow. She tucked it under her butt and crisscrossed her legs. And she looked really cute doing it.

"Ah," she sighed, pulling her hat from her head and unwrapping the scarf. "That's nice."

Dillon joined her, choosing another pillow and facing her with enough space to lay the game board out between them.

"Ladies first," he said, after he'd spread the board out and they'd positioned their markers. He handed her the die, and she rolled.

Nothing happened on Kit's first move, but Dillon rolled a four, which meant he got to climb a ladder.

Kit said nothing as he leaned over the board and braced his hands on the floor on either side of her knees. He leaned in and murmured, "So hard to decide where to start kissing you. So many awesome options." He pressed his lips to hers, mentally counted to ten—and then three more—before leaning back.

She blinked her eyes open slowly, then without a word, she reached for the die and tossed it again. And got nothing. Dillon also simply moved spaces on his next turn. They played without talking, without any noise except the crackling of the fire and the sound of the die hitting the board.

"Screw this," Kit said when she rolled yet another number that gave her no chute or ladder. She grabbed the jar of apple cider and unscrewed the top, tipping the Mason jar for a long drink.

She looked up at him as she swallowed. He'd been watching the whole time.

"What?" she asked, wiping her mouth with the back of her hand.

He shrugged. "Cute."

She frowned slightly, then shook her head. "It seems that everything I do that's something you've never seen me do before is cute."

"It does seem that way."

She hesitated, then took another drink of cider. She swallowed and asked, "So do you like cute me better or the usual me better?"

Dillon was sure his surprise was evident on his face. Wow, so she was starting the questions and without even having the game as an excuse. He leaned over and looked at the board. He moved his game piece to square forty-seven, the top of a chute, and then slid it down to number twenty-six.

"That's cheating," Kit pointed out.

"But I slid back down."

"But you're now on space twenty-six, and you were on twenty-one before."

He shrugged. "Okay, we can wait for me to answer that question until I get to a slide for real." He picked up the die and started to toss it.

"Wait," Kit interrupted.

He looked up, fighting a grin. "Yeah?"

"Fine. You can have space twenty-six."

"You really want the answer to that question, huh?" he asked. It was an easy one. He'd expected her to delve into his need to work in high-pressure, fast-paced, sometimes grim situations, or his need to constantly ruffle her feathers, or if he was really happy being back in Chance.

She just looked at him.

"Okay, the answer is both."

She blinked. Then shook her head. "No way. You have to actually answer the question."

"That is the answer. I like both sides of you."

"Fine. But which do you like *best*?"

He leaned forward, resting his elbows on his knees. "Okay, honestly? Before today, I would have said the kick-ass, take-no-shit, knock-me-on-my-ass-sexy side. But now, I realize it's only because I thought I'd seen you let your hair down and relax. But I've never seen you actually tilted off your axis. Until today. And yeah, Kit, I like it. A lot."

She studied him, as if trying to gauge how sincere he was being. And he let her look. Because he meant every damned word. This Kit he could happily hang out with every day forever. The other one—hell, he could hang out with her, too, but it wasn't until he was sitting in a blanket fort playing Chutes and Ladders that he realized how much energy it took to keep up with her, to be on his toes, to be ready to spar with her at any moment. He loved the idea of taking it easy with her, just having fun. Like lying in a hammock with her plastered against his side on a warm summer day. Or sitting with her hand in his in a movie theater. Or tucking her into a booth next to him at the bar while they hung out with friends. Or playing a silly game in a blanket fort during a snowstorm.

They'd worked together, they'd argued with each other, they'd had off-the-charts sex, they'd hung out with groups of friends and attended the same social functions from weddings to fund-raisers to house parties, but they'd never played. Not just the two of them. They'd never had just a normal, fun day together.

Until now.

And while he'd been pretty wrapped up in her before, he was now officially addicted.

CHAPTER SEVEN

Kit could *feel* the danger in the air. The feeling of being the only two people in the world because of the storm, and the feeling of playing house, were both strong and made her want things she hadn't let herself admit before. But now . . . Dillon Alexander, the doctor who had worked in the aftermath of hurricanes and in the midst of civil unrest in Africa, the brilliant mind who had designed emergency-room protocols that were being used around the country, the charmer who had her entire hometown celebrating his return, and the man who could melt her with a look across a crowded room, was now sitting with her in a blanket fort in the middle of her grandmother's living room.

She had never wanted him more.

"I'll be right back." She was scrambling for the gap in the blankets before she even really thought about the need for escape. It wasn't the first time she'd felt overwhelmed by Dillon, but it was the first time she couldn't get away from him completely, and she was feeling a little claustrophobic and like she might start screaming at any second.

Or begging him to take her right there in that blanket fort in the living room she'd been having birthday parties and family movie nights and Christmas mornings in for as long as she could remember.

Once safely in the kitchen—and thank God Dillon didn't follow her—Kit took huge, gulping breaths and did the self-talk that she taught to patients with anxiety issues. After a few deep ins and outs, she felt her heart rate slowing and the spinning in her mind straighten out.

Part of what she was feeling had to be the fact that this was a house where she had a million good memories and where she was completely comfortable and could be herself. Was she showing Dillon a new side? Yeah, maybe. Okay, yes, for sure. One of the things she believed firmly was that how you saw yourself dictated how other people saw you. She dressed professionally, always tried to look put together and sophisticated and in charge because it helped her *feel* those things, and she knew it helped others feel those things about her, too.

Dillon had seen her flustered and stressed and confused at times, but he'd never seen her . . . dressed in five layers of her grandmother's clothes, trying not to freeze to death, depending on flashlights and firelight to see, and sitting in a blanket fort playing a board game.

What had possessed her to suggest the fort thing?

It had seemed practical on the one hand. The tent did trap more heat. But it had also seemed fun. And she'd wanted to see if he'd go along with it. And . . . she'd forgotten to project the always-got-it-together thing that she usually wore like a suit of armor when he was around.

She'd figured out in high school how to keep him at arm's length. She'd had to. She couldn't let on how she felt. She couldn't feel anything for Dillon that he didn't feel for her. Somehow that seemed like a contest he'd win, and she couldn't let that happen.

Kit ran a hand through her hair, letting all those remembered emotions wash over her. How much she'd wanted him. How much she'd wanted him to want her. How hard she'd fought those emotions. And then how all-in she'd been when she finally decided to stop fighting it.

She hadn't been trying to steal Dillon from Abi. She'd just been trying to get under Dillon's skin. And it had worked. All of a sudden. She'd been flirting with him just because . . . she could tell it drove him crazy. She'd always liked winning contests between them, and for some reason, their senior year of high school, the contest had been to get Dillon to admit that he was attracted to her.

Probably because she was so incredibly attracted to him, but he was such a good guy and the perfect boyfriend to Abi. She'd hated herself for wanting a guy who had such a great relationship with his girlfriend. She'd hated herself for wanting *Dillon*. Of all people. There were several guys who did want to date her, but she was always comparing them to Dillon, and they'd come up short. And she'd hated that the only reason Dillon ever paid attention to her was because she was competing with him.

So the night they'd been prepping for their debate competition, she'd gone a little nuts. That was her professional diagnosis—temporary insanity. She'd done everything she could to seduce him, to make him crack, to make him do *something* that showed he wasn't, in fact, perfect.

And it had worked. She'd leaned over to reach past him for something, and it was like he'd snapped. He'd pulled her into his lap and kissed the hell out of her. They'd gotten to third base before they'd pulled back. In all the mess of those memories and emotions, she was proud of that. They'd both stopped. She'd been relieved even then.

And then he'd stalked out and, apparently, gone straight to Abi and confessed.

They'd had a huge fight, and the next night Dillon had been back on Kit's doorstep—yelling at her. He'd told her, loudly, that he'd been doing great resisting her for two years. Two *years*. Kit had been stunned. And then, in the middle of asking her why in hell she'd had to wear *that* body lotion and why she'd had to dress in *that* tank top and shorts and why she'd had to sit so close to him, he'd kissed her again. He'd backed her up against the wall in her parents' foyer and *kissed* her.

While Abi's car was crashing into a ditch two miles outside of town.

His phone had rung just as he'd gotten Kit's bra off.

If it hadn't been for the call about the accident, it was possible that he and Kit would have had sex while Abi was fighting for her life in the emergency room ten blocks away.

Kit felt her chest squeezing. God, they'd screwed up. She hated that they'd done that. They'd been kids. They'd made a mistake. The guilt was normal. But succumbing to their feelings and hormones had been normal, too.

All her crazy, mixed-up feelings for Dillon and about Abi's death and how she'd handled everything were what had pushed her in the direction of mental health in medical school. They'd done some self-inventories that had interested, and concerned, Kit, and she'd found herself fascinated by the human mind and all the emotions and coping mechanisms that the mind could create. Then she'd tried to give herself a break about Abi. And it had kind of worked.

She wasn't proud of the times that she and Dillon had fallen into bed—or up against a wall or in the middle of a floor—since then. Every time it had been prompted by intense emotions and stress and being thrown together for an extended period. Alone. But it had never been for this long. And she'd had an escape. And she'd used it. Now there was nowhere to go, and the longer they spent together, the faster her walls came tumbling down.

Dillon was very much *not* at arm's length now.

Kit dragged in a deep breath. He wanted to talk. The game was just a vehicle for it. A way of making it happen with less pressure than just staring at each other and confessing everything.

Talking was probably a good idea. Lord knew she should be the one advocating for it. But she didn't want to talk. She really didn't. She knew what she was feeling and why. Guilt and a huge dose of doubt. Yes, she wanted him. Yes, she felt things like affection and respect and pleasure with him. But she wasn't sure what was behind it all. Dillon had been her adversary and her motivation for as long as she could remember.

Did she really want to be with him, or did she just love the high of sparring with him? And the rush of winning? Because if getting him to crack had been the whole goal, then she should have sent him firmly in the other direction when he'd pulled up at the curb outside her house three days after Abi's funeral.

She'd tried. He'd said, "Get in," and she'd said no. Then he'd said, "Please," and she'd gotten into his car. And she'd let him sit without saying anything, staring at the river. And she'd let him tell her about the funeral. And about Abi's mom crying on his shoulder about the wedding they would now never have. And about all the people who kept telling him they were sorry and that they were there for him and that life would go on. And she'd let him take her clothes off. And then she'd gone a little crazy. The first sex of her life had been some of the hottest.

In retrospect—in her first psych class in college—she realized that she'd needed that closure, that chance at what she'd started the night she'd kissed him, to be the one he wanted, for whatever he'd needed at that moment. And he'd needed to feel connected to someone. He'd planned to have a future with Abi, and he was mourning her and the loss of that future. He'd been lonely and sad, and Kit had been there, offering him an outlet for his emotions. Not to mention a huge distraction. So he'd taken it. Why not? He had been an eighteen-year-old kid dealing with emotions and loss that no one his age should have to experience.

And since then, Kit had told herself that she was glad she had been there for him. The sex had been great, but she also knew that she'd comforted him, in a way, and that was a good thing.

Then he'd gone off to Army National Guard basic training with Jake and Max right after graduation, and she'd spent a summer in Chance without Dillon around driving her crazy. For the first time since third grade. And she'd hated it.

Then she'd gone off to college. They'd run into each other here and there on visits home, but they'd never been alone. Not until Christmas break of her sophomore year when she'd had too much to drink and he'd offered to take her home. Her parents hadn't been home from their holiday party yet, and she'd crawled into Dillon's lap in the front seat of his truck and given in to everything he'd still made her feel.

Then she'd gotten dressed and gone inside as soon as it was over.

Same in medical school when they'd been studying and all the stress and being cooped up with him in his apartment, and all the feelings she *still* wasn't over, and all the frustration about still not being over them, had all mixed into a combustible concoction of desire and desperation, and they'd found themselves naked in the middle of his living room.

And then she'd gotten dressed and left.

She'd also been the one to leave after they'd had sex against the wall in the deserted second-floor hallway in the high school during their five-year class reunion.

And when they'd been trapped together in the storeroom at the hospital in last June's tornado, they'd been *this* close to losing their clothes again. The only thing stopping them had been the sound of running feet in the hallway outside and Dillon's phone beeping incessantly in his pocket the second the tornado had passed.

She'd still been the one to walk away first.

She hated that, as an adult, mature, intelligent woman and a highly trained and damned-good-if-she-did-say-so-herself psychiatrist, she couldn't deal with her after-sex-with-Dillon emotions. But she couldn't.

She'd dealt with her guilt over kissing Dillon in high school, and breaking up him and Abi, and her feelings that she'd contributed to Abi's accident by being the cause of her emotional turmoil, in therapy of her own. But she couldn't quite shake how she felt about Dillon and the need to hide it.

So, they'd already had sex tonight. Fine. She could survive that. It was the talking about their feelings that she wasn't sure she could emerge from unscathed. She could not tell Dillon that she was in love with him and always had been. She couldn't tell him that she *didn't* love him and wanted only to compete with him, either, because she wasn't sure that was true. But sex and their game of one-upmanship were really what they were best at. She should stick with that. Definitely. So she'd distract Dillon from the talking. And there were two surefire ways to do that.

Pick a fight. Or take her clothes off.

And she didn't want to fight.

Usually, she kind of anticipated fighting with Dillon. But the guy was sitting in a blanket fort wearing her grandfather's suit jacket and telling her she was cute.

Yeah, she definitely wanted to take her clothes off.

As she thought about that, a chill went through her, and she realized the house outside of the living room was definitely cold. She glanced down the hallway. She was *not* sleeping in that bedroom. She'd share the couch with Dillon. Or they could just stay on their pile of blankets. Another little shiver went through her that had nothing to do with the cold.

Okay, seduction it was. Though she'd never actually *seduced* him before. She didn't think it would be difficult, exactly, but they had always just kind of jumped on each other in the past. She probably could simply go in there and strip down. But for some reason the idea of teasing him sounded like fun. Kind of like fighting but without the insults.

Kit thought quickly about their setup. And she suddenly had the perfect idea.

She returned to the fort and ducked under the end blanket.

"I thought maybe you'd—" Dillon stopped as she dropped back onto her pillow, spilling her armful of supplies.

He took inventory of the graham crackers, chocolate bars, bag of marshmallows, and the stick for roasting said marshmallows.

"Hungry?" he asked.

She smiled. "Just making our fort perfect. We always made s'mores when we did this when we were kids. Do you like s'mores?" she asked.

"Who doesn't like s'mores?" he asked. He passed her the Mason jar of cider. "Had a little bit of this while I was waiting."

Even better. Her grandmother's cider would take the edge off . . . anything and anyone.

"Your turn," he said, handing her the die and then grabbing the bag of marshmallows. "I'll get a couple of these going."

Kit rolled. She got a three. Which put her at the base of a ladder. She happily climbed from space twenty-one to forty-two. She picked up the Mason jar, since that was supposed to be her reward for ladders. But then she had a second thought. "I think I like your ladder idea better," she said, going up on her knees. She leaned toward him before he fully realized what she meant. She'd planned to put her lips against his neck. There was one spot along his throat that made him make the most delicious groaning sound. But he turned his head, and her lips ended up on his chin.

She made the most of it, though. She licked over the skin made rough by end-of-the-day whiskers before meeting his mouth. He didn't move except to part his lips, but ten seconds easily turned to twenty or so before she pulled back. Then she licked her own lips.

His eyes were locked on hers, and she decided, *What the hell.* She reached for the zipper on her hoodie and had it down and the sweatshirt tossed away when the smell of burned sugar hit her nose.

"Shit!" Dillon pulled the stick with the smoking marshmallows on the end out of the fire. "Shit!" he said again as the blackened bits of sugar continued to smoke. He stuck them back in the fire and shook the stick until the blobs of marshmallow fell into the flames.

Kit started to giggle. She'd distracted Dillon from the simple job of roasting marshmallows. She wasn't sure why, but she felt proud of that.

He looked at her. "That's funny?"

"That you can't multitask when I'm kissing you?" she asked. "Yeah."

The next thing she knew, he'd pulled her into his lap. He held her cradled in one arm, while his other hand splayed over her stomach. "I can't do other things while you're kissing me, huh?" he asked. Then he lowered his head to within millimeters of her lips. "Kiss me, Kit."

She slid her hand into the hair at the back of his head and pulled him down. Sure, she might have stretched up toward him, but he took her lips in a slow, deep kiss. While his hand on her stomach slid under the three layers of clothing she still wore to glide over her bare skin.

Bare skin in the currently cold house should have produced chills and goose bumps. But there wasn't one inch of her body that was cold as Dillon ran his hand back and forth over her stomach, sliding ever higher. She did have goose bumps, though.

Kit felt her arms reaching to wrap around his neck almost without a conscious decision on her part. It was like that was where they wanted to be. She clung to him as he cupped one breast, running his thumb over her nipple as she whimpered into his mouth.

God, she was so . . . needy. And overcome. And at his mercy.

He lifted his head, his thumb and finger tugging at her nipple as he watched her eyes. "Need more proof?" he asked.

She, because of the overwhelmed and needy thing, nodded.

He gave her a wicked grin. Maybe not exactly surprised but definitely pleased. He ran his hand down her belly and under the edge of the sweatpants. And then the second pair of sweatpants. And then the leggings she'd been wearing before.

And suddenly she was overheating. Her skin burned wherever he'd already touched her, and when his fingers slid over her mound and then into her hot, wet core, she swore she was going to turn into a burned, melty, gooey mess like the marshmallow.

And she didn't care.

She arched up against his hand and breathed his name.

That seemed to spur him on, and he pumped his two fingers deep. Kit pulled his head down for another kiss. As their mouths met and their tongues stroked, Kit knew that she was showing every bit of her hunger for him. But this was so much better than talking.

Or, worse, confessing.

Then again, kissing Dillon while his fingers worked their magic on a spot that no other man had ever seemed to quite reach was pretty much better than anything.

Kit realized that she was going to get another orgasm out of this setup. Dillon didn't seem inclined to stop. And Kit would have had to kill him if he did. He kept up the exquisite torture as they kissed. Her fingers drove into his hair, holding his head tightly so she could taste every millimeter of his mouth. Her knees parted, and she pressed against him wantonly. And she didn't care.

That was the thing about being with Dillon. He made her care about everything, more than anyone else did. Until he touched her. And then all she wanted was to let him have his way.

In a very, very tiny corner at the back of her mind, she knew that should alarm her. But she'd realized it a long time ago and had gotten used to it. Or had gotten used to tamping all that down in the face of having Dillon's fingers exactly where they were now. Or his mouth. Or his . . . anything else.

Dillon moved his magical fingers exactly the way she needed him to, and Kit felt her orgasm building. Then he muttered against her lips, "I still have a question for you."

His thumb pressed on her clit, and Kit moaned. He still wanted to talk? Dammit. She needed to get her hands on parts of him to fully distract him.

She wiggled, careful not to move so much that his hand shifted from where it was, and got her hand between them, right over the hard cock that was pressed against her hip.

"Kit," he said, his voice low, "I know what you're doing."

"Trying to shut you up?" she asked, stroking him. She shifted again, wedging her hand behind the elastic band of the sweatpants he was wearing and then into his boxers. "You're right."

"That only makes me want to ask this question even more," he practically growled, circling her clit and stroking deep.

She almost forgot what she was doing with her hand as the sensations flooded her nervous system. But she managed to wrap her hand around him. "The only thing I want to hear from you is *Get on me*," she said.

He pulled in a ragged breath. "You can't run away this time," he reminded her.

Yeah, like she'd forgotten. "If you keep your hand right there, there's nowhere I'd rather be," she said, trying to ignore the fact that as soon as this was over . . . But it wouldn't be over. Because she was stuck in this house, and if Dillon really wanted to talk, eventually it would come around to their feelings, and she was going to have to fight like hell to hold back what she really wanted to say.

"Let me ask my question or I'm not going to let you come."

Of course, the sex was hardly one-sided. "There's that *let* thing again," she said.

Which was a tactical error on her part, it turned out. He moved his hand out of her pants.

"Seriously?" she asked.

"Feel free to do it yourself. You know how ridiculously hot I find that."

She did know, in fact, and she remembered how ridiculously hot *she'd* found doing that with him watching. She drew in a shaky breath and willed her competitive streak to kick in.

It did. Kind of. And she managed to push herself off his lap. "Actually, I'm okay."

Dillon gave her a grin that said he wasn't buying that at all. "Don't worry, Doc. I fully intend to take one of those melted marshmallows and smear it all over your gorgeous tits and then lick them clean. But I want to talk about something first."

Her traitorous nipples tingled with his words, and she swore she could already feel the gooey warmth of the marshmallows followed by the wet heat of his mouth.

She was glad for the many shadows under the tent to hide her reaction to that. "You're boring me with all this blah, blah, blah, Alexander."

"Okay, I'll keep it short and to the point."

She sighed, wishing she could just turn off all the reactions and feelings.

"Will you go on a date with me tomorrow night?"

She blinked at him. "What?"

"A date. You and me. Out on the town."

"The town? Chance?"

He gave her a little smile. "Yes. That town."

She shook her head slowly at first, then picked up the pace. "Why?" she finally asked.

"Because I want to date you."

He wanted to *what*? "Have you lost your mind?"

"Not even a little."

"But why? I drive you crazy. And I'm already having sex with you."

"Because . . . you drive me crazy. And I love it. And I want to keep having sex with you. But I want more than the sex, Kit."

She felt emotions flittering around in her chest, but she wasn't sure what they were. It felt a little like excitement. But there was a fine line between excitement and panic.

Okay, moment of truth. There was more here than a simple "Want to go out?"

"Do you know that you're the only person in the world who makes me doubt who I am?" she asked.

He looked confused, then surprised. "What do you mean?"

"I mean, I know what I think and how I feel and what I want out of every person and situation in the world. Except you."

That was the honest-to-God truth. And she wasn't sure if it was a good idea to fill him in on the major impact he had on her life. Her instinct, honed by years of working to be kick-ass and tough where he was concerned, was to hold back anything that might make her seem—or feel—vulnerable. But what the hell? Maybe this talking thing would work out, after all. Maybe he'd decide that the sex-only thing was what he actually wanted. All the emotional stuff wasn't really his thing.

"You don't know how you feel about me?" he asked. "Or you don't want to *admit* how you feel about me?"

She took a breath and took the plunge. "I don't know how I feel about *me* when I'm with you like this. And I don't like that. Usually I feel revved up and confident and totally ready to take on the world. But that's because you're giving me a hard time, and I'm wanting to show you up. But when we're like this"—she gestured between them—"I don't know what this is. I'm relaxed and having fun, but then I think that's not really me. But then you really like this side of me. This . . . messy side. But that's not who I usually am."

"Maybe it's who you really want to be. Who you are when you're the most you," Dillon said, his voice husky.

She felt tendrils of heat swirl in her stomach. He seemed almost affectionate when he said that. But Kit shook her head. "I mean, sure, I take off my heels and put my hair up in a ponytail and wear sweats sometimes, but I don't . . . build blanket forts, and I haven't had s'mores in years."

Dillon didn't say anything for a long moment. But then he asked, "Do you like blanket forts and s'mores?"

She nodded. She did.

"And have you done this with any other guy?"

She shook her head. No way.

"Do you think it means something that you did it with me? Something that you like but that you don't let yourself normally do?"

She just looked at him for a few seconds.

Crap.

Yeah, it did. Something she didn't want to analyze. "I thought this was supposed to be short and to the point." And she'd thought he was supposed to not be good at being insightful.

"I asked you on a date. Short and to the point," he said. "You're the one making this more interesting."

"You think this is interesting?"

He pinned her with a look that said he understood a lot more here than she wanted him to. "Very interesting," he told her.

"Okay, so what do you think it means?"

"I think it means that you really want me to know a side of you that no one else gets to know. That you're more comfortable with me than you realize. And that you were testing me."

To avoid studying the rest of that, she asked, "Testing you?"

"Seeing how I would respond. If I would like this side. Because if I didn't, this was a great way to push me away, right?" He leaned in. "But I'm not sure I've ever wanted to be closer to you."

"And now you think that you won somehow?" she asked, wishing she felt more irritated by all this. Instead, she felt herself softening toward him. Either he'd been hiding this more perceptive side, or he was just discovering it himself. She suspected the latter, and that absolutely made her feel softer. The idea that she could help him get better at something was almost as much of a turn-on as his promise for those marshmallows. She made herself frown slightly, though, because she needed to know what he was thinking here. "You think that I threw this out as a challenge, and because you didn't run, you win?" That wasn't what she'd done. At least not consciously.

His eyes narrowed, clearly not overly concerned with her frown. "Maybe. Maybe I'm the brave one. The one who's willing to take a chance here. The one who can see how fucking amazing this could be."

She swallowed. Could it be amazing? Was this something more than her wanting the upper hand with him somehow? More than her using sex appeal to keep him off balance? Was it possible that she'd made *everything* between them a contest over the years because she was afraid of making it real and *actually* losing?

She knew he was baiting her with the "I'm the brave one" bit. And she was going to bite.

"I've wondered for a long time if I really wanted you in high school or if I just wanted to *get* you," she said. "You were a huge challenge. With our constant battling and . . ." Was she going to say it? "And how much you loved Abi and everything." Yeah, she was.

Abi's name, his feelings for her, the fact that Kit had wanted to tempt him simply to prove that he was tempt-able and not perfect and not above all the complicated emotions Kit was dealing with, all needed to be out there between them if they were going to actually talk about things like doing more than spreading marshmallows over interesting body parts.

But Dillon didn't even blink. Not a flinch, not a frown, not a grimace. "I know," he said. "And you never got to see what really having me was like. Abi died, and I was supposed to be the grieving boyfriend, and then you and I both left town."

Kit nodded, unable to get words past the tightness in her throat. And, horrible person that she was, the wad of emotion in her throat was less about Abi and more about the missed opportunity between her and Dillon. The accident had been tragic and had shaken the whole town. Including Kit. She'd known Abi since preschool. But yeah, she also mourned losing Dillon in that way.

She was going to hell for sure.

"But you can have me now," he said. "All of me. For as long as you want me."

His words took her breath. That surprised her. It was weird because she'd anticipated him saying almost those exact things, but hearing them out loud, in his gravelly, low voice, with his eyes locked on hers, inside their tent, with them in their crazy clothes and the rest of the world far, far away . . . it quite simply took her breath away.

All of me. For as long as you want me.

And she knew in that moment that maybe back in high school it had been about knocking him off his very high pedestal and proving that he could be ruled by hormones and could be a bad guy if pushed far enough—lots of not-very-nice things. But the second he'd kissed her, it had become all about him. All of him.

Then something he'd said came back to her. "What do you mean you were *supposed to be* the grieving boyfriend?" she asked.

Instead of answering, he asked, "If I were your patient, what would you tell me about Abi's accident?"

"That it wasn't your fault," she said easily. "That even if what happened between us upset her and contributed to the accident, that wasn't your fault. You were honest with her, and people argue and upset each other sometimes. That you were right to tell her."

Kit believed all of that. She also knew that it wasn't as easy as it sounded.

"And what about our making out the night she was killed?"

She sighed. "That we shouldn't have done it, but that we were kids and it didn't make us bad people. We didn't do it to hurt her."

He nodded. "That's pretty much what my shrink said."

"You talked to someone?" she asked. She hadn't known that.

"Yep. And it helped a little."

"Just a little?" She was surprised and pleased that Dillon had sought counseling, but she wanted it to have *really* helped him. Because she cared about him, and because, if she was totally honest, she wanted him to believe in what she did for a living.

He shrugged. "I just don't process emotions the same way everyone else does. I've figured that out. It's what makes me good at triage and trauma. I don't get that emotionally involved."

Kit knew her eyes were wide, but she was trying to understand what he'd just said. "You don't think you process emotions normally? What does that mean?"

He shrugged. "I don't feel things like I should."

Kit frowned. "Give me an example."

"Abi."

Kit felt her heart thump. "You mean because you could make out with me while in love with her?" she asked. "Dillon, we were kids. We had a bunch of feelings and hormones that we didn't really know how to handle. That doesn't make us bad people, and it doesn't mean you don't have emotions."

"It wasn't that," he said. "Or maybe it was also that. I didn't really feel guilty about that. I went and told her about it because she deserved to know, but I didn't feel guilty about wanting you. And then . . ."

He trailed off, and Kit leaned in. This was her thing. And Dillon was a subject she'd been fascinated with, on many levels, for a long time. "Then what?"

"I wasn't devastated," he said. "After she died. I was shocked. I was sad. Of course. I missed her. But I wasn't . . . devastated. I didn't want to just go to my room and never come out. Hell, three days later I was on *your* doorstep."

Kit swallowed hard. She had to be a professional here. That's what he needed. Counseling. She had to try to keep her own feelings out of it. "You came to me because you were lonely and needed closure with what had happened between us."

He frowned. "No."

No? Just no? "What do you mean by 'no'?" she asked.

"I didn't want closure. I wasn't lonely." He leaned in, pinning her with a look that seemed to penetrate to her very heart. "I didn't come to you because I missed Abi, Kit. I missed *you*. I wanted to be with you."

"You . . ." She cleared her throat. "At the river that night, you talked about the funeral and everything."

"Yeah." He nodded. "I was trying to process the fact that everyone seemed to expect me to be curled into a little ball in the corner, unable to talk or smile or eat or sleep. And the fact that I didn't feel any of that. I was sad. I hated that fucking funeral. But the worst part was everyone treating me like *my* life was over . . . and not feeling that myself. And wanting to see you." He took a breath. "I tried to tell myself that I could just pick up where you and I had left off. In my head, that made sense. It seemed insensitive. But I didn't *feel* that. Things with Abi and me were over in my heart *before* I kissed you. Definitely before her accident. I was sad she was gone; I felt horrible that her life had been cut short. She was amazing and would have done amazing things. But I didn't feel like *my* life had been cut short."

Kit let his words roll around in her head. She studied his face. He seemed . . . okay. Maybe a little perplexed, even all these years later, by the reactions of others and *his* reaction. Or lack thereof. But he seemed okay.

She was a pro at compartmentalizing. It was, in her opinion, a necessary part of her job. *She* couldn't get caught up in the emotions herself when she was talking with and listening to patients. She had to stay objective. So she firmly put her feelings for Dillon and about Abi into a box and locked it. She leaned forward, in full professional mode.

"And you feel, because you didn't react the way everyone seemed to think you should, that you don't process emotions normally?" she asked. "Is that right?"

He nodded.

"And you think that's why you're a great trauma and emergency physician?" she asked.

"It's why I went into that field. Not getting emotionally involved is key."

She nodded. That made perfect sense. "And you think that's why your bedside manner . . ."

"Sucks," he supplied with a half smile. "And yes."

Kit felt the emotions she'd locked away banging against the side of the box, trying to get out. She stubbornly added a second lock. This wasn't the time to realize how very completely crazy she was about him.

She took a deep breath, in and out, and carefully formulated her very professional response. "Dillon," she started, "that's all . . ." She blew out a breath. "That's crap," she finally said.

He lifted an eyebrow. "I'm sorry?"

It wasn't professional, but this was Dillon. He'd see through all her fancy words and carefully constructed explanations anyway. "That's all crap. You do *not* lack emotions or the ability to process them normally. That is not why you're amazing at trauma, and it's not why your bedside manner sucks."

"Is that right?"

"It is. You are a *very* caring person. You care about people you don't know and haven't even met. People you'll never really get to know. It doesn't matter to you if they are friends and neighbors—you want everyone to be healthy, happy, and safe, and you are willing to do whatever you can to make that happen. *That* is why you went into trauma and emergency medicine. That and the fact that you're incredibly bright and can think on your feet and take command of a situation and that you have an amazing natural leadership ability. And the only reason your bedside manner sucks is because you haven't worked on it. In part, because of the settings you've worked in up until now, and in part because you've been *telling* yourself that you aren't good at it."

He shook his head. "I don't know. I mean, I *should* have been devastated, shouldn't I?"

Kit again had to tighten the lid on the personal side of this. She hated that Dillon doubted himself. Ironic, really, considering she'd been working, in one way or another, to best him for years, to make him stumble, to take away some of his swagger. But deep down, the cocky, sure-of-himself, brilliant-and-I-know-it guy was the one she had fallen for . . . and had never really gotten over.

The swirl of panic that tried to rise up made Kit sit straighter and swallow hard. Falling. That's what they called it. *Falling* in love. And when you were falling, you were out of control. It meant that you'd lost your balance or let go of what was holding you up. Kit loved balance. And she didn't really let go.

Besides, it hurt when you landed.

"However you felt was how you felt, Dillon," she said, her professional tone of voice firmly in place. "There's no right or wrong way to feel."

"But she was my girlfriend. For a long time. She was sweet and amazing and . . . loved me," he said after a brief hesitation.

Ah. "So Abi would have been devastated if *you* had been the one in the accident."

Kit felt her stomach knot. It wasn't the first time it had occurred to her that if Dillon hadn't been with *her*, he might have been in that car, too.

And *she* would have been devastated.

"She would have," Dillon said. He took a deep breath. "Yeah, I guess that's part of it."

"Dillon," Kit said firmly, leaning her elbows on her knees, "you're awesome. You feel things. You process emotions. I promise you, you're fine. *I* would definitely tell you if you weren't."

That caused his mouth to curl slightly. "I guess that's true."

"I am a professional, after all."

"Right." He gave her a bigger smile this time.

She nodded. "And, of course, I've been making a list of your imperfections for a long time. If emotionless psychopath were a part of your character, it would be on that list."

He even gave a soft laugh at that. "You have a list of my imperfections?"

"I do."

"Because I'm your nemesis?"

She could tell by the look in his eyes that he didn't mean that—and didn't think *she* meant that.

"Because I've been trying to not like you for a long time."

"And that list helps?"

"It's supposed to."

They sat looking at each other for a long moment, and Kit realized that no, that list didn't help much at all, actually.

"You know," she said, "the fact that you were even trying with Sarah, in her room earlier today and then on the phone, is pretty amazing. You think you're not *able* to be good at this, but you're still trying. That's growth."

"You're proud of me?" His tone indicated he was teasing, but the look on his face was serious.

"I am."

"You think there's hope for me?"

She nodded, her eyes locked on his. "Definitely. I mean, you're *already* the person you want to be. You just need to realize it."

He didn't say anything to that.

"Going through bad things can actually make you a good person, Dillon."

He nodded at that. "And if anyone else said that to me, I'd take it with a grain of salt, but when you say it, I totally trust it."

Kit felt a warmth spiral through her. All of her and Dillon's past, all of the bickering, all of the pushing, had gotten them here, where she could help him. That was ironic, too. And wonderful.

"You've always been amazing at the feeling thing," he said. "You helped people through all kinds of stuff in high school. I remember you holding many 'sessions' during study hall."

She shrugged. "Teenage girls are teeming with emotional angst."

"But you were one of those teenage girls, and you still really helped some of them. Angela had an eating disorder. Jade had a very emotionally abusive boyfriend. You helped them both."

Kit sighed. "And then there was me with my unrequited crush on the most ungettable guy in school . . . who was also my sworn enemy."

He gave her a grin that did funny things to her insides. And made her flash back—not to the deliciously dirty things he'd done and said to her over the years, but to that first kiss. When he'd leaned in, his eyes going over her face as if seeing her for the first time, and the gruffness in his voice when he said, "I can't believe this is happening."

At the time she'd taken that as an *Oh shit, I'm in trouble.* But now she could hear, and see in his eyes, that it was *Thank God this is finally happening.* She felt a thickness in her throat and willed herself not to cry.

She wasn't so good at the feeling thing, after all.

"Not unrequited, Kit," he said softly.

Kit pressed her lips together.

"Are we really just going to skip past the part about me being in love with you back then, and that that's what made it possible for you to get to me? And that knowing you had feelings for me, too, was what actually broke up Abi and me?" he asked.

She pressed her lips tighter, but finally couldn't keep the words inside. "So you really were perfect. You never would have cheated just for the physical stuff."

"Well, I should have told Abi *before* you and I made out. Obviously."

"But you did pull back before it went too far, and you did go and tell her about it right away."

"I did."

She sighed. "And this is why I had that stupid crush in the first place, while still wanting to punch you in your perfect face."

He laughed at that. "You could never have been crazy about someone who didn't challenge all of your own ideas about how things should go and what was right and wrong."

The truth of that seemed to hit her directly in the heart. Things weren't black and white. She knew that, especially in her line of work. There were all kinds of colors in the world. But with Dillon, he made her look at *her* world and how things lined up and how they worked. Dillon made everything she helped other people with personal for her.

Because he was the only guy she'd ever been in love with.

And the only thing that she hadn't been able to set her mind to and accomplish.

He was her greatest passion. And her greatest frustration.

"So you did leave Chance, and stay away, because of Abi's death," Kit said.

He nodded. "I wasn't grieving the way everyone seemed to think I should, so being away from it all was easier. Then they didn't know that I'd moved on quickly, and I didn't have to think about how heartless I was."

She took a deep breath and asked an important question. "And how about now? Being back, seeing Abi's family, seeing her house, seeing the butterfly sanctuary?"

Her family had planted a garden of flowers that attracted butterflies in the spring and summer in her memory. It was huge, taking up the entire east edge of the park. It was beautiful. And a constant reminder of Abi. Which was, of course, the point.

"I'm okay," he said. "I think about her. Of course. But I'm ready to move on."

Kit gave a soft laugh at that. "You've moved on, Dillon. You've been far away, doing amazing things, for years now."

"I mean in a relationship," he said, not allowing her to laugh it off. "I haven't been serious about anyone, no long-term thing with anyone. I've had some girlfriends, of course."

Kit rolled her eyes. Of course. Dillon Alexander was the full package. No doubt there had not just been girlfriends but women who'd hoped it would advance to the diamond-ring stage.

"But I haven't had anything serious. No one I could imagine being with every day, for the rest of my life."

Kit felt a tightness in her chest listening to him talk about being that serious with someone. Another advantage to his being in Houston . . . and Africa, for that matter . . . was not seeing him with other women. "It takes time, Dillon," she said, desperately reaching for her psychiatrist cap. "It takes a number of relationships, sometimes, to figure out what you're looking for."

"I kept waiting for them to make me better," he said. "And none of them did."

She mentally pulled her hat down more firmly. "Make you better?" she asked, kind of wishing for her notebook.

"Make me a better person, a better doctor, a better thinker. Someone who would make me try harder and who wouldn't let me get by on just being good-looking and charming." He paused and gave her a grin. "It's amazing what I can get by with."

It wasn't that amazing at all. Dillon was a good guy. He was intelligent and caring and treated women with respect and consideration. That made him better than 90 percent of the men out there on dating sites and meeting women in bars. Add in the fact that he had no addictions, could cook, and made good money, and he was most definitely a catch.

"What's amazing is that you could fit that big head inside this little tent," she said, instead of pointing out all the reasons he'd had women falling at his feet.

"There. That," he said, pointing a finger at her nose.

"What?"

"That. That's what none of them gave me."

"The truth?"

"An ego check."

Kit let that sink in. "You were looking for someone to keep you humble?"

"No. I'd already found her." His voice had dropped to a sexy, low rumble. "And I've compared every woman to her since."

She cleared her throat, but her voice still sounded scratchy when she said, "That's pretty smooth."

"Yeah," he agreed, looking completely unapologetic. "But I don't feel bad because it's also true. You make me a better person, Kit."

She couldn't respond to that. It was . . . really nice. And she could easily say, "Ditto."

"And the sex with you is the best I've ever had."

She couldn't help it—this was a sweet, even romantic moment, but she felt a surge of *Damn right* when he said that.

"And you're very fucking cute."

She sat looking at him for a long moment. His face was so familiar. His voice, his smile, the way he said certain things, the way his hair laid in the front, the shape of his hands—she'd studied, and absorbed, all of it for so long. She swore she could pick his hands out of a lineup.

"Yes," she finally said.

"Yes, you're fucking cute?" he asked.

She shook her head. "Yes. I'll go on a date with you."

He took a deep breath, then gave her a single nod. Then he reached for the marshmallows and the roasting stick. She watched him put two on the end and then extend them toward the fire.

"So, that's that, then," she said.

"That's that," he agreed. "Why don't you start taking your clothes off now?"

Heat shot through her. "Oh?"

He looked over. That sexy, mischievous twinkle in his eye that made her want to do whatever was going through his creative, naughty mind. "I told you about the marshmallows and your tits. Let's go."

She laughed. It was like all the emotions that had balled themselves up in her chest and gut suddenly dissolved into an effervescent explosion of bubbles that rose up within her and made her feel light and happy.

It was either her grandmother's hard cider. Or it was Dillon.

And either way, she had plenty of both for the rest of the night. And the talking was over. Thankfully. Though she couldn't quite work up to being sorry it had happened. Dillon had supposedly been in love with her in high school.

"Why haven't you come back before now?" she asked. Then bit her lip. She was keeping the talking going? When he had marshmallows in the fire?

He looked over. Then pulled the stick from the fire. "Because I loved it. I loved my time in the Guard, I loved med school, I loved the work in Africa and the craziness in the ER."

While the idea of being the only thing he wanted out of life was romantic, Kit appreciated that he truly had found work he was passionate about and that he was honest about that. "But you're here now. It's not as challenging and crazy now."

"I'm good with less crazy. And it's challenging in a new way," he said. "Taking care of people you've known your whole life, seeing their entire lives—their families, their work—seeing the way what you do for them, or can't do for them, impacts all of that is a different kind of challenge." He pointed at his chest. "It challenges me here. In the ER, the battle is just keeping them alive. Here, it's about what being alive means to them."

Kit stared at him. Everything was now crystal clear. Scary, but crystal clear. She wanted to go on a date with him. For the rest of her life.

She reached for the bottom of her top shirt and stripped it off. Dillon returned the marshmallows to the fire, without looking away from her for an instant. She pulled off the second, third, and fourth shirts as well. She had just tossed her bra to the side when Dillon pulled the perfectly toasted marshmallows from the fire. He blew on them as he studied her.

Then he said simply, "Come here."

CHAPTER EIGHT

She crawled toward him, feeling decadent with the fire warming her naked skin. And Dillon's eyes warming all of her.

He pulled the crispy outer crust off one marshmallow and held it out. She took his finger and thumb between her lips, sucking the toasted sugar onto her tongue and letting it melt in her mouth. She sucked on his fingers, then ran her tongue over the pads of each. He made a soft growling noise that made heat slip from her chest, through her stomach, to settle between her legs. She moved onto his lap, straddling his thighs, putting her breasts right there for him.

Dillon slid the sticky white glob from the end of the stick. He spread the marshmallow over her right nipple with one hand while the other splayed between her shoulder blades and brought her up to his mouth. He licked and sucked until the sugar was completely gone. Or at least, Kit assumed it was gone. She'd lost her mind, and her ability to care about anything but Dillon's tongue, back around the time he'd said, "Nothing has ever tasted better than your skin."

She arched closer, murmuring things she hoped sounded encouraging. Because she definitely wanted to encourage him. But wasn't quite able to make full words.

After sucking more marshmallowy goodness from her other breast, Dillon shifted, and she found herself on her back with her wrists over her head and held in one of Dillon's big hands.

"I can't take the time to toast another one, but I'm going to pretend I've got one spread out all over the rest of you." And he proceeded to strip her of her pants—all of them—and her panties. Then he dipped his head to her navel, kissing and swirling his tongue around her belly button, from one hip bone to the other, and then over her mound, finally settling on her clit.

Kit came fast and hard, and before she'd even caught her breath, Dillon shifted over her and between her legs. He looked down at her with a crazy mix of cocky and affection, and Kit was more grateful for snow than she'd ever been in her life.

He started to roll on a condom, evidently having brought them into the tent with him at some point. Kit wanted to just lie back and let him have his way with her. But then it occurred to her that she wasn't quite done with the marshmallows. Or making Dillon crazy.

She looked up at him. "Lie back," she said, her voice husky.

He paused. "I'm dying a little here, Doc."

"Good." She was sure her smile conveyed every bit of what she was feeling—playful, needy, and naughty.

He let out a long breath. "Okay, I'm giving you five minutes before I need to be inside you."

That hot, swirly thing that he caused so easily happened, and she almost said, "Never mind." But Dillon lay back on the blankets, his big, hard body stretched out and all hers. Yeah, she could wait five minutes. Or maybe three and a half.

She reached for a marshmallow and stuck it on the end of a stick. She leaned her chest onto his, stretching to reach the fire. Dillon didn't ask what she was doing, but he also didn't just lie there. He reached for a nipple and rolled it, making desire pulse between her legs, and she willed the fire to go faster. Then his other big hand settled on her butt, and his fingers slid lower, between her legs, playing with her, heating her core, making her wiggly and wet and hungry for him.

"Dillon," she moaned.

One thick finger slid into her, and she dropped her head to his chest, her breathing turning to panting.

"I so want to pull you up here and bury my face in your pussy," he told her gruffly.

Yeah, she definitely wanted that, too. She started to shift, but then she remembered the marshmallow. She pulled it from the fire and blew on it. She plucked it from the end of the stick, biting into it and exposing the melted center. Then she sat back. "I think you're going to like this, too," she told him, her voice breathless.

He watched her, his eyes hot, as she dragged a finger through the melted sugar and then lowered her hand to his cock. She painted the marshmallow along his length and then lowered her head. She'd used her hand on him before, but she'd never done this, and if the taste and feel of him wasn't enough, the low, growling noise that came from his chest as she touched her tongue to him for the first time was enough to make her never want to move.

She licked, and sucked, and licked again, her tongue gathering every bit of the marshmallow but then continuing to move up and down the hard shaft. She felt his hand thread through her hair, she heard the "Fuck, Kit, your mouth is heaven," and she knew she wanted to take him all the way like this.

Kit pulled the tip into her mouth, sucking, then moving lower, taking him deeper. Dillon's thighs clenched, and his fingers tugged on her hair. She moved her hand to cup his balls, stroking her thumb back and forth, and she heard the *"Fuck"* that sounded ripped from his throat. He lifted slightly, sliding farther into her mouth, but it felt like he was holding back.

She lifted her head. "I want this, Dillon. Please."

His fingers tightened in her hair again as he stared at her, his mouth open as he breathed raggedly. She stroked her hand up and down his length, squeezing slightly, convincing him.

"You want me to come in your mouth, Kit?" he asked, his voice hot and heavy.

"I do."

"You want me to fuck the pretty mouth that sasses me and tells me when I'm being a dumbass and says some of the most inspiring things I've ever heard? The mouth that's been making me *crazy* for twenty years?"

She swallowed hard and nodded. The dirty talk was going to be the death of her.

He let out a rough laugh. "You have any idea how many times I've thought of that?"

"Have you?" That thought sent a shaft of heat through her. She'd stayed awake many nights thinking of the ways he made her nuts, but also with plenty of fantasies. The idea that he'd done the same definitely made her hot.

"Babe, give me your mouth."

Gladly.

He guided her head back down, and she took him in her mouth, pleasuring him with even more determination. She sucked, licked, fondled, and reveled in the noises he made, the way his hips bucked, the way his hand stayed on her head as if holding her to him. But there was no question who was in control here. She wasn't giving him her mouth; he was giving her his desperate need.

He thrust faster, and she added her hand to the base of his shaft, squeezing and stroking, and soon he was warning her that he was coming. And she just sucked harder.

When he erupted, Kit felt a wave of pleasure that surprised her. It was his orgasm, but the realization that she'd done that to him was an intense aphrodisiac. The sense of power was incredible, but so was the feeling of giving.

After the ripples in his body had quieted, she lifted her head. He was staring at her with wonder, and a desire that didn't seem to have been quenched.

He tugged on her hair, encouraging her to slide up his body. He locked his mouth on hers, kissing her deeply, his hand cupping her head. They kissed for several long minutes, then he tucked her against his side and sighed.

Kit rested her cheek on his chest, her hand on his stomach, and wondered if there was any way to stay here in this tent in her grandmother's living room forever. It all seemed easy here. Tomorrow they'd be dug out and would head back to Chance. And it seemed that things were pretty complicated there. How would people react to their being together? How would Abi's family feel? And how would she and Dillon work together? Everyone was used to them arguing and sparring and one-upping. Would they continue to do that? Just because they'd admitted to having feelings for each other didn't mean they would always agree. Or even agree often. She and Dillon just did things differently. Or would they finally be over that? And then there was the free-clinic scheduling and staffing and supplies and, of course, paying for it. She and Dillon had been arguing everything from what to call it to if it should be supported by private donations or government grants. And who was going to handle the lobbying efforts needed for the grant support.

And suddenly, she didn't care.

Well, that wasn't entirely true, but the details they'd been picking over didn't seem important. Did it matter what they called it or how they supported it, as long as it was there for the community? She knew—had known all along—that some of their disagreements were truly just because that was their go-to move. If Kit said she thought community support was more important than government funding, then Dillon said he disagreed, partly just out of habit.

But if they did want government support, at the state or federal level, she and Dillon should be lobbying together. They brought expertise on two sides of the medical needs of the community, and they both had connections and impeccable reputations in their fields.

"Stop," he admonished quietly. Then he yawned.

"Stop what?" she asked, not looking up.

"I can hear your mind working from here. Just relax. It's all going to be okay."

She sighed. "You sure?"

"I'm sure that I'll do whatever it takes to keep getting blow jobs from you. Damn, girl, that was amazing."

She rolled her eyes but smiled. "The marshmallows made me enthusiastic," she lied. "I really like toasted marshmallows."

"Honey, that's a big can-do. Marshmallows are cheap."

"You don't have a fireplace."

"I'm knocking down a wall and putting one in tomorrow."

She chuckled. Of course this wasn't just about blow jobs, but maybe he had a point. How they made each other feel, how they fit together personally—now that they'd admitted it—had to influence how they worked together. It would all be fine.

"Well, in that case, I'm no longer concerned," she told him.

He yawned again. "And I'm not done with you yet, so rest up."

The only problem was going to be trying to work while sleep deprived. Kit was actually smiling as she drifted off to sleep.

Dillon woke up with his arms empty.

And that was not okay.

He stretched and glanced at the fire. It had burned down enough that he figured he'd been out for a few hours. He crawled over and stoked it. Then scrubbed a hand over his face. Okay, so where was Kit?

For one, he hadn't been kidding—he wasn't done with her. He needed her again. He couldn't get enough of her.

For another, he fucking hated that she'd run again. Every time in the past, she'd hightailed it away from him the minute she had her panties back on. But he'd thought they were past that now. They were to a whole new point now, a place where they'd finally been totally honest and were on the same page.

The same page. That was a place he and Kit hadn't spent a lot of time together.

He pulled on a pair of sweatpants and ducked out of the tent. There were only so many places she could be. He'd find her and bring her back in here and make her crazy all over again. And if they needed to start back at square one about how they felt and what was going to happen when they got dug out and back to Chance, then they'd start back at square one.

He should have expected it to go this way. Kit Derby had never made things easy on him. But that was why she was the one for him. When she challenged him, she made him realize what was important to him, what was worth fighting for. And she was worth fighting for.

As he neared the kitchen doorway, he heard her voice. And then a long pause. And then her saying, "I do want it. I just don't know that I've thought of everything. I mean, it seems like it should be fine, but there could be a million things that could go wrong."

Dillon sighed. He stepped into the kitchen to find her sitting on the floor under the rotary wall phone, the receiver pressed to her ear, the flashlight set on its end, illuminating the area around her like an electric candle.

She looked up at him. "Crap. He's here," she said into the phone.

He walked over and squatted in front of her. He took the receiver from her hand and brought it to his ear. "Bree?"

"Hey, Dillon," Kit's best friend said.

"I'm going to take Kit back to bed now. She'll talk to you tomorrow."

"Sounds good." He could hear Bree's amusement. "She's kind of worked up."

"She wouldn't be Kit if she wasn't," he said.

"I'm on your side, for what it's worth."

He appreciated that, but he sighed. "We still have sides, huh?" He was watching Kit the whole time.

She was chewing on the inside of her cheek and looking part sheepish and part annoyed.

"Not sure the world can survive with you and Kit on the same side all the time," Bree said with a light laugh. "That's way too much brainpower and drive and being right all tilting the same way. It would throw everything off."

Even at three a.m. in a freezing-cold kitchen in the near dark, Dillon saw what Bree was saying. And he thought that maybe she was right.

"So then we're definitely good."

"Totally good," Bree agreed.

"Good night, Bree."

"Sleep tight. Or whatever," she said, with a touch of glee in her voice that made Dillon smile as he hung up the receiver above Kit's head. "Let's go." He bent and scooped her up into his arms. "You're going to freeze to death while overanalyzing this thing. How about you wait until tomorrow when you've got some heat and coffee?"

"You think I'm overanalyzing it?" But she didn't fight for him to put her down.

"Of course you are." He headed for the living room and set her down next to the tent. He held up the one side for her to duck under.

She'd pulled on sweats and her hoodie again, and he couldn't help but wonder how many layers she had on underneath.

As he joined her in the tent, she said, "We're in a surreal situation here, and everything seems easy and good and possible. But the light of day and real life might have a way of changing things."

Dillon settled back on the pile of pillows and linked his hands together behind his head. "You realize that we've been together in the light of day in real life four billion times, right? I'll give you that tonight has been unusual, but nothing that we're thinking or feeling is anything that hasn't occurred at two p.m. on a bright sunny day in the middle of a hallway in the hospital. It doesn't get much more real life than that."

She was worrying her bottom lip, but finally she nodded. "Okay. Let's have sex."

He laughed, and couldn't deny that his cock stirred at the offer, but he knew that she needed something a little more normal than the lose-their-minds-it's-so-good sex they always had. "How about you just come here?" he asked, extending an arm.

She didn't even hesitate, which he loved. He pulled her on top of him, her body stretching along his. And yes, his body loved that and wanted far fewer clothes between them, but he put a hand on her head, pressing her cheek into his shoulder, and settled the other on her lower back. He stroked her hair and hugged her close and said nothing. After a few minutes, he felt her relaxing.

As her body melted into his, she sighed. "This is nice."

It was. And he wanted this just as much as he wanted her beautiful body spread open to him. As much as he wanted her sassy mouth and quick mind and sharp wit across the conference table from him. As much as he wanted her eye-rolling when he was screwing something up. As much as he wanted her big grins and laughter and blushes when he was successfully charming her.

He wanted it all, and he was going to have it. Even if she fought him. Because fighting with Kit was one of his specialties.

They woke up to the sound of Dillon's phone ringing, the kitchen phone ringing, and the rumbling sound of a diesel engine outside.

Kit was still draped over the top of him, and she was slower to wake up. As she wiggled and stretched, Dillon's body instantly responded to the feel of her soft curves rubbing against him.

He put both hands on her ass and pressed up into her, trying to ease a bit of the ache. "Morning."

She brushed her hair back from her face with one hand and blinked at him. "Morning."

Was she going to freak out? The whole in-broad-daylight thing?

He removed his hands and let his arms drop to his sides. If she wanted to bolt, he'd let her. For now.

But she didn't bolt. At all. She lowered her head and kissed him. The ringing phones, the engine outside, the *everything*, faded away as he cupped her head and kissed her back.

Waking up like this for the rest of his damned life was exactly what he wanted.

When had he been so sure about something before? It had been a really long time. He'd felt a definite sense of *yes* when he'd stepped out of the bus to begin basic training next to his two cousins, his best friends in the world. He'd felt a gut-deep sense of rightness when he'd gotten off the plane in Africa. He'd felt a surge of *Hell yeah* when his first patient had rolled into the ER in Houston on day one. And he'd felt a contentment clear to his soul when he'd pulled the moving truck that was transporting him and all his possessions into Chance.

But this—kissing Kit in the morning light after talking, playing, and loving all night—beat all of those rolled together. *This* was where he was supposed to be.

The phone in the kitchen stopped ringing. Then started again.

Kit lifted her head. But did nothing to move her body off his.

"Guess we should get going," she said.

"Probably."

She pressed her hips into his. "In a little bit?"

He squeezed her ass. "Or a long bit."

Their lips had just met again when a loud pounding started on the back door. A moment later, there was a loud *whump*, and Dillon winced. Whoever had come banging on the door had knocked in the already-kicked-down thing.

"Or maybe we pick this up later," he said. He gave her a little swat on the butt and then moved out from under her.

"Dammit," she muttered, but she followed him out of the tent.

By the time Dillon and Kit got to the kitchen, Max and Jake were coming through the door from the front hallway.

They grinned widely. "The cavalry is here," Max announced.

"How did you get out here?" Kit asked.

"I have some pull with the mayor's office," Max said with a wink. "He let me borrow a snowplow."

Max—and Jake and Dillon—were the mayor's wife's first cousins. The guys were also three of Frank Harvey's favorite people. Hell, they were three of the town's favorite people. It didn't surprise Dillon a bit that Frank had let Jake and Max bring the snowplow out here.

"You're my heroes," he said drily. If only they'd waited maybe thirty minutes longer.

"Well, the town needs its two best doctors," Jake said with a shrug. But Dillon could see his cousin taking in every detail of the situation. Namely that he and Kit had come into the room together, were both wearing a strange combination of clothes, and that Kit looked . . . rumpled.

Dillon didn't know if Jake would find that as adorable as Dillon did, but he was sure his cousin would find it fascinating. No one ever really got to see Kit as anything other than completely polished and put together. And the strangest part here was that she wasn't fussing with her hair or hightailing it down the hall. She didn't seem to care that the guys were seeing her this way.

There had been some times after the tornado and during the cleanup that she'd had a smudge of dirt on her face or her hair had been coming out of its ponytail or her boots had been muddy. But that had been par for the course. You couldn't really clean up a town after an F4 twister without getting a little dirty.

This was different. This was just-out-of-bed rumpled. And more, this was had-hot-sex-all-night, just-out-of-bed rumpled.

Dillon couldn't help the grin he felt stretching his lips. He liked that look on her because he'd put it there. And he didn't care who knew it.

"You didn't even bring doughnuts?" Kit asked. "Or coffee?"

Jake and Max looked at each other and then back to Kit. "Sorry. We should have done that," Max agreed.

"I'll let you buy me a cup when we get back to town," Kit said.

"Deal," Max said with a nod.

Kit extended her hand. Max looked at it and back up at her. "A ten should cover it," she said with a smile.

"A ten? Where are you buying coffee?" Max asked.

"I might need more than one." She glanced at Dillon. "I didn't get much sleep last night."

Max chuckled and dug a ten from his pocket. "You don't want me to take you for coffee?"

Kit plucked the bill from his fingers. "Sure, Max. If you want to sit with me across a small coffee-shop table and *talk* for an hour or so, I'm game."

Max's eyes widened. "Uh, no thanks, Dr. Derby. My noggin is just fine."

She laughed and turned toward the hallway leading to the bathroom. "Well, you know where to find me."

"The shower?" Jake quipped.

She looked back at him. "For now, yes. But Dillon's the only one invited in there. And it won't be his *noggin* that I'll be interested in." She actually *winked*. And then disappeared down the hallway.

Max and Jake watched her go, grinning like idiots.

"Hey," Dillon said, snapping his fingers, "eyes over here."

They swung to look at him in unison.

"Holy shit, Dillon," Jake said.

"Yeah, what Jake said," Max agreed.

Dillon frowned. "What? You knew we were out here together, and Bree had to have told you what happened after she and Kit talked."

"Well, yeah, we knew you'd gotten her naked," Jake said. "But . . . damn."

"What?" Dillon asked again.

"You must have been goooood," Max said, drawing out the word.

Dillon looked at them, then down the hall where Kit had exited. "Yeah? What do you mean?"

"I've never seen Kit look like *that*," Max said. "Ever."

Jake nodded. "Ever."

"Like what?" So her hair was messy, and she was barefoot, and she'd just admitted to being interested in not-his-noggin. Dillon had to grin. That was . . .

"Cute," Jake said.

"Tousled," Max said at the same time. Then he looked at Jake. "Cute. Yeah, that."

Dillon felt himself nodding. "She is, isn't she?"

Jake shrugged. "She really is. And all teasing and laughing even though we saw her with her hair messed up? Dude, that's . . . so not Kit."

"Careful what you say about her," Dillon warned.

"He just means that she's usually so put together." Max jumped to Jake's defense. "She's never . . . messed up, and as far as I know, she only kids around with the girls."

He liked that, too. Kit loved Bree and Avery. If she was feeling that comfortable with him and his friends . . . that was huge.

Jake went on. "Yeah, there's a lot about her to really like and admire. But until this just now, she didn't seem like a—" Jake suddenly stopped.

"Like a *what?*" Dillon said firmly, crossing his arms.

Max saved Jake again. "A girl to get dirty in the shower," he said, almost apologetically.

Dillon just stared at the other two men. "Seriously?" How had he always seen her that way? Yes, she gave off all kinds of cool bravado, but the fire in her eyes was clear. The passion in her personality, the fervor when she argued for something she believed in, the flash in her eyes when he disagreed . . .

Yeah, okay, maybe the guys hadn't seen all that because they hadn't been on the receiving end of any of it.

"Everyone feels that way?" he asked of the other men in Chance. It was *fine* by him that he was the only one to see the firecracker behind the composure.

"When she dates, it's guys from other towns," Jake confirmed. "Nobody here's got the balls to tangle with her."

"Except you," Max said with admiration. "You've always been willing to take her on." He waggled his eyebrows.

"And I gotta say, it looks good on her," Jake said, glancing toward the hallway again.

"What does?" Dillon asked.

"That contented, glowing thing."

"The contented, glowing thing?" Dillon repeated. "She *looks* different this morning?" And was it okay for him to feel proud of that? It was probably really chauvinistic. But he couldn't help it.

Both men nodded. "Oh yeah," was Jake's answer, while Max gave him a "Definitely."

Dillon looked down the hallway toward the closed bathroom door. She *looked* contented this morning. That was something. Something big. Something that made him want to march down that hallway, strip down, and take her from behind while the shower pounded down onto them both.

"Let's go get the snowmobile dug out," he said instead.

The guys were here. He needed to check in at the hospital.

And mostly, when he took a shower with Kit for the first time, it was going to be in his own shower. Followed by his bed, his couch, his living-room floor, and his kitchen table. Not necessarily in that order.

He intended to keep that soft, glowing thing going. And going. And going.

The guys were outside when Kit stepped out of the bathroom. She quickly dressed in what she'd worn to the farm yesterday and then cleaned up the house.

She poured the chili into plastic storage bowls and put two in the fridge for her grandma for later, then stored the rest in the freezer. The power had come back on at some point in the night, so she turned things off, put the fire out, reset the digital clocks, put all the clothes she and Dillon had borrowed either back in the closet or in the laundry room with a note, and returned all the blankets and pillows to their rightful places.

It made her a little sad to tear down their fort, and she saved the Chutes and Ladders game until last. They hadn't gotten far on it, yet it felt like they'd gone a long way.

By the time the guys came stomping back in, declaring the driveway, the path to the barn, and the road passable and the snowmobile ready to go, Kit was ready to leave.

Kind of.

Part of her never wanted to leave. The farmhouse had turned into a haven of sorts, and she was, quite frankly, worried about what the return to town would mean.

"Stop overthinking it," Dillon said in her ear as she stood by the snowmobile, strapping her helmet on and looking at the house.

She looked up at him. "How did you know?"

"I know you." He bent and kissed the end of her nose in what was quite possibly the sweetest gesture ever. "But you know me, too," he said. "And remember—I never give up when I want something."

He wanted her. Enough to never give up. She pulled in a deep breath. Okay. She could do this happy, in-love thing. Hell, she'd felt it for a long time. The only thing that would be different now was that she could show it. That would be . . . great.

Kit climbed onto the snowmobile behind Dillon and was able to stop worrying about what their new normal would be. Kind of. Instead, with her arms wrapped around him, her body pressed to his, her eyes closed against the sun glinting off the new, bright-white snow, all she could think about was that Dillon had never backed down from something he wanted to accomplish.

And that nagged at her. Was that part of the attraction? That he didn't *have* her? He'd been the ungettable one in high school, and she'd told herself that was part of why she wanted him. Now, in retrospect, she knew that wasn't true. But she couldn't help but wonder about

Dillon. They'd both thrived on taking the other one down. He'd admitted to a lot of emotions, which went back a long way, last night. But it was definitely possible that on some level, dating her, making her fall completely head over heels for him, was another contest that he wanted to win.

They pulled up behind Dillon's truck, and the guys went to work digging it out. Soon she was perched in the passenger seat again. It was amazing to her that it had been less than twenty-four hours since they'd driven out here together. So much had happened. And changed.

Dillon adjusted the vents to blow on her and turned the truck out onto the highway. It was at least thirty degrees warmer today than it had been yesterday, and with some nostalgia, Kit took the gloves and hat he'd given her yesterday and tossed them behind the seat.

"You want me to drop you at home?" he asked as he pulled the truck onto the highway.

"Where are you going?"

"To the hospital."

Of course he was. She wanted to check in on Sarah and see if her husband had made it. The highway was cleared of snow, and the sun was shining. No doubt the interstate had been clear early that morning, and Tim was either on his way or already in Chance. But she needed a shower. And her regular clothes. She simply wasn't her usual composed, I've-got-this girl when she was in sweatpants. When she was, she talked about shower sex. Yeah, she needed her pantsuit.

She wasn't embarrassed about making the crack about sex in the shower to Jake and Max. It was Jake and Max. Very little fazed either of them. But it had definitely been out of character. That had been a laid-back, teasing version of her that neither of those guys had seen before, she was sure.

Bree already knew that she and Dillon had slept together, which meant Max knew. Which meant Jake knew. Which meant Avery knew. And that didn't really bother Kit. Their friends weren't the gossiping types—except with one another. But Avery and Bree didn't know about her and Dillon's history. She didn't think Max and Jake did, either. They probably all thought last night was like the storage room at the hospital during the tornado—a spur-of-the-moment thing brought on by adrenaline and close proximity. They didn't know that it was actually the culmination of years of mixed-up emotions and attraction.

But Kit knew it was time she talked about it with someone. And her two best girlfriends, who were madly in love themselves with men with whom they had long, somewhat complicated histories with, were the perfect ones to understand.

"You can take me to the hospital. My car's there," she finally answered Dillon as he pulled up to the stop sign that required a decision of right for the hospital or left for her house.

"We have that meeting at noon," he commented as he took the right. "What do you have going on before that?"

"I have a couple appointments," she said. "The first is at nine." And she needed to see if Bree and Avery were free for coffee before that. She looked at her watch. That didn't give them much time. Maybe they could have drinks later.

"Well, I'm going to clean up in the locker room," Dillon said, pulling into his space in the parking lot. "I've got stuff all day." In other parts of the country, thirteen inches of snow would mean a few days off. In the middle of Nebraska, it meant that you'd better have your snow boots and four-wheel drive in gear. Life didn't stop for a little bit of snow. It was just inconvenienced for a while.

She nodded and reached for the door handle.

"Kit."

Dillon's low voice stopped her. She glanced back.

"I want to see you later," he said.

It wasn't really a request, and Kit had the fleeting thought that she should mind that. But she didn't. And she'd have to think about *that* later.

"Are we taking this public tonight?" she asked, a mix of excitement and trepidation swirling in her chest. Were they going to really date? Show off what they were doing for the whole town?

He looked at her for a long moment, then reached for her as he leaned in. His hand cupped the back of her neck, and he pulled her in for a long kiss. When they separated, he rested his forehead against hers.

"I need to get my hands all over you again as soon as possible. What I have in mind may not be appropriate for public."

Heat danced through her, and she nodded. "Okay."

"Okay." He kissed her again, hard but sweet, and then let her go.

Kit made her way to her car, waiting until he'd disappeared through the sliding doors to the ER before putting her hand over her pounding heart. She hadn't been this worked up over something in a long time. The last time had been . . . Dillon.

It was always Dillon. Whether she was worked up over their latest argument, or pissed off about something he'd said in a meeting, or annoyed because he'd been right about something she'd disagreed with, or because he'd made some innuendo that had gotten her revved up.

Dillon was the only person, the only *thing*, that shook her. She didn't like being shaken. She didn't like not feeling totally stable. She was the emotional rock of this community.

And that was part of why she'd chosen mental health. She liked being the rock. She did not like *being* rocked.

Dammit.

And speaking of being the rock . . . She found her phone lying on the front seat of her car. Thank God. She quickly checked her messages. Only one made her worry. Lisa Shear. Her husband, Travis, had been dealing with a lot of issues since the tornado. Travis and Lisa had lost everything—their house, most of their possessions—and he'd sustained a back injury. He'd been making some money working for one of the contractors during the rebuilding, but now that it was winter, he was having a hard time paying his bills. Travis was the kind of guy who could use the free clinic to get through the tough times. They really needed to stop having their freaking meetings and just get the damned thing running.

Kit had been meeting with Lisa first, dealing with her stress and anxiety, but had eventually talked Travis into coming for a few sessions. She was far more concerned about Travis at this point.

The message from Lisa said that Travis had been drinking lately, and they'd been arguing.

Kit called Lisa, wanting to get them in for a session. She was sent to voice mail, and she left a message asking Lisa to call her right away. She also sent a text.

At home, Kit showered and changed into a black pantsuit, sweeping her hair up into a twist on top of her head. But looking in the mirror, she felt something was off. She changed into a red pencil skirt, white blouse, red jacket, and red heels. It was an outfit she wore often and loved. It made her feel in charge. But it wasn't quite right, either. Which was ridiculous. She needed clothes on. Professional clothes. Period. She didn't need to look a certain way.

But she went back into her closet anyway. The next thing she put on was perfect. A pair of silky black pants, a peach top, with a multicolored sweater and scarf. And she kicked off her heels and stepped into a pair of flats. Then she pulled the pins from her hair, letting it fall down around her shoulders. When she wore her hair down, she generally straightened it. But today she left in the gentle waves.

She arrived at the hospital feeling good but feeling . . . softer. That was the best way she could describe it. She still felt professional and confident, but she felt happy and upbeat. Almost tipsy. Maybe that was it. Maybe this comfortable feeling was just that she was sleep deprived.

From having great sex all night. The endorphins from that were powerful, she knew. That had to be it.

She thought about her friends. Bree and Avery were newly in love. Not like yesterday-in-love, but they were only about six months in. Well, if you didn't count the ten-plus years of loving Jake and Max without realizing it—or admitting it. And yeah, she could say that they both seemed different. Happier. More content. She needed to pick their brains. Maybe they could get away for lunch. She pulled out her phone. Thank God she'd found it lying on the front seat of her car and it had not turned into an ice cube.

"Are you *humming?*"

Kit looked up from texting Bree. Megan, the receptionist who handled the front desk for the specialty outpatient wing where Kit's office was located, was watching her with eyebrows up.

Kit glanced around. There was no one else in the immediate vicinity, but that wouldn't last long. Her office was alongside the clinic where cardiology, orthopedic, neurology, and pediatric specialists all saw patients on their weekly visit to the hospital. Chance was a small town, but they served a wide area of rural Nebraska. They didn't have a patient population large enough to support full-time specialists, and even Kit's practice was part-time, but the access to specialists on a regular basis saved residents from making the two-hour drive to the nearest metropolitan health centers.

Some people questioned why such a little town needed its own psychiatrist, but again, she served a larger geographical area than just Chance, and, frankly, *everyone* needed mental-health services to be available. She worked in a town that had been ravaged by more tornadoes than anywhere else in the country. The tearing-down and rebuilding process took its toll physically and emotionally on its citizens. Travis and Lisa were a great example. Then there were the people with stress and anxiety, the need for family counseling, grief counseling, as well as diagnosed mental illness. No place was really too small for a solid mental-health program.

"I was humming?" Kit asked.

"You were. And I'm ninety-nine percent sure that you were humming 'It's in His Kiss.'"

Kit felt her cheeks heating, then willed her body to not give her away.

Of course, maybe she should stop humming if she didn't want people wondering what was up with her. She never hummed.

"'It's in His Kiss'?" she repeated, and then scoffed. "I barely know that song."

Megan gave her a strange look, but said, "Okay."

"But yes, I'm in a good mood this morning," Kit said. She couldn't totally deny her sunny disposition, or Megan would be watching extra carefully to try to figure out what was going on. And Kit wasn't sure she could completely hide that something big had happened. In fact, right at that very moment, she was fighting a smile.

"Yeah, I can see that you're feeling good today," Megan said with a nod, watching Kit closely.

"Oh?" Kit said nonchalantly.

"You definitely look different. Kind of . . . soft."

Kit focused on Megan more fully. "I look *soft*?"

"Yeah, like you're just really . . ." Megan shrugged. "Happy. You look happy."

"And that's different for me?" Kit asked. But she knew what Megan was getting at.

Kit had strolled down the hallway. She never strolled. She walked with purpose. The clicking of her heels on the tile floors usually gave her a strange feeling of determination. But today, in her soft leather flats, she'd felt lighter. And like strolling. And she'd been humming, evidently.

"You're just usually super focused and ready to go the second you walk in here." Megan glanced at the clock. "Of course, you're usually here early."

Kit followed her gaze to the ornate clock in the waiting area. And as she noticed it was two minutes to nine, she also noticed Marcia Jackson—her first session of the day. The woman was seeing her for grief counseling after losing her husband of sixty years, and had just walked in. Which meant Kit couldn't follow up any further with Megan on how she looked different today. But she didn't really need to. She *felt* different.

Crap. If she was going to do this thing with Dillon, she was going to have to get her stuff together.

CHAPTER NINE

Dillon pushed the elevator button that would take him up to the floor where he could check in on Sarah and Caleb and Tim and tried to push thoughts of Kit from his mind. She'd been distracting him all day. But he couldn't help but grin about it. She'd distracted him before. Every time she wore her red skirt, for instance. And every time she got on his case about something. And every time he got close enough to smell her. And every time she gave him one of her signature eye rolls.

But today was different. Today he was grinning the grin of a fool in love. And he didn't mind. Three people had already commented on his great mood, and Janice had caught him whistling earlier.

It wasn't that he wasn't a happy, upbeat guy usually. But he was serious at work. He joked, he smiled, he tried to praise the staff when he could, and he always tried to be honest but optimistic with patients. But he wasn't the type to stroll down the hallway, hands in his pockets, whistling.

But right now he was definitely strolling toward Sarah's room and biting back the urge to whistle.

Earlier when he'd gone to check on the new mom, the nurses had told him she was still asleep after a long night with a newborn who had his days and nights mixed up. Tim had arrived around eight and had instantly taken over with Caleb, and Sarah, knowing he was there, had fallen into a deep sleep. Tim was fixing things—exactly as Dillon had predicted.

Dillon had been pleased to find that Sarah had turned it all over, and the nursing staff had given Tim a list of things they needed him to do, from bathing to filling out paperwork to just holding his son. They were a small hospital and didn't have a dedicated nursery staff, so most babies stayed in the mother's room. Which was fine. Unless the mother desperately needed sleep and the baby refused to cooperate.

As Dillon knocked on the door frame to Sarah's room and peered inside, the sight that met him made his chest feel suddenly tight. Tim was sitting on the edge of Sarah's bed, where she held their son. The look on Tim's face hit Dillon hard. *That* was a man in love. With his wife. With his son. With his life.

"Hi, Dr. Alexander," Sarah said, looking up.

"Hey, everyone." He sauntered into the room, trying to seem totally casual about being hit between the eyes by the family moment. And the want that it shot through him.

The way Sarah was looking at Caleb, the way she smiled when she looked up at Tim—she had a softness about her. A glow.

He wanted that. He wanted it on Kit. He wanted her soft and glowing the way she had been that morning, every morning. Because of him. Because he made her happy and gave her fulfillment that she couldn't get anywhere else.

"Any chance I can take these two home today?" Tim asked.

Dillon had been expecting the question. "Medically, everything looks great, but I want to check road conditions and weather reports before you head out," he said. "The last thing you need is to be stranded by the road or stuck in a hotel with a newborn and postpartum wife." He gave them both a smile.

"I would never take them if I wasn't sure it was completely safe," Tim said quickly. "But I also want to get them home. I can take better care of them there."

Sarah reached up to touch his cheek, and Dillon couldn't look away as she said, "You're our hero."

He wanted *that*. He wanted to be Kit's hero. The one who made her look at him like that. The one who deserved her looking at him like that. He'd always loved ruffling her feathers and riling her up and making her grit her teeth. Because he couldn't have anything else.

Now he could. Now he could have this—this love, this sweetness, this feeling of *We're in this together*.

They'd done a ton of projects together over the years, and they'd turned out amazing. Sure, they'd fought their way through it, but together they could do anything. He knew it. So the next project was building a relationship. A *life*. And they were going to make it incredible.

"I'm going to look through your chart one more time," he told Sarah and Tim. "And I'm going to make a couple calls to be sure things are safe. But if it's all a go, you can head home today."

"Thanks, Dr. Alexander." Tim stuck his hand out, and Dillon shook it.

"Just take care of them."

"Of course." Tim looked over and smiled at Sarah. "That's my whole job."

Amazed by the tightness he suddenly felt in his throat, Dillon headed for the hallway, pulling his phone from his pocket. He hit Bree's name in his contact list.

"Dr. Go All Night, what can I do for you?" Bree answered on the second ring.

Dillon laughed. "Hey, Officer Smart-Ass. I need an official road report between here and Chicago." He had to admit, getting teased about last night felt nice. Like this was official.

"Only if you and Kit promise to come out with Max and me and Avery and Jake Friday night," she said.

But he could hear her typing on her end and knew she was checking the official reports. He could find the road conditions in Nebraska easily enough, and Iowa and Illinois, for that matter. But he knew the highway patrol would be putting out warnings to troops that would be more detailed, and Bree would be able to access it all faster than he could.

Plus, okay, maybe he'd reverted to a fourteen-year-old boy who wanted to hear if the girl he had a crush on had said anything about him to her best friend.

"We were probably going to stay in," he told Bree.

"Oh my God!" Bree exclaimed. "You had twelve straight hours of sex last night! You've got tonight and tomorrow and Thursday night. And you can take her home Friday night afterward. Can't you take a couple hours off?"

"I don't know. That's a couple of *hours*," he said, grinning.

"No. That woman needs to eat if you're going to keep going like this. Bring her to A Bar at seven Friday night." A Bar was the only bar in Chance and was actually named Sorry Mom, We Bought A Bar, but the shorter name had caught on quickly.

He sighed dramatically into the phone. "Okay, but only long enough for her to eat. And don't you have your own up-all-night guy who you're dying to stay home with?"

"Yes, but that man understands the importance of my having a regular cheeseburger. I'm amazing when I have some good meat in me."

Dillon let the pause after her words go on a little extra long. Then he said, "Can I please say it?"

"Do you have to?"

"I think I do."

"Well, go ahead, then."

"I'll be sure that Kit has some good meat tonight, too."

Bree chuckled. "That wasn't as bad as I expected."

He grinned. "I'm the nice one of the three of us," he said of him and his cousins.

"Um, no, I don't think that's true. Jake's the charmer, Max is the goofball, and you're the big badass. Huh," she said. "Look at that. None of you is nice."

He was the big badass? He supposed he could see where that came from. But he was feeling a little softer lately, too. Since he'd moved home, and certainly since last night. "Then it might surprise you that I was whistling today at work."

He strode to the nurse's station and grabbed Sarah's chart.

"I don't know—what were you whistling?"

"That matters? It's *whistling*."

"Of course. If you were whistling the Darth Vader theme song, that's not quite as *nice* as something like 'Zip-a-Dee-Doo-Dah.'"

He chuckled. "You've got me there. Let's just say it was more along the lines of the latter."

"You can't say 'Zip-a-Dee-Doo-Dah' out loud?" she asked.

"I'd rather not."

"Because it would ruin your big badass thing."

He whistled the main *Star Wars* theme as he opened Sarah's chart and grabbed a pen.

Bree laughed. "Nice. Okay, the roads look good. Some slight snow coverage once you get past Des Moines, but traffic is moving at a normal rate, and crews are out."

"So I can send my new mom and baby home without worry?" he asked.

"I think they'll be good," Bree said.

"Great. Thanks."

They were quiet for a moment until Bree finally said, "Kit included two smiley-face emojis in her text message earlier."

Dillon smiled. He really liked Bree. "She usually only uses one?"

"Kit Derby doesn't use emojis, Dillon," Bree said.

He liked that, too. "And her text said, *Best I ever had*, right?"

Bree snorted. "It said, *Drinks later?*"

Hmm. Well, at least there were emojis. "Ah, so that's when she'll give you the best-I've-ever-had info," he said. Though he really did want Kit to tell her friends that.

"You're kind of pathetic, Dr. Alexander," Bree informed him. "I love it."

Yeah, okay, maybe he was. But that didn't bother him. "We'll have a sign," he told her instead of confirming or denying. "When I just happen to show up at A Bar later on."

Bree snorted again.

Dillon smiled and continued. "If she says I'm the best she's ever had, when I see you, you pull on your right earlobe. And if she says she's crazy about me, you itch your nose. And if she says she's ready to run off and elope, you put your hand over your heart."

Bree was quiet, probably taking notes on his directions, for a few seconds. Then she said, "And do you know what it will mean if I put my finger up by my temple and rotate it a few times?"

"What?"

"That *you're* crazy," she said with a soft laugh.

"You think I'm crazy?"

"I think that you don't need signs to figure out how she feels, Dillon," Bree said, her tone gentler now. "Kit is good at projecting an image. Except when it comes to one thing—you. It's always been easy to read how she feels about you."

"It has?"

"You know that. You've seen it, too," Bree told him. "That's why you keep at her."

"I keep at her because driving her nuts is really fun."

"Exactly. And if it weren't fun, you'd stop. And if she'd ever *really* given you an indication that she didn't like it, you wouldn't think it was fun."

Dillon thought about that. "You know, hanging out with a shrink might be rubbing off on you."

"I know." He could picture the mildly disgusted look on Bree's face. "Sometimes I just want to drink and bitch, you know? But I always end up with *advice*." She said it as if Kit were trying to give her brussels sprouts instead of help.

It was Dillon's turn to snort. "Well, *I* appreciate *your* free advice," he said.

"Who said anything about that being free? I expect a large order of onion rings to go with my burger when you just happen to show up at A Bar later on," she said.

When Dillon arrived at the noon meeting, everyone else was already there.

He slipped into the room and then took the chair next to Kit as Don Rickert, the hospital's CEO, got the meeting started.

Kit shot him a quick smile—that almost knocked him on his ass—but he knew she was surprised he'd sat right next to her. He always sat across the table. It was a better position from which to argue with her. But it made smelling her difficult.

In the past, that had been a good thing. Smelling her made it nearly impossible to concentrate on anything else. But today, he definitely wanted to smell her. And maybe touch her. And maybe lean in to whisper something in her ear.

She always smelled good, but today it seemed that she was drawing him in, pulling him closer, tempting him. And all she was doing was sitting there.

But there seemed something different about her. He couldn't put his finger on it at first, but then he realized it was how she was sitting. She was leaning back in her chair, one leg crossed over the other, one hand resting on her lap and one on the tabletop. She was listening to the reports from around the table—nursing, radiology, pharmacy—and that's all she was doing. She wasn't taking notes; she wasn't asking questions. Typically she sat up, both elbows on the tabletop, a pen in hand.

He rolled his chair back slightly, wanting to take in the whole picture.

"Dillon, where are we at with your stuff?" he heard Don ask from the head of the table.

Dillon stopped as everyone turned to look at him, including Kit.

"Well . . ." It would be really helpful if he knew what the hell they were talking about. The meeting was about the free clinic. Other than that, he wasn't sure what they were discussing. All the department heads and then Kit and Dillon, as the instigators of the idea, had been meeting twice a week over the past two months, trying to get things lined up.

"Have you changed your mind about offering walkers and canes and braces?" Kit asked, meeting his eyes.

Right, the equipment. She'd just saved him. Dillon had been asked to look at how to cover the equipment he wanted to provide as a part of the clinic.

"If we want to make equipment available, we'll have to shift funds," he said.

Kit frowned at that. "We'd have to shift funds? Meaning we won't have enough to cover everything?"

Don nodded. "Our projected starting budget is short."

"What kind of shifts are we talking?" Kit asked Don. Frank Harvey, Chance's mayor, sat to Don's right. The free clinic was a big deal for the whole town, and Frank was fully on board. He'd been a big part of early fund-raising. To Don's left sat Shelly Walker, the woman in charge of the hospital's foundation.

Shelly spoke up. "We just might have overreached. At least to start. The whole program is impressive, of course, but we just don't have the resources to do everything you and Dr. Alexander have proposed."

Kit didn't look at Dillon, but he knew what she was thinking. This was one more thing they'd always had in common—wanting more and pushing beyond what everyone else could even imagine. They'd done that with their sophomore-class community-service project. The class had wanted to pick up trash or plant flowers at the park. Kit had suggested raising money by doing odd jobs for people around town and using the money to put in some handicapped-accessible equipment in the park instead. Because his mission was to always one-up her, Dillon had added on to the idea and suggested they also do pet care—dog walking, dog washes, dog sitting—and using that money to put a dog park in on the north side. By the time they were done going back and forth, the plan had included a community garden, a new gazebo, and a sand volleyball court.

And in the end, they'd ended up with enough money to add some ramps to the park, and a fence around a square of ground where dogs could run.

"If we shift some of the funds for the geriatric follow-ups, we could cover the equipment," Dillon told them. They just had to pick out the most important stuff to do first.

"We cut actual medical services?" Karen, the director of nursing, asked.

"No," Dillon said. "We just need to prioritize where we start. We can do this in stages." Just like they'd eventually bought a swing that would accommodate a wheelchair and a volleyball net. It had gotten done, and he and Kit had learned a lesson in patience. "We will still see to the primary needs. But the six-month follow-ups can be covered with a class setting. We bring everyone in together and go over education and questions that way, instead of one-on-one."

Everyone at the table turned to look at Kit as one.

She just blinked at them.

"Kit?" Don asked. "What do you think?"

Right, because this was where she usually jumped in and played devil's advocate no matter what Dillon said. Dillon prepared himself, fighting a smile at how cute she looked right now. No one ever had to ask her what she thought. She volunteered the information—invitation or not.

"I think it sounds like an acceptable, temporary solution," she said. "We'll want to get the follow-ups back into the plan as soon as possible, but if Dillon—Dr. Alexander—thinks the equipment is a primary need, we have to listen to him."

The entire room was quiet for five beats. Dillon tried to remember the last time he and Kit had agreed on something in one of these meetings without at least two weeks of debate. He couldn't come up with one.

Don cleared his throat. "Okay, then. Dillon and Kit, can you look at which things to shift where, and we'll redo the budget. Shelly has a foundation board meeting at the end of the week, so if we could get that before then, that'd be great."

"No problem," Dillon told them.

Everyone stood and gathered their pens, papers, and folders. Dillon hung back and was pleased to watch Kit cap, uncap, and then recap her pen four times. She was stalling.

When the last of the committee finally stepped through the door, Dillon turned to her. She had already taken the step that separated them, and as he shifted to lean back against the table, she moved in, against him. Dillon took a huge deep breath and tangled his fingers in her hair, tipping her head back and moving his lips to hover just above hers.

"I made the mistake of sitting next to you," he said. "I couldn't wait to see you, and when the seat was open, I went straight for it. Huge mistake."

"Yeah?"

"I couldn't sit still or focus. All I could think about was how fucking gorgeous you look and how much I wanted to touch your hair and run my hand up your leg and how I wanted to whisper in your ear that I can still taste you on my tongue."

Kit drew in a long, shaky breath. "Wow. This could be a problem."

"It could." His eyes traveled over her face. "God, you look so beautiful."

"You like my hair down?"

"Yes. But I like your hair however you wear it. When it's down, it reminds me of it spread out on the pillow next to me. When it's up, it makes me want to pull it down and mess it up. But it's not your hair I'm talking about."

"What is it?" she asked softly.

"You're glowing."

"I'm . . ." She lifted a brow. "I'm glowing?"

He nodded. She was. And he wanted her more than he ever had before. "You are. You look soft. And happy."

"Oh." She wet her lips. "I *feel* soft and happy."

"Because of me," he added.

She nodded, and Dillon felt satisfaction burst through his chest.

"This is happening really fast," she said.

"The fuck it is," he said quickly. "This has been happening since we were eight."

She smiled up at him. "Well, maybe eighteen."

"Sixteen," he countered.

"Really?"

He nodded. "We were the leads in the school play." They hadn't gotten to kiss, much to his disappointment, but they'd had to dance together. "You were graceful and gorgeous and never missed a mark or a line. And then you kicked my ass in the math competition that year.

Those two activities alone pretty much illustrated that you're the whole package. How could I not start falling for you?"

She looked at him for a long moment. Then said, "It was sixteen for me. When you pulled over and changed my car tire in the rain."

"The soaked shirt did it for you?" he asked with a grin.

She shook her head. "The fact that you pulled over at all. That afternoon I'd called your paper on FDR juvenile. In front of the whole class."

He remembered the flat tire and the rain. He hadn't remembered the insult. "That didn't matter. It was raining; you had a flat. Of course I pulled over," he said.

She nodded. "And that's why I started falling."

He stroked a thumb over her cheek. How had it taken them this long to get to this point? "Let me take you to dinner sometime this week," he said. "I want to go public. I want to do dirty things to you all night long, too, but after."

"I'm suddenly really interested in staying in all the time, though," she said, lifting onto her toes and kissing him.

How many times had he wanted to kiss her in the hospital in the middle of a workday? A thousand. Easily.

Dillon's hand threaded through her hair, and she gave a soft moan that made him pull her closer. Her belly pressed against the hard length behind his zipper, and he groaned.

"*This* could be a problem," he said gruffly as he pulled his mouth away from hers. "Now your lipstick is smudged, and I've got a raging hard-on to hide."

She couldn't help the sly smile she gave him as she ran her fingers around her lips. "Sorry." She stepped back, and he stretched to his feet.

He swatted her butt and laughed. "No, you're not." He folded her hand in his, and they started for the door. "Oh, by the way, Bree says we have to go out with them Friday night."

"Yeah, she told me."

"And you still got me all riled up about staying in?" He pulled the door open and held it as she walked through. "I believe you said *all the time.*"

"Oh, I would totally cancel on Bree for you," Kit said. "I've been waiting to text her that the meat at A Bar has nothing on what I have at home."

Dillon laughed and pulled her close to kiss the top of her head. "I love you."

And then they both froze. Completely, instantly still.

They didn't make eye contact. They still held hands, but Dillon could feel hers was stiff in his.

His thoughts spun. Should he say something more? He wouldn't take it back, but yeah, he was as surprised as she was that it had just fallen out like that.

Five seconds ticked by. Then ten.

Finally, Kit said, "I'd better go," pulled her hand away, and headed down the hall.

"Yep. Okay, me too. See you later."

But she was too far away to hear that.

Dillon dragged in a deep breath and thrust his hand through his hair. Well, shit. That hadn't gone as planned. Not that he'd *planned* to say "I love you" at all. At least, not anytime soon. And he certainly hadn't planned to just drop it into the middle of a conversation in a random hallway in the hospital.

He'd freaked her out.

But how did she not know that he loved her? Because he did. That realization hit him almost instantly. Hell, he'd *told* her that he'd been in love with her in high school. That was kind of like what he'd just said.

But it wasn't. That was in the past and a long time ago and they'd been kids. This was definitely different.

Okay, so what? Maybe he would have preferred to tell her over a romantic candlelit dinner or breakfast in bed. But how could he not love her? And he was the type of guy to say exactly what he was thinking and feeling. Especially to Kit Derby. Besides, in the middle of the day at the hospital after a meeting where they'd agreed to something that would move a mutually beloved project forward actually seemed like the perfect time for them. They weren't really the romantic-dinner type of couple. They were a fight-like-hell-and-go-to-bed-to-have-amazing-makeup-sex-afterward type of couple.

So she was freaked out now. Fine. He'd fix that. He'd repeat the words, and he'd let her rant about how it was too fast and how he was crazy and how he should have done it differently. And then he'd say the words again. And he'd tell her all the reasons it was true. And he'd kiss her until she melted against him. And said the words back to him.

Dillon took another deep breath and nodded. Yeah, it would be okay. Because he and Kit made a hell of a team, and he fucking *loved* it. All of it. All of her.

And she was just going to have to deal with the fact that he'd won the first-to-say-I-love-you race.

Kit headed for her office with her heart pounding and a very strange urge to cry. And she didn't know what she was crying about—was she upset or happy?

It really felt like a little bit of both.

She sat down behind her desk, put her hands palms-down on the cool desktop, closed her eyes, and took a deep cleansing breath. Deep breaths were almost always a good idea.

After about three, she opened her eyes.

Okay, so Dillon had said he loved her.

That was hardly a tragedy. That was . . . kind of amazing. Dillon was an amazing guy. He could have his pick of women. And yet, he had a thing for Kit.

That was pretty cool.

It was also . . . progress. Dillon wasn't her patient, but he was someone she'd studied for a long time. He had lost someone significant in his life. He'd left town and his family because of that loss. Now she knew that there was more there than grief or guilt. And it really broke her heart to think that Dillon would ever question his capacity to care and love. But this . . . Falling in love with someone else, *telling* that person how he felt, that was big.

If she didn't think too hard about the fact that the person was *her*, she could truly appreciate Dillon's growth from a very professional perspective.

Of course, it *was* her . . .

Kit pulled out her notebook and made some *professional* notes about what falling in love and being able to really pursue it and admit it and express it meant for Dillon.

Then she closed her notebook, closed her eyes . . . and freaked out a little.

Dillon was in love with *her*. Dillon had worked through his issues, realized that he *did* process emotions, and then he'd turned those emotions to *her*.

Her heart pounded, and her thoughts spun.

Finally, Kit picked up her phone. Everyone, even shrinks, needed people to talk to sometimes. Both Bree and Avery were at work and couldn't just drop everything. Especially because this was hardly a crisis. This was just . . . unexpected.

She texted them both. Dillon's in love with me.

Avery's reply took only about five seconds. We know.

Bree took a little longer, but her answer was all Bree: Duh.

Kit looked at both answers. And breathed again. Then felt her mouth curling into a smile. Okay, so maybe this wasn't so unexpected. It wasn't crazy, she supposed. She and Dillon had a long history. They had mutual respect, they shared a lot of similar interests and

---

passions—medicine, helping people, Chance, their friends and families—and they had amazing chemistry.

Kit thought about Avery and Bree. They'd both fallen for guys they had long, pretty complicated histories with, too. And they were happy. She had no delusions that things were always perfect and that the guys didn't still drive them nuts sometimes—and vice versa—but they would rather be with Jake and Max than without. That Kit knew for sure.

And she knew that now that Dillon was back in Chance, living and working and playing and making her crazy, she wouldn't want him to ever be anywhere else, doing anything else.

She wet her lips and texted him—I'm definitely canceling on Bree Friday.

His response was almost immediate. You'll want to cancel any early-morning plans, too.

She smiled. Then laughed. Out loud. Then she sent a message to Megan to move her Saturday-morning appointments back two hours.

"We're calling an emergency meeting for noon today," Helen Litner told Kit two weeks later as Kit scrolled through her e-mails at her desk.

"Oh, I'm sorry, Helen, I can't make it."

There was a beat of silence from Helen, but finally she said, "You can't make it?"

"I'm sorry. I already have a meeting at noon today." Kit smiled as she looked at the two dozen yellow roses on the corner of her desk.

They had arrived that morning with a card that said simply, *I meant what I said.*

They were, of course, from Dillon, and even though they'd said a lot of things in the past two weeks, Kit knew what he was referring to.

The *I love you.*

He hadn't said it again. She hadn't said it to him yet. But they'd both sure as hell been acting like it.

They'd been out to dinner in Chance four times. They'd hung out with their friends. She'd gone to Sunday brunch at his grandmother's house. He came to her office for lunch every day—her noon meeting today—and they were just generally sickeningly happy and all over each other.

And no one—not friends, not family, not neighbors—acted surprised. At all.

"But we're going to be deciding who's in charge of the various events for Founder's Day," Helen said, as if that would sway Kit's decision.

"I know. But I can't make it," Kit repeated.

"You don't want to be in charge of anything?"

Helen's tone of voice indicated that she had never heard of such a thing. And, frankly, she probably hadn't. Kit was always in charge of something. Or everything.

"We have many good leaders on our committee," Kit said. "I know that the Founder's Day celebration will be fabulous no matter who's in charge."

It, admittedly, felt a little strange to say that. Kit had a small notebook full of notes she'd taken after last year's Founder's Day that would make this one so much better. But she had a lot going on. With the free clinic and the disaster resource center and—

There was a knock on the frame of her door, and she looked up to see Dillon leaning against the doorjamb looking gorgeous. She felt the huge grin that stretched her face.

Seeing him in his scrubs and lab coat did something funny to her insides. She'd seen him earlier in the hallway, and he'd given her a private smile and wink, and she'd been stunned by how turned on she'd gotten. Because that morning he'd pulled her into "their" storage closet, the one where they'd taken cover during the tornado six months ago, and had dropped those scrub pants and rocked her world.

"Helen Litner," she mouthed to Dillon.

He rolled his eyes as he stepped across the threshold of her office. She watched as he shut the door, pressed the lock, and shrugged out of his lab coat.

Her pulse began hammering as he approached.

"Helen, honestly, I'm happy to help however I can," she said to the older woman as Dillon stopped by her chair and rotated it to face him.

"Donna thinks that she can take over the cook-off *and* the parade, but we both know that won't work," Helen said.

Dillon dropped to his knees in front of Kit and uncrossed her legs. Her breathing instantly went ragged.

"Everything will be fine," Kit told Helen.

Dillon's hands settled on the outside of her thighs, and he started inching her skirt up. Her eyes went wide, but he wasn't looking at her face.

CHAPTER TEN

Meeting up with Kit for lunch every single day was awesome. Dillon barely remembered what he'd done for lunch before he'd started dating her—and it had been only two weeks.

Dating her. Man, he loved that. They should have absolutely done this a long time ago.

His turkey sandwiches tasted better, he felt more energized when he went back to work, his bedside manner had improved—and they'd only had sex about half of those lunch breaks. He just fucking liked being with her.

But going down on her in her office while she was on the phone was, quite frankly, a fantasy come true.

He knew Helen. He even liked Helen, mostly. But he didn't feel one bit of guilt as he slowly slid Kit's skirt up her legs and parted her knees.

It was this red pencil skirt. That was part of it. He loved this skirt and had imagined this, and so much more, numerous times when she'd worn it in the past. He was now in heaven.

She was wearing silky red panties to match, and as he kissed up the inside of her thigh, he pulled them to one side, loving the way her breath hitched and she completely forgot what she was saying to Helen.

"Yes, I can do that," she said, definitely breathless.

Dillon ran a finger over her clit and kissed the inner thigh muscle that tensed as he did it.

"Of course," she said into the phone.

But when he looked up, her head was tipped back, her eyes were shut, and her fingers were digging into the arms of her chair.

He grinned. So much fun.

He licked a path from her thigh to her center, pausing ever so briefly on that sweet spot that made her gasp. She'd pulled the phone away from her mouth and was watching him, her cheeks pink.

"Dillon," she whispered.

"Finish your phone call," he told her, his voice low. "So I can finish you."

"Helen, I'm sorry, something just came up; I need to go." She didn't even pause for an answer before she slammed her phone down on the receiver. "I can't believe—"

But he put his mouth back on her, and she stopped talking. And started moaning.

He licked and sucked, added a finger, then a second, until she was desperately gasping his name, trying to stay quiet, as she went up and over the edge of her orgasm.

Dillon let her come down from the clouds before sliding his fingers free. He made sure she was watching him as he lifted them to his mouth and sucked her sweetness from each one. Slowly. Thoroughly.

"I can't believe you just did that," she said.

He leaned in and put his mouth to hers. "Kiss me," he commanded softly.

She did, sliding forward in the chair, bracketing him with her knees, pressing her body against his.

Everything was lips and tongues and sighs for the next several moments. As Kit clung to him, Dillon undid the tie at the front of his pants, eased down his scrubs, rolled on a condom, and then grasped her hips and pulled her forward, sliding home.

"*Yes,*" she moaned against his mouth.

She rubbed and rotated, moving against him as if she couldn't get close enough and he couldn't get deep enough. He quickly found a rhythm and, cupping her ass in his hands, pounded into her. There was just something so damned hot about taking Kit apart in her office. This was the place where she was the most put together, the most in charge. But now she was making delicious sounds that wound him tight and made him want to pound his chest. That Dr. Derby could be reduced to nothing but hot need by his hands and mouth in the leather chair in her polished, perfectly neat office gave him a shot of cocky confidence that he couldn't replicate any other way.

He felt the climax tightening deep in his gut, then the electricity racing up his spine as her inner muscles clamped down on him, and he let go with a shout he muffled against her lips.

Holy shit. He wanted to stay right here, forever.

Dillon dragged in a huge gulp of air and leaned back to look into Kit's eyes. "Happy lunchtime," he said, brushing her hair back from her face.

"This is a hell of a diet plan you've got me on, Dr. Alexander," she said with a laugh.

He kissed her and pulled back, taking care of the condom in the trash can under her desk while she straightened her clothes. He hoped the cleaning lady didn't inspect the contents of Kit's wastebasket. But then he grinned. He didn't care. Everyone knew he and Kit were sleeping together, and more. And no one was a bit surprised.

"You need to eat," he said. "I shouldn't take up your entire break."

She grabbed the front of his shirt as he started to stand, pulling herself up with him. "I'm fine, Dillon. You don't have to worry about me or take care of me. I'm eating just fine. In fact, I've discovered a new love of cheeseburgers, *and* I had dessert last night with Bree and Avery."

"You girls went to Bree's after dinner?"

Kit nodded.

"Well, gee, let me guess," he said. "Ice cream?"

Kit laughed. "We did. She has, like, six varieties."

"I've never met a person who eats so much ice cream," Dillon said. With Kit pressed up against him, he could hardly stay on the topic of Bree's dessert preferences, though. He palmed her butt, grinding into her. "Tell me we can be alone tonight," he said.

"We were alone . . ." She scrunched her nose as she thought about it. "Three nights ago."

He sighed. "This thing where we're both from here and have friends in common and stuff?" he said. "It's putting a crimp in my getting-you-naked time."

"You've had me naked every night," she said, rubbing against him like a cat. "And most noontimes, too."

"I didn't have you naked just now," he protested. "I had *parts* of you naked, but not everything. And I love nothing more than to spread you out, totally bare, where I can get at every inch, and go from head to toe and back again."

She shivered in his arms. "Yeah, I know."

"So tonight, just us."

"I told Bree we'd meet them for a drink."

Dillon groaned.

"I know," she said. "But after, I'm all yours, and you can spread me out wherever you want."

He groaned again, but for an entirely different reason. "Really?"

"Really."

"Well, let's see . . . we've done the bed, of course, the kitchen table, the coffee table, the living-room floor . . . oh, washing machine."

Her eyebrows rose. "Washing machine?"

"Oh yeah. And we'll turn it on. All that rumbling and vibrating?" He waggled his eyebrows, and she laughed. God, he loved her laugh. More, he loved *causing* it.

"So you're all mine after drinks?"

"Yes." She kissed him. "And I'll even be the one to cut things off at A Bar. I was late for my first appointment yesterday because you kept me up too late the night before."

He kissed her again and let her go. "Yeah, I heard."

"You were *there*," she said.

"But I heard about it once I got here, too," he said. He made sure everything was tucked in where it was supposed to be and then took one of the chairs facing her desk. He started to rummage in his lunch bag.

"Wait, you heard that I was late for an appointment?" she asked, sitting and spinning to face him.

"Yeah. They were talking about it in the break room on the second floor." He grinned. "And then Janice looked right at me and said, 'Gee, I wonder why.'"

"Oh my God."

He looked up. Kit was definitely not smiling. "What?"

"The whole hospital knows that I was late? Because we were having sex all night?"

"You weren't late because we were having sex all night," he said, biting into his sandwich. "You were late because we had sex that morning."

"Because I woke up late and didn't really have time for sex that morning because I overslept because we'd been having sex all night," Kit said.

Dillon took another bite.

She just watched him chew. When he'd swallowed, he asked, "What?"

"People know I was *late* for a *patient* because of *sex* with *you*," she said slowly, as if he were learning a new language.

191

"Kit," he said, setting his sandwich down, "everyone knows we're together. Everyone. Every single person in this town. And they know what we're doing at night. And in the morning."

"That's not the point! They know I was *late* because we're together. I'm *never* late! And certainly not because of something like sex!"

Dillon knew that he shouldn't feel a little smug about that. He definitely knew that he shouldn't *show* that he was feeling smug about that. "Was the patient upset?" he asked.

"It was only ten minutes, and I let our time go over by fifteen."

"Then what's the problem?"

"That you are a very bad influence." She sat back in her chair and crossed her arms.

Dillon picked up his sandwich again. "You're letting loose a little," he reasoned. "No one's perfect, and I would guess most of the town will be relieved that applies to you as well."

"Dillon," Kit said firmly, "it is not okay for me to be late to appointments. Maybe I need to start going home after we . . . you know."

He grinned at that. "Considering where my mouth just was, I think it's okay for you to say the word."

She actually blushed at that, and Dillon laughed. He really did love her. He was careful not to say it again. They weren't quite there yet. But he had to bite it back on a daily basis. And he loved waking up with her. So there was no way in hell she was going home after they you-knowed.

"Maybe I need to be paying more attention to things," she said as she pulled her salad from her lunch bag.

"What things?" he asked.

"Well, for instance, Helen has me signed up to do something for Founder's Day, and I have no idea what it is," she said drily.

He finished off his sandwich with a grin. "The best thing about that," he told her, "is that you've already done everything on that committee at one time or another, so it doesn't really matter where she signed you up."

"But I'll have to admit that I don't remember what I agreed to. And I never forget things."

Yeah, she never forgot things or was late to things or blew things off. But damn if he didn't love being the one to throw her off her game a little.

"I'll find out for you," he said. "I'll see Helen at the diabetes education class tomorrow. I'll ask her then."

"You'll just go up to her and ask her what I signed up for?" Kit asked.

"I'll tell her I want to sign up for the same thing so we can work together."

"You've never worked on Founder's Day before."

"If you're working on it, I'll work on it. It'll be great."

She frowned and stabbed some lettuce. "You don't have to do that."

"I know. I want to."

"No, really, it's okay," she said. "I'll just do it on my own."

"Let's do it together." He was frowning now, too. What was the big deal here? He wanted to be with her, and he didn't mind helping out with something so important to the town.

"I'd rather do it on my own," she said, stabbing more lettuce with excessive force.

He opened his mouth, but just then his phone beeped. Dammit. He pulled it out and glanced down. "ER. I've got to go."

She nodded. "I know."

He rose but kept his eyes on her as he wadded up his paper bag. "I'll see you later."

She looked up. "Okay."

"And you're spending the night tonight," he felt compelled to say.

"Fine."

Fuck. Something was up, but he had to go. And he couldn't be distracted once he hit the ER.

He plucked the card out of the roses that sat on the corner of her desk. *I meant what I said.* He flipped it onto her desk planner, right in front of her.

Her eyes landed on the card, and she took in a deep breath.

That was going to have to be enough for today.

But not for much longer.

Kit barely tasted her lunch as she ate, thinking about Dillon and trying to pinpoint why she felt restless suddenly. Or why she didn't want him on the Founder's Day committee with her.

But she wasn't even done eating by the time she had the answer—she wanted to do it by herself.

That didn't seem like a huge revelation, of course, but considering how the last two weeks had gone and the fact that she had definitely fallen for him, it bothered her.

But you haven't said you love him back yet.

No, she hadn't.

And why not?

He seemed all-in here, had confessed how he felt, had made it clear to the whole town that they were together. Why hadn't she returned the *I love you*? And why did she *not* want him on the Founder's Day stuff? They'd been working on the free clinic and the resource center together. They'd done everything together for the past two weeks. They'd eaten almost every meal together, slept in the same bed, come into work and gone out with their friends.

And that was it, right there.

Kit wasn't used to sharing everything in her life with someone. Particularly with Dillon. She hadn't been giving committee work and meetings 100 percent of her attention lately, she could admit, but she'd chalked it up to the honeymoon phase of her relationship and figured it would pass.

But this was Dillon. He gave all he had to the things he cared about. And he cared about most of the same things she did. And now, he cared about *her*. He was always going to want to be a part of everything.

Kit slumped down in her chair as a cold knot of reality settled in her gut. His commitment and passion toward causes was one of the things she liked best about him. But it was what she liked best about herself, too. So why did it feel like she was losing some of that?

With her thoughts spinning, Kit almost didn't hear the knock on her door. She frowned at the wooden frame. "Yes?" she called. She didn't have an appointment for another hour.

She couldn't have been more surprised by who poked her head into her office a moment later. Kit sat up straight, nearly dropping her salad bowl, as Shelby Harvey stepped through the door.

Shelby was the mayor's wife. The mayor's bubbly, optimistic, blonde, twenty-eight-year-old wife. Shelby had grown up in Chance and had never been more than fifty miles away from it, that Kit knew of. She was Dillon, Jake, and Max's cousin, part of one of the most beloved and influential families in town, and loved the town with an unmatched passion. She was a force to be reckoned with and nearly impossible not to like.

Kit braced herself.

Shelby had never, ever come to Kit's office for any reason. And Kit didn't think Shelby was here for therapy.

"Shelby, hi. What a surprise." Kit set her lunch to the side and quickly ran her tongue over her teeth, hoping she didn't have anything in them.

"Hi, Kit," Shelby said with a big smile. "I don't mean to interrupt, but I really need to talk to you."

Okay, maybe she was here for therapy. Or at least for advice. Kit straightened further and smiled. "Of course."

"I'm so happy about you and Dillon," Shelby said, dropping into the chair her cousin had recently vacated.

Kit hid her sigh. This wasn't about Shelby. And they were going to just dive right in. "Thank you," she said. Because what else was she going to say? She was happy about her and Dillon, too. Mostly.

Kit frowned as that last word flashed through her head.

"But I'm concerned."

Kit made herself focus on Shelby. "You're concerned? About Dillon and me?"

Shelby set her purse on the floor next to the chair, crossed one trim leg over the other, and gave Kit a sweet smile. "Of course, like everyone, I knew it was inevitable that something was going to happen between you two."

Inevitable. Well, there was a big word. Kit couldn't deny that a lot of what was happening felt inevitable, but she didn't love how that made her feel a little out of control. "Dillon is . . ." Kit trailed off, not sure what word to put in there exactly.

"He is," Shelby said with a light laugh. "And I love that there is finally someone who has him wrapped around her little finger."

Kit shifted on her chair. A month ago, she would have liked thinking that she might have some power over Dillon. Not that it was a particularly adult way to feel, but Dillon had always had the ability to make her feel and act crazy, and she liked knowing she could affect him, too. But now, the way Shelby said it, it made Kit uncomfortable. She didn't want his feelings for her to change how he acted or reacted.

And that's when it hit her—she didn't want her feelings for him to change how *she* acted or reacted, either.

"I would never use our relationship to influence him," Kit said carefully.

"But it will," Shelby said matter-of-factly. "Important relationships in our lives *do* influence us. You can't be in love with someone and share your life with him and not expect to be affected by him."

Kit couldn't argue that. Besides, Shelby had more experience in relationships than Kit did. She and Frank had been married for nearly four years, and they were definitely Chance's version of a power couple. They'd done a multitude of amazing things for the town, were involved in several initiatives on a state level and, in spite of their age difference, had a strong, loving relationship. And it was clear that their shared passions for community service and betterment were a big part of their bond.

"Which is why I'm here," Shelby said.

Kit was *not* going to try to talk Dillon into whatever Shelby had in mind. Dillon was his own person. He could make his own decisions, and while she might share her opinion with him, she would never expect him to change to do things her way. "Shelby, Dillon can—"

"I'm concerned about you."

Kit stopped and blinked at her. "I'm sorry?"

"I'm concerned about you," Shelby repeated.

"Yes, I heard you. But I don't know what you mean."

"You can't give in to Dillon all the time just because you're in love with him," Shelby said.

One thing Kit had always appreciated about Shelby was how straightforward the other woman was. "I don't intend to give in to Dillon all the time," Kit said.

But she felt a strange niggle in the back of her mind.

"Good," Shelby said. "Because Frank told me about the meeting a couple weeks ago, where you went along with Dillon's idea rather than fighting him, and it concerned me."

The thing about shifting funds from the follow-up checks to equipment. Kit remembered it well. It had been the morning after the farm. She certainly hadn't been her usual self that day.

Have you been your usual self since then?

She ignored that nagging voice and focused on Shelby. "Dillon and I argue and disagree," she said. "A lot," she added. "But we do listen to each other and respect the other's opinions. I want what's best for the clinic, but so does Dillon. I believe that. So there's a point where I have to just trust that. And him."

Shelby nodded. "Okay." Then she leaned in, resting an elbow on her knee. "We need you, Kit. Chance needs you. You've *always* been one of our leaders. You get stuff done. You make sure it's right. You love this town. I'm thrilled to death that you and Dillon are finally admitting how you really feel about each other, and I want you to be happy, but we can't lose you."

Kit felt her throat tighten slightly. She wanted to be important to this town. Yes, she liked to be number one and be regarded as successful, but more, deeper, she loved this town and wanted to be a part of making it great.

"Dillon is important to me," Kit said. "But nothing will change all of that."

Except that the past two weeks had been full of changes.

"Helen Litner told me that you've decided to head up the rooster races," Shelby said. She tipped her head to the side. "Rooster. Races. Where last year you were in charge of the entire Founder's Day celebration."

The rooster races? Seriously? Kit took a deep breath. "Helen caught me at a bad time. I'll talk to her. I can do more than that."

Well, at least she didn't need Dillon to find out what she'd been assigned to now.

Shelby nodded. "Thank you. Helen and Donna absolutely cannot handle Founder's Day on their own. Or, at least, we can't handle the results of them handling it on their own."

"It's not a problem," Kit assured her. "I'll be at the next meeting, and I'll be sure everything is on track."

Shelby nodded, then stood, pulling her purse strap up on her shoulder. "I have no worries if you're in charge," she said.

That made Kit feel good, if slightly embarrassed that she'd needed to be encouraged to be more involved.

Shelby made it to the door before she turned back. "And some advice from someone who's known Dillon forever and loves him dearly but can be a little more objective, since he's not making me late for things with hot morning sex," Shelby said.

Kit fought the urge to groan. *Everyone* knew about that. Dammit.

"Yeah?" she asked, knowing there was no reason to give excuses.

"Dillon is used to charging into things and doing what's most important, what's right in front of him at the moment. But he's not as good at thinking about consequences down the road. That's usually someone else's issue."

"What are you saying?" Kit asked.

"In the Guard, in Africa, in the ER—he has to make quick decisions based on his gut. What comes later, the long-term effects, are less of an issue," Shelby said. "Being in love with you and wrapped up in all of that is what's right in front of him, and he just acted on it. But I don't know that he's aware of the consequences."

"Like softening me up to the point that I don't do all of the things I should be doing?" Kit asked, feeling a weariness start to settle on her shoulders.

"And the way that you being softer will affect him," Shelby said.

"What do you mean? He'll probably love that."

Shelby shook her head. "You and Dillon balance each other," she said. "Like the scales where you have to put equal weights on each side to keep it level. Dillon is used to being the one everyone looks to for decisions and opinions and advice and action. Everywhere else. But not here. Here, he has to share that with you. In Chance, you keep him from taking everything over, and you're the one who ensures the times he does take over are because he's really the best one to do it."

Frustration seeped into her. She'd given in on *one* decision about the free clinic. Just one. But she hadn't so much as asked a question about it. She rubbed her forehead. "So I need to keep fighting with him?"

"Not necessarily. Just do what you've always done."

"Hold him back? Bitch at him?" she asked.

"Make him work at it. He needs that. And he knows it. Why do you think he finally came home to settle down? He knows, on some level at least, that this is where he's best. In large part because of you. But if you go over to his side of the scale, it will tip."

Kit took a deep breath. Which was harder than it should have been with the band of emotion around her chest. "I hear what you're saying."

"Good." Shelby nodded. "And I have a couple ideas about the rooster races, so call me when you're ready to work on that."

Then she swept out of the office in a twirl of blonde hair and perfume.

CHAPTER ELEVEN

Kit let out a breath and slumped back in her chair. She had an appointment with Gwen and Larry Thomas for marriage counseling. She couldn't do anything about Dillon right now, and she would *not* be further distracted from the things she should be doing.

But she reached for her phone.

Being the very experienced and highly professional mental-health expert that she was, she realized she needed some therapy of her own. And everyone knew that a doctor should never diagnosis or treat herself.

"I need to talk," she told Bree when her friend picked up.

"Where and what time?" Bree asked.

In spite of her churning emotions, Kit smiled at that. That was a true friend right there. And she knew Bree would be practically bouncing in excitement to get to give Kit advice for a change. Kit talked, but she was rarely the topic of conversation.

"A Bar," she said. "How's three o'clock?"

"Drinking at three in the afternoon?" Bree asked. "Count me in."

"I just want to avoid a big crowd. You're not on duty?" she asked her friend, one of Chance's finest, and next in line for chief of police.

"I'm off at two."

"Then let's make it two," Kit said. She didn't have any appointments later that afternoon, and the research paper she was working on would never happen with her currently scattered thoughts. "You think Avery would be available?"

"I'll make her available," Bree promised before disconnecting.

Avery was the fire chief, but as long as she had her phone and didn't drink, it wouldn't be a problem for her to stop by A Bar for a little bit. At least, Kit hoped that it would take only a little bit to sort all of this out.

How long could it take? Kit was an expert at understanding human emotions and reactions to trauma and drama. There was just something that Avery and Bree had more experience in than Kit—being in love.

Well, okay, she was experienced at being in love with Dillon. From afar. Without his knowing. Without *anyone* knowing. Without him feeling the same way. And certainly without him sending her flowers and giving her just-for-her smiles in the hallways and locking her office door at lunch and making her lose her mind.

That thought made her heart pound and her throat thicken with emotions she couldn't name. Because those lunchtime trysts weren't just sex. They weren't just hot. They meant something. They meant that . . . even her lunch breaks had changed. And she liked it.

God, was she happy or upset? She didn't even know. But in that moment when Dillon had said, "I love you," almost as if it were just a given, something he'd been saying to her forever, something they always said when they parted ways, she'd been hit by a giant wave of . . . want. Yep, that was what it was. She wanted that. She wanted him saying that as easily as he said "Have a good day" or "See you later."

She knew that people sometimes felt that *I love you* was used too casually, that people said it without thinking. But there was a difference between proclaiming love for chocolate cake and love for Beyoncé and love for family. She didn't think Dillon had said it casually, exactly. The fact that he'd said it *easily* was what had rocked her.

And the fact that he hadn't said it again. As if he knew that she was adjusting and that it was big. But he'd sent the flowers with that card. The card he'd flipped onto her desk as he was leaving today. Reminding her of it, even without saying it. And that was something else she wanted—to know it. To just *know it*. No matter what.

Just like she wanted to *know* who she was, no matter what.

And the woman who had been late, and distracted, and easy to get along with, and unconcerned about Founder's Day, and was now in charge of the roosters . . . that was *not* her. That was not her normal.

For years, her normal with Dillon was to not see him more than three or four times a year. Then, for the past six months, it had been to butt heads all day and then go home separately.

Now it was . . . She really didn't know. She saw him throughout the day, all day, every day. Then they went home. Together. What had happened to the middle part where they were supposed to butt heads? That hadn't happened for two weeks. And there was a new middle part—where they kissed and teased and flirted and . . . said *I love you*. Kind of.

Yeah, she had no idea what to do with all of this.

Which was why she was at A Bar fifteen minutes early for her therapy session with Bree and Avery.

"Hey, Kit," Brenda, one of the twin sister owners of A Bar, greeted as Kit came in.

"Hi, Brenda."

"So you and Dillon at your grandma's house, huh?" Brenda said with a huge grin as she took a glass and filled it with iced tea, Kit's go-to.

Kit realized she hadn't seen Brenda since then. She'd been in A Bar a few times, but Brenda's sister, Becky, had been manning the bar. "Uh, yeah," Kit said with a shrug. "We went to check on Grandma and decided it was safer to stay till the storm was over. Because it was dark. And then the wind chill and all." Kit took a drink of her tea so she would stop talking.

"Smart move," Brenda said.

Kit nodded. "We thought so."

"Then again, *any* move that results in being cuddled up with Dr. Alexander is a smart move in my book." Brenda gave her a wink. "I woulda climbed on the back of his snowmobile, too."

"Oh, it wasn't—" But Kit bit off her protest. Her go-to reply was "It wasn't like that," but the thing was, it had been. She'd climbed on the back of that snowmobile because she trusted Dillon. And because she'd wanted to. She hadn't known they'd end up stuck together, and lip-locked, and other-things-locked, but even if she had, she still would have climbed on his snowmobile.

"You're already one drink in?"

Kit swiveled to find Bree and Avery coming through the door. "Iced tea," she said, holding up her glass.

"Still, I'm gonna have to catch up," Bree said with a wink. "Beer, please!" she called to Brenda.

"How about you, Avery?" Brenda asked.

"Soda. I'm on the clock," Avery told her.

"Thanks for coming," Kit said.

Avery lifted an eyebrow. "I wouldn't miss this for the world."

Kit sighed. She should probably be proud that her having an emotional meltdown was so unusual that it meant her friends would do anything to witness it.

They took a table toward the back of the main room. There was a party room with pool tables and dartboards, and even a dance floor behind them, but during the week, the main room was more than large enough to accommodate the lunch and drinks-after-a-long-day-of-work crowds.

"So tell us *everything*," Avery said as Brenda set down their drinks, including a refill for Kit.

"Can I get a cheeseburger?" Bree asked Brenda. "And onion rings."

Kit looked at her. "You didn't have lunch?"

"I had lunch," Bree said, as if that was a dumb question.

Kit had always marveled at the way her friend ate. Bree was trim and fit yet had a penchant for junk food, especially ice cream. Of course, she also ran and biked and mountain climbed, and a million other very physical activities. Not to mention that she had an energy about her that Kit had never seen in another person. She was quick to laugh, always seemed to be moving—whether she was bouncing a foot or drumming her fingers—

And was always ready to go, up for anything.

But as Bree slumped back in her chair, crossed an ankle over her knee, and tipped her beer back, Kit also realized that Bree seemed less animated lately. No, that wasn't the right word. Bree was as upbeat and lively as always. She just seemed more—at ease. Or something. She still seemed happy, but she wasn't fidgeting or on the edge of her seat.

"So what's up?" Bree asked.

Kit sighed. "I'm in charge of roosters because I'm in love with Dillon."

Avery just blinked at her. But Bree nodded, not seeming a bit surprised.

"*Roosters?*" Avery asked. "As in male chickens?"

Kit nodded. "Founder's Day."

"Why did you sign up for that?" Avery wanted to know.

"I didn't. Exactly. I was distracted by Dillon and just agreed to it."

"To roosters," Avery said.

"Yes."

Avery leaned in. "*What* is going on?"

Kit looked at her other friend. Avery, too, seemed different. She had always been quieter—though it wasn't hard to be quieter than Bree—and more content to observe than participate in their girl talk. None of the women had been friends in high school. They'd all been far too different. While Kit had been leading everything from committees to the honor roll, with Dillon right on her heels, Bree had been sneaking out of school and studying only enough to get by. Avery had been the quiet, shy girl with a rough home life who had followed the rules but hadn't participated in anything but classwork.

After they'd all ended up back in Chance, working jobs in major leadership positions—fire chief, psychiatrist, and police officer—they'd found a bond, though, and now Kit couldn't imagine her life without these two women.

And there was a definite difference in them both since they'd fallen in love. "You and Jake used to drive each other crazy," Kit said to Avery. "How is it now that you're together?"

Bree and Max had always been friends, even before realizing they were in love. They'd traveled together and had seen each other once a month for their adrenaline adventures—skiing, rafting, hiking. Avery and Jake had definitely not been friends. They'd actually not been much of anything other than acquaintances and classmates, until graduation night when things had suddenly combusted between them. Then Jake had left town, and they'd spent ten years driving each other crazy whenever they saw each other. Until the tornado in June. They'd been stuck together in a shed, and . . . things hadn't been the same since.

They'd been so much better.

"What do you mean?" Avery asked. "We still drive each other crazy." She got a faint blush on her cheeks as she said it, and her smile was wide but soft.

Kit blew out a breath. "So it's not different for you?" *Dammit.* Was she the only one who was having these crazy changes in habits and personality?

"It is different. But it's also the same. I mean, everything that was there before is still there. All of those feelings haven't gone away, but it's different because we know where those feelings are coming from now," Avery said. Then she frowned. "That sounds confusing, doesn't it?"

"I just . . ." Kit sighed. "Before, Dillon and I fought all the time. About everything. But now that we're together, I'm going soft. I'm late for things, I'm not going to meetings, I'm distracted. And Dillon is making stupid decisions about the free clinic. And who knows what else? I'm not sure how to be sweet and supportive and in love with him but also fight with him."

"Well, first off," Bree said, "you're not going to be able to pull off sweet, so just stop trying. Second of all, there's a very good reason that you and Dillon always fought. And that hasn't changed."

Kit knew the reason. She was enlightened enough to at least recognize a lot of her bickering with Dillon for what it was. "For a long time, it's been my way of not showing how I really feel," she admitted. "When he was with Abi, I couldn't let on how I felt because he was spoken for."

Bree nodded. "Okay, maybe. But what about before Abi? And after?"

"Before Abi?" Kit asked. "He started dating Abi when we were sophomores."

"And you had no feelings for him then?" Bree asked. "Really? Because every other girl in school did."

"You did?" Kit countered.

"A little bit," Bree said with a grin. "He was always hanging out with Max, and Max was always hanging out with me, so I was around Dillon. He was awesome, even back then."

Kit frowned, recognizing that being jealous about a crush that hadn't turned into anything and had happened almost fifteen years ago was ridiculous. But she felt a little stab anyway.

"What is it *really*?" Bree pressed. "Why have you been afraid to admit your feelings, to let up on Dillon a little bit, to maybe even go for it when it's so obvious there's chemistry and major history between you?"

Kit took a long, deep breath and looked at her two closest friends. These women knew her. Had seen her at less than her best. And they cared about her anyway.

But as those thoughts went through her mind, she realized they weren't her *closest* friends, actually.

That was Dillon.

He knew her, better than Bree and Avery even did. That was the thing about having a nemesis—you had to study him, learn his strengths and weaknesses, catalog his best and his worst moments. Dillon *knew* her. He'd seen her at her bitchiest, at her lowest, at her most embarrassed—because all those things had happened when she'd been up against him. But he'd also seen her shine, seen her succeed, seen her proud and happy.

And he'd said that he loved her.

In spite of it all.

"Because I was afraid of giving him that control," she finally said. "He already made me feel out of control. He can stir up my emotions faster than anyone. And I always hated that he had that power. I guess I thought I had to keep fighting him. Fighting those emotions and everything."

Bree and Avery both nodded.

"You think I'm right?" Kit asked.

"Listen," Bree said. "Dillon and Jake and Max—they're all kind of larger than life. They take over a room, a conversation . . . and yeah, your heart, when you let them. And that can be kind of scary. Until you realize one thing."

Kit felt her heart hammering. Wow, being on the other side of advice was hard. "What's that?"

"That none of them have ever done anything without the best intentions," Bree said. "None of those guys are out for themselves. They want the people and the world around them to be better."

Avery reached over and took Kit's hand. "And that when they love, they do that with all of the passion and energy and heart with which they do everything else. They all came back to Chance, they helped rebuild this town, they started a resource and teaching center for other communities, they're here for their families, and they are here for *us*. Being loved by those guys is overwhelming at times, but it's so worth it."

"It's like a tornado," Bree added with a grin. "It'll get you all twisted and tangled up, but when you're on the other side, you realize what's truly important because it's what you were clinging to while the storm was raging."

Kit swallowed hard. She'd been clinging to Dillon—literally— during the tornado, just like Bree and Avery had been clinging to Max and Jake. And during the snowstorm, she'd been safe and happy because she'd been with Dillon.

She looked at her friends—two of the strongest, smartest, most confident women she knew—and took in their in-love smiles and the general air of contentment around them. But they were still kicking ass, doing their jobs, taking care of the things that were important to them.

"Except that I can't do anything, evidently, by my own motivation and drive," she said. "Dillon has to be challenging me and pushing me and making me mad for me to get off my butt and do something."

"What are you talking about?" Avery asked.

"As soon as I admitted how I felt about Dillon, I went all soft, and now I'm blowing off commitments and passing up leadership roles and generally not getting anything done."

"That's ridiculous," Bree declared, signaling their waitress for a refill. "You're fine. You're amazing." She ordered another beer and then three shots.

"I was late for an appointment the other day," Kit said.

Bree lifted a brow. "And?"

"I'm never late for appointments."

"And you were suddenly late because now that you're having hot sex with Dr. Stud, you've lost the will to do anything else?" Bree asked.

Kit chewed her bottom lip.

Bree burst out laughing. "First, good for you. Second, give me a break."

"I'm *serious*, Bree. I don't know if I'll ever accomplish anything else if Dillon is nice and sweet and . . . in my bed."

"Oh my God." Bree shoved a shot glass toward Kit. "As much as I'm enjoying *you* being a mess for a change, this has to stop. Dillon Alexander is not the reason that you're accomplished and respected, Kit."

"I said no to heading up Founder's Day."

"So what? You fucking do *everything* around here, and you always have. You deserve a break."

"That is *not* the point. I'm losing my edge. I need to be challenged, and when we're together and getting along and saying things like 'I like you no matter what,' then . . . I guess I stop caring about the other stuff."

"Okay, Doc, listen up," Bree said, leaning in to rest her elbow on the table. "Here's the thing. Dillon didn't make you a type A, over-achieving, kick-ass chick. He made it *okay* for you to be a type A, overachieving, kick-ass chick."

Kit looked at her friend. "What do you mean?"

"I mean, Dillon being who he is didn't make you do amazing things. Hell, he hasn't even been here for ten years! He just made you realize that it was okay to do amazing things."

Kit felt her heart hammering against her ribs. She picked up one of the shot glasses and tipped back the sweet-and-spicy cinnamon schnapps that was Bree's go-to.

"And do you know why he's the one who made you understand that?" Bree went on. "Because you're the same person," she said without waiting for a response from Kit. "He's the same type A, save-the-world, be-on-top person you are. And he basically gave you permission to conquer the world . . . because he was doing it, too. You guys push each other, but more than that, you complement each other." She sat back in her chair again and crossed her arms. "You would make anyone else fucking miserable."

Kit stared at her friend. And thought about what she'd said. Crazy, adventurous, down-to-earth Bree McDermott had just psychoanalyzed her. And done a good job at it.

"You wouldn't date Dillon?" Kit asked. "He's adventurous. He could totally keep up with all your craziness."

"Hell no," Bree said with a laugh. "He might jump out of an airplane with me, but he'd be telling me everything I was doing wrong and wanting to prove that he was *better* at it than me. I'd smother him in his sleep. After the really amazing hot sex, of course," she said with a wink.

That didn't bother Kit a bit. Bree was madly in love with Max. No way did she have feelings, or even a true attraction, to Dillon.

She looked over at Avery. "You agree?"

"That Dillon would drive me bonkers if I were involved with him?" Avery asked. "Absolutely."

"Jake's completely cocky," Kit pointed out. Max was, too, for that matter, but he more or less worshipped Bree. Jake liked to rile Avery up. "Doesn't he ever rub you the wrong way?"

Avery laughed. "Of course. But he's . . . Okay, he's an overachiever, too, but it's like . . . he can't help it," she said with a little frown. "That doesn't make sense. I mean, Dillon obviously has tons of natural talent and intelligence and a natural leadership style. But he also *tries* and pushes." She finally shrugged. "I think Jake is more content than Dillon is. Jake does his thing and, yes, gets cocky about it, but Dillon seems to always be looking for more."

Kit nodded. That all made a lot of sense. And she got it in Dillon. That made the most sense. Bree was right. She understood Dillon because . . . she was just like him.

"So are we okay here?" Bree asked. "You okay to be in love with Dr. Save the World?"

Kit took a deep breath. "I don't know."

Avery nodded. "That's okay. You know that, right? You don't have to be sure of everything all the time."

"But you do have to be willing to take a chance," Bree said.

Kit finally lifted her iced-tea glass and toasted her friends. "I'm glad you've been paying attention all of the times I've advised you. You've picked up some good stuff."

Bree laughed and clinked her glass with Kit's. "See? Even making *our* amazing advice about *you*. You're perfect for Dillon."

Kit opened her mouth to reply, but just then, the door opened, and three big, cocky, good-looking guys strode in. Jake led the way, followed by Max, then Dillon.

Jeez, she felt revved up just looking at him.

The guys took over the space and the conversation, just as Avery had said they did. Jake picked up Avery and took her chair, pulling her into his lap. Max grabbed two more chairs and shoved one at Dillon while he turned the other and straddled it, putting him right up next to Bree. Dillon dragged his chair over to Kit and sat, dropping his arm over the back of her chair and settling in. As if he'd been doing it forever.

The heat from his body soaked into her side, and she felt him toying with the ends of her hair as Jake launched into conversation as if the guys had been there all along.

"Just got word that five different communities will be attending our preparedness weekends in March and April," he said with a huge grin.

"Awesome." Bree leaned over and high-fived him. "I've got my manual almost done."

Jake, Avery, Max, and Bree had been working on turning Chance into a living, working resource and training center for tornadoes and other emergency situations in rural areas. With Jake's emergency-management background; Max's construction and building experience, along with his expertise as a storm chaser; not to mention Bree and Avery being in major leadership roles in a small town that had been hit by a record number of EF4 tornadoes over the years, the training they could provide to other communities was unparalleled. Dillon's experience in medical assessment and treatment after disasters, and Kit's expertise in dealing with the emotional and psychological effects disasters could have on people, especially children, were also being tapped for the project. The six of them working together were certainly a force to be reckoned with, and Kit felt a familiar thrill at the amazing things she and her friends had, and would still, accomplish.

"So these towns will be sending their leaders—their mayor, fire- and police-department reps, contractors, doctors, whoever they think should be involved. We'll run them through educational sessions, some hands-on training, have them observe all of us," Jake went on. "Each group will get a weekend of their own, so we can really get down to what they specifically need and want to know. But they'll be arriving Friday afternoon and leaving Sunday evening, so we have a lot to get done in about forty-eight hours."

"We'll be fine," Avery said, wrapping her arm around Jake's neck. "It's the six of us. We can do anything."

"Damn right," Max agreed.

Bree linked her arm with Max's. "You know how I get all tingly when you talk about weather," she said. "I might not be able to sit through your sessions."

Max took her chin in his hand and pressed a kiss to her mouth. "I'll have you listen to me practice at home. Then we can take care of those tingles, no problem."

Kit didn't know if she should look away from the blatant PDA or study it. She would have never guessed tomboy, tough-girl Bree McDermott for the type to go all googly-eyed at her boyfriend or kiss in public, but there she was.

Same with Avery. Avery led a crew of men, ran into burning buildings, and argued with anyone who dared suggest cuts to any public-service programs, and yet there she was, sitting on Jake's lap, his hand splayed possessively over her ass, smiling at him like he'd hung the moon.

The girls had definitely changed since falling in love. And that same thing would happen to Kit. She'd soften up and relax and . . . let Dillon have his way more because she wasn't trying to keep him at arm's length.

But . . . then who would she be? She'd always been Kit Derby—the crusader, the advocate, the one who didn't back down from a fight—no matter what. The winner. She'd always been the one who came out on top. Okay, so maybe it was right behind Dillon some of the time, but still, striving to outdo him, to be better and do more . . . that was what put her up there. Without that competition, where would she be? Fifth? Tenth? Would it even matter? And if she was having amazing sex and he was kissing her in the conference room in the middle of the day, would she even care?

"You're overthinking again," a deep voice said in her ear.

She turned her head to look at Dillon, finding his mouth millimeters from hers. "Am I?"

"I can see the smoke coming out of your ears as you try to figure out whatever you're figuring out," he said. "Relax." He settled his hand on her shoulder.

But instead of comforting, it felt heavy.

"I, um, need to go." She pushed back from the table and stood.

Everyone looked up at her in surprise. "You have to *go*?" Bree asked. "Go where?"

"Back to my office," Kit said, jerking her purse strap up onto her shoulder. "I have a research paper to work on."

Bree didn't looked convinced, Avery looked concerned, and Dillon looked . . . knowing.

Dammit, she hated when he looked knowing.

"I'll walk you out," he said, stretching to his feet as well.

At least he wasn't trying to talk her into staying. Or saying things like *Relax.* "You don't have to."

"I know." But he stepped back to let her pass in front of him, obviously fully intending to follow her out.

Well, whatever. She'd dealt with Dillon in the past when she hadn't wanted to. Why would this be any different?

Because he loves you.

No. That should *not* make a difference. She should be the same person whether Dillon loved her or not. Hell, Dillon should love her for *being* that person.

Kit worked on her breathing as she headed for the door. She was overreacting. She knew that. But it really was so much easier to identify and *rectify* things like this in someone else.

When she got to the door, she felt his big hand wrap around her upper arm and steer her down the short hallway to the right. And directly into the storage room.

She turned to face Dillon. "Another storage room?"

"I'm not letting you leave without at least trying to talk about this," he said, dropping his hold on her arm. He moved so that nothing was between her and the door.

She recognized that she had every opportunity to just go. He was giving her the choice to stay. She sighed. The adult, mature, healthy thing was to talk this out with someone who would understand and whom she could trust. If nothing else, Dillon fit those two qualifications.

"Fine," she agreed.

"Then shut the door."

"What?"

"Shut the door, Kit."

And there was that low, firm voice that always stirred her. She took a deep breath. "I don't think that's a good idea."

"We always shut the door before we yell," he said.

Now she turned to face him fully. "We're going to yell?"

"We always yell. At least a little bit."

"I just thought that maybe now that we're sleeping together and . . . d-dating . . ." Yeah, okay, she tripped over the word a little. It was just a new one to be using with Dillon. His eyes had narrowed, but he didn't say anything. "I just thought maybe we should try getting along."

He moved swiftly to the door, shutting it firmly. It wasn't quite a slam, but she had no doubt that anyone on the other side knew that he wasn't happy. Even without that, no way in hell would anyone in A Bar come in here if they knew Kit and Dillon were in here together.

He turned on her then. "We're not going to stop fighting just because we're sleeping together."

Kit knew both of her eyebrows were up. "You realize that sounds crazy, right? People who date and fight all the time are the types of people I counsel before they head to divorce court."

"That's them. This is us." Only a couple of feet separated them, but he moved closer anyway. It felt like he was taking up all her oxygen, too. "We fight because we're better that way."

"We are?"

"Of course we are. My idea to shift the money from follow-ups to equipment in the free clinic? The one that you agreed with the other day during our meeting? That sucks. So now patients with new type 2 diabetes who can't afford clinic visits are going to have to wait for a class and risk circulatory issues and possibly even amputation so that someone can get a knee brace for arthritis?"

This was exactly what Shelby had brought up. "Did you talk to Shelby today?" she asked.

He frowned. "No, why?"

Okay, so he'd come to this conclusion on his own. That was interesting. "Knee braces for arthritis aren't important?" she asked.

"Of course they are! They're also a fraction of the cost, and there are a number of other options," he said. "If we have to make cuts, the funding should stay with medical care."

"It was *your* idea, Dillon!" she exclaimed. "I was just trying to be supportive."

"Well, don't support me when I'm being a dumbass!" he shot back. "I count on you to keep me from doing that!"

She stared at him. Then her gaze dropped to his mouth. "I'm not on my game lately," she admitted. "I'm beyond distracted."

"Me, too," he said, running a hand through his hair.

"I've been distracted for two weeks. I don't want to do anything but be with you. That's not fair to my patients or the town or the committees that count on me."

"And I suggested we defund a medical program."

"So if I'm supposed to be keeping you in check and *not* thinking about kissing you while in session with patients, maybe we need to—"

"Don't say it." His voice was husky as he took her face in his hands. Dillon's mouth claimed hers in a deep, hot kiss. One hand slid around to cup the back of her head; the other palmed her hip, bringing her up against his body.

And Lord help her, she wrapped her arms around his neck and arched into him.

His tongue took possession of her mouth, and she responded to every stroke, nibble, and groan. She wanted him. She wanted all of this. The things he made her feel, the way he made her think. But she couldn't lose herself in this.

Kit pulled back, breathing hard, and pushed against his chest. "I have to go."

He took his hands off her, shoving them into his pockets, but his gaze wouldn't let go. "After all this time, after everything, *now* you run?"

"What's that supposed to mean?" she asked.

"I mean, you've stood toe-to-toe with me, time after time after time. You've never backed down from something I've challenged you to do. Until now."

"What are you challenging me to do?"

"Love me."

Kit felt the air whoosh from her lungs.

"Be in love with me, Kit." He took a deep breath. "Do this relationship thing, this forever thing with me."

She pressed her lips together and shook her head. She felt the tears stinging. "I'm just . . . I don't know how to do this with you. We've been a certain way for so long."

"I want to keep being that way," he said.

Kit could tell that he was battling to keep his hands in his pockets. He wanted to reach for her, he wanted to hold on to her, but he was giving her space.

She shook her head. "How do we do that? How do we fight in committee meetings and then get along at home?"

"We do it because we respect the fighting. We understand it. We *need* it. We're both better when we're pushing each other."

"You really think we can sustain that?" she asked. "Because I'm not sure I can. When I'm with you, I'm softer. I'm sweeter. I want to cuddle in blanket forts and make out in conference rooms more than I want to fight about funding the free clinic. That's not good. I want to be the woman who fights." She grimaced. "I know that sounds bad. But what I like best about us"—she took a deep breath—"is that you're my best opponent. No one makes me work as hard as you do. And that work matters to me. It's important."

He studied her face, as if trying to decide how sincere she was. She knew it sounded horrible, but she needed Dillon to fight with her. Maybe more than she needed him to love her.

He blew out a breath. "Neither of us has ever *not* gone for something we wanted. We've both failed, I'll give you that. But not very often. And never together."

"We've come up short," she said softly. "The other day when Shelly said that we'd overreached on the clinic, I couldn't help but think maybe we're overreaching on this. Maybe we're expecting too much."

"Too much? Being together is too much?" Dillon thrust a frustrated hand through his hair. "We're both here. We both want this. How can this be the wrong thing?"

"Because I don't want to change!"

He frowned at her. "Change? Why would you change?"

"I've already changed! I'm 'softer,' I'm humming at work, I let you have your way in that meeting, I'm giving up committees, and I'm running late and forgetting things!" She was as frustrated as he was. She was the person people came to for answers, to work through emotional issues. But she wasn't sure how to fix this one.

"I would never want you to be different, Kit," Dillon said, his voice rough, his face miserable.

"But when you're different with me, I am different," she said, feeling just as miserable. "When you . . . love me, I'm different."

Dillon dropped his hands to his side and blew out a breath. "So what do we do, Doc?" he asked. "Because this addiction to you might be a problem, but I don't want to get over it."

Her heart melted a little at that. She did love him. He loved her. She just wasn't sure she'd be good at loving him. Or being loved.

"Just . . . give me some time," she finally said. "I'm going to go. I'll take a drive. I just need to think."

"No," he said quickly. "I'll go. You need to be with your friends." He gave her a sad smile. "That's how this works, right? I upset you, and you go talk to Bree and Avery, and then you figure out how to kick ass again?"

She shook her head. "I don't talk," she said softly. "I make everyone else talk."

"Well, then . . . go do your thing," he finally said. "It's been working all this time."

She watched him turn and pull open the door, then disappear around the corner. And she slumped against the wall behind her.

Because "her thing"—ignoring how she felt about Dillon and *not* talking about it—*had* been working all this time. But, as usual, Dillon Alexander was making her rethink everything.

CHAPTER TWELVE

Dillon reclaimed his seat at the table and grabbed Max's beer. Damn Kit Derby and storerooms and tornadoes and blizzards.

He took a long swallow, then set the beer mug back down with a *thunk*.

"Everything okay?" Max asked, shooting a look at Bree, who looked equally concerned.

"Nope," Dillon said flatly.

"Kit left?" Bree asked.

"Yep."

"You going after her?" Jake asked.

"Nope."

"You sure?" Jake asked.

"When have I ever been sure about anything where Kit is concerned?" Dillon asked.

They all just nodded as he made that very good point.

"Should we go after her?" Bree asked Avery.

Avery shrugged and looked at Dillon.

He held up his hands. "Hell if I know what she needs." But he did know. Kit needed *him*.

Dillon felt itchy as he made himself stay put in the chair.

Kit was worked up, and he wanted to fix it. But he didn't know how. Besides insisting that she keep kicking his ass, he wasn't sure how to assure her that everything would be fine and that this could work.

But damn, he needed her to be the Kit she'd always been, too. He needed her to argue with him and make him look at things differently and challenge him to defend his stance on things.

Because of Kit, he knew what was important to him. Was getting along with people and cooperating and working together toward a common goal important? Of course. But without Kit questioning and holding him accountable and making him defend his choices over the years, he wouldn't know what he believed in with the confidence he had now.

Could she be both soft and kick-ass? He hoped so. He couldn't give up either side.

"We need to talk about something else," he said. "*Anything* else."

They all dutifully launched into further conversation about the community disaster resource center. But none of it was new. They all knew the plans backward and forward. But that worked for Dillon. He needed a topic of conversation that he didn't have to concentrate on.

Bree's phone rang a few minutes later, and she pulled it out without looking at it. "Officer McDermott." Then she sat straight up in her chair. "Where?"

Everyone at the table stopped talking and focused on her. Bree was staring ahead and listening to whoever was on the other end.

"She's not here," Bree said. "Have you tried her cell?"

She listened again, and Dillon felt a knot of tension tighten in his lower gut. She had to be talking about Kit.

"Yes, try that number, and I'll start calling, too." Bree started toward the door. "I'm on my way."

Dillon was up and out of his seat and on Bree's heels. Max was right behind him.

Bree disconnected the call and starting dialing another. Dillon didn't say a word as he followed her to her car and climbed in the back seat. She glanced at him but didn't say anything. She just got behind the wheel while Max got into the front seat. Jake and Avery were heading for Jake's truck.

A moment later, she hung up with a "Dammit" and then dialed again. "Kit's okay," she said over her shoulder to Dillon as she started the car. "They're trying to find her for one of her patients."

Dillon felt some of the tension leave his body. "Thank God."

Bree looked up into the rearview mirror. "The guy's holed up in his house with a gun. He's shot his wife—she's alive but bleeding—and he's saying that he's going to kill her and himself if Kit doesn't get there in the next ten minutes."

All the air whooshed out of his body. *"Fuck."* He jammed a hand through his hair. It felt like an anvil had settled on his shoulders, pressing him into the seat, into the very floor of the car. At the same time he felt like every one of his nerve endings was jumping and zapping. He needed to *move*, to *do* something.

"Dillon," Bree said firmly, "start calling her. Over and over again until she picks up."

He nodded and pulled out his phone, his thoughts spinning. Kit's phone went to voice mail. He hung up and redialed. Bree was on the phone with someone new a moment later. The dispatcher, Dillon assumed from her questions and answers. There was a gun and a distraught patient who needed Kit. That was the bottom line.

Kit couldn't go to that house. He couldn't let her walk in there. He couldn't lose her.

But she had to go.

That realization smacked him in the face as he started to push the button to dial her number. His thumb shook, but he made it press the phone.

She had to go. That's what she did. She took care of things. She took charge. She made things better.

But *damn*. How could he watch her walk into that? Could he talk her out of it? Plead with her?

Maybe.

But he wouldn't.

"Kit!"

His head jerked up as Bree spoke into her phone. Kit's phone had gone to voice mail for him. He hung up. He didn't know what to say anyway, and it wasn't like she was going to be listening to her messages for the next while. But he had *so much* to say. So many things he needed to tell her. So many things she *had* to know.

"Breathe, Dillon," Max ordered, turning to look over the seat at him.

Dillon pulled in a long, shaky breath and gripped his knees with his hands, squeezing, trying to anchor himself.

Bree was talking to Kit, filling her in on the address and situation. Dillon caught only single words here and there, but it was enough. *Travis, Third Street, one gunshot wound, shoulder, Lisa, threat.* And most of all, *Kit.* That last word was the only one he needed to hear.

Bree pulled up the car and slammed on the brake. They were on Second Street. Dillon made himself look around, then focus on Bree's conversation.

He had to help. Somehow. In any way. Sitting in the back seat, struggling to breathe, and thinking of all the ways this could go sideways was not doing a damned thing for anyone.

He forced all the panic, all the adrenaline, all the what-ifs to the back of his mind and focused. He could do this. He'd done it a million times with patients and coworkers, and it had never been more important than it was with the woman he loved out there in the middle of the heat.

Bree was still talking to Kit as she climbed out of the car. Dillon followed her to the trunk. She popped it open, unlocked the gun case inside, and loaded her weapon. Dillon's heart lodged itself firmly in his throat, but he had control now. He had his shit together, and it would stay together until this was over.

Until Kit didn't need him anymore.

Bree's eyes went to his. "Travis is going to let you inside," she said into the phone to Kit. "He's going to let you treat Lisa's shoulder, and he wants to talk. But it has to be only you, and he doesn't want you to even be on the phone with anyone."

She paused to listen, still watching Dillon.

Dillon paced back and forth along the back of the car while Bree talked to Kit.

"Go straight up the front walk," she told her friend. "He's waiting for you. Don't take anything in." Again her gaze found Dillon's as she listened to Kit. "You'll have to find stuff inside to treat her with."

With that, Dillon's mind instantly clicked into triage gear. There was a woman inside with a gunshot wound to the shoulder, and Kit would be going in without supplies. Grateful for a reason to use the part of his brain that wasn't filled with *I need her, I can't live without her, she has to be okay, I have to be sure she's okay,* he generated a list of common household supplies she could use. A gunshot wound, if it was clean, wouldn't be hard to control until they could get Lisa treatment at the hospital. If the bullet was still in her shoulder, it could get harder. And the location in the shoulder was critical.

"Just do what you can for her shoulder," Bree said into the phone. "But you have to talk him down. The fact that he wants to talk to you is big. He didn't shoot anyone in a public place. He hasn't shot himself. This is all good."

Dillon could tell that Bree was mostly just talking. Those things *were* all positive, but they could also change rapidly. And it was possible that Travis had a beef with Kit, and he was bringing her into the house to settle up.

Dillon's heart plummeted, and he forced himself to breathe. He had to be here for her. He couldn't freak out.

"Is she there?" he asked Bree.

She nodded. "Outside the house. Across the street."

Bree had parked one block over. Travis had insisted Kit be the only one to come to his house, and they didn't want to spook him. But Dillon moved quickly down the sidewalk. Between two houses, he could see what he presumed to be Travis's house on the next block. And Kit's car parked directly across the street from it.

His throat tightened. She was right there. He could get to her before she made it up the front walk. He cared about her far more than he cared about Travis.

Dillon instantly shook his head. It might be true, but it didn't matter. Kit's job was to help that man. Travis needed her. Lisa needed her. And Dillon knew Kit would fight him to go in.

Fight him. She'd fight him. *That's* what she needed.

He stalked back to Bree and held out his hand.

Bree frowned and shook her head, clearly understanding he was asking for her phone.

"Let me talk to her, Bree."

"No way."

"Bree." He used his best doctor-in-charge voice. "Give me the fucking phone."

She covered the mouthpiece and glared at him. "*No.* Dillon, she can't be shaky right now. She's going in. You and I both know there's no other option in her mind. But she has to be *on.* You've mixed her all up. She can't be soft right now."

"Bree," Dillon said, calm, cool, and absolutely determined. There was only one woman who could out-stubborn him. And she was about to walk into a volatile situation that he *needed* her to walk out of. "I know you love her, but I promise you that there is *no one* on this planet who needs her to come out of this in one piece more than *I* do." Dillon held out his hand again. "Give me the phone."

Bree frowned, then took a deep breath. And handed over the phone.

"Kit?"

"Dillon?"

Her voice almost sent him to his knees. She sounded scared. He couldn't remember the last time he'd heard that in her voice. And that wasn't Kit. She was tough and in charge and always knew the right thing to do and say.

"You know exactly what's going on with this guy, right?" he asked, tamping down every urge to tell her he loved her and that he wanted to marry her and that he knew she didn't like big dogs but that they were going to have a black Lab and he already knew the dog would like her best.

"I . . ."

She trailed off, and Dillon swore silently.

"Dr. Derby," he said firmly, "do you or do you not know what's going on with your patient inside that house?"

He heard her take a deep breath. "Yes," she finally said. Then firmer, she repeated, "Yes. Of course I do."

"Then what the hell's taking so long?" he asked, making himself do this when he really wanted to rush to her side and hold her. "I have a patient inside there, too, and until you deal with yours, I can't treat mine."

Again he heard her pull in a breath. "Yours is a clean bullet wound. Mine has a few bigger issues," she said.

Dillon felt relief bloom in his chest. There she was. His fighter. Almost.

"So can you handle this or what?" he asked. "I'm going to need you to do some triage for the gunshot, too. Is that going to be too much?"

He could almost picture Kit pulling herself up tall and lifting her chin. He'd seen that four million times in his life. And he could imagine her doing it when she was eighty-six with gray hair, meeting his gaze with her sharp brown eyes and saying, "I love you, Dillon, but you're wrong."

He wanted to be wrong with her for the rest of his life.

"Of course I can handle it, Dr. Alexander," she said.

He heard her car door slam and knew she was out of the car and on her way up the walk. He willed his heart to quiet so he could at least hear the rest of what she was saying.

"First thing is getting that fucking gun away from him, Kit," he said, knowing that some of his emotions had spilled into his voice.

"I know," she snapped.

"And then you need to stop any bleeding."

"I'm aware."

"And I know that shoulders aren't really your thing. If she's still alive, he missed the carotid, but the brachial plexus—"

"Dillon," she broke in, "I did take anatomy. The same class you did. Do you really think that I studied the shoulder complex at any point in my life and am not aware of the circulatory issues at stake here?"

Dillon felt his smile spread. He hadn't expected to be smiling for quite some time. He nodded. "There's my girl," he said softly.

He knew he shouldn't say anything softly. He shouldn't be sweet. She couldn't let her guard down now. But he couldn't help it.

There was a long pause on the other end. Then her voice came to him softly as well. "Tell me you love me, Dillon."

He swallowed hard, his throat so tight suddenly he wasn't sure he could. But of course he could. "I love you, Kit. So fucking much."

He heard her breathe deeply and then, "I love you, too. And I know that doesn't make me soft or weak or less than I was before. It makes me stronger. More sure. It makes everything I do mean more."

"Damn right it does," he told her. He paused. "And now I'm going to need you to go into that house and deal with this situation because I need to take you home and celebrate you finally saying that to me."

She didn't say anything, but he could picture her nodding.

"Go get 'em, Kit," he said.

"I'll see you soon," she told him thickly.

They disconnected, and Dillon gripped the phone tightly in his hand, breathing in through his nose and out through his mouth.

"I'm going to need that back."

He opened his eyes, not having realized he'd squeezed them shut until Bree spoke. He handed her the phone.

"You did good," she told him.

"You sure?"

"You've always pushed her just enough," Bree said.

"And I've always loved her just enough."

"No, you've always loved her way beyond that." Bree took the phone and tucked it in her back pocket. She had her gun drawn. "You need to stay here," she told him as she started across the grass between the houses. "Ambulance is on its way with no sirens or lights. They're coming to you right here."

"You're going in there?"

"I'll be in the front yard, ready," she said, indicating the huge tree in the front yard of Travis's house. "This is going to be okay. Just hang tight."

Dillon nodded. Okay, ambulance. Emergency medicine for Lisa. That's what he could concentrate on.

Max came up beside him. Dillon scrubbed a hand over his face, "Jesus, how do you let her go in like that?"

Max clapped him on the shoulder. "Because she'd be miserable if she didn't go in," he said. "And she's a hell of a shot."

Dillon let out a small laugh. It wasn't much, and it kind of hurt his chest, but he did it.

"Kit's a hell of a shot, too," Max said. "Maybe not with a gun, but she knows how to get to the heart. She'll figure this out."

Dillon knew he was right. Kit wouldn't want to be anywhere else but in the middle of this, and she was the best one for it.

That made it a little easier to stay outside and wait. Not much, but a little.

Thirty agonizing minutes later, the front door to Travis's house opened, and he walked out, his hands up in the air.

Bree moved in immediately, with two other officers who'd shown up. She quickly got Travis to the ground and cuffed.

"And then there's that," Max said, letting out a long breath that showed he'd been as wound tight as Dillon had. "It's pretty hot when she cuffs someone."

Dillon didn't say anything. And he didn't remove his stare from the front of the house until Kit stepped out, helping another woman with an arm around her.

Relief washed over him so intensely that he had to lean back against the hood of Bree's car to stay on his feet.

Bree looked over her shoulder as the two other officers escorted Travis to their squad car down the block. Kit nodded and waved to her friend.

Dillon couldn't hear any of it, but he knew she was okay.

"Go," he told the EMTs, waving them forward.

They pulled around the corner and up in front of the house, blocking Dillon's view of the yard. Pulling in much-needed oxygen, he took two steps to test the stability of his knees before he broke into a run. He rounded the front of the ambulance a moment later. Lisa was already on a stretcher. He glanced at Kit, and she gave him a smile.

For the first time—maybe in his life—his own needs nearly overrode those of the patient. But he forced himself to turn to Lisa. She was conscious and even smiled at Jeremy, the paramedic taking her blood pressure.

They rattled off numbers to Dillon, who took them in and processed them automatically. He lifted the edge of the dish towel on Lisa's shoulder. The wound had missed anything vital and was as clean as it could be coming out of a kitchen.

"I'll meet you up there," he told the EMTs as they rolled Lisa into the rig. Then he swung around and stalked toward Kit.

"I'm—"

That's as far as he let her get. He crushed his mouth to hers, gathering her into his arms and drinking her in. He absorbed the feel of her against him, the way she immediately clung to him, the heat of her, her weight in his arms, the way she smelled and tasted.

He didn't let her up for air for several long moments, completely ignoring Bree's throat clearing and Max's "Uh, dude." It wasn't until the police chief, Dillon's uncle Wes, said, "Okay, break it up," that Dillon finally lifted his head.

Kit stared up at him.

Dillon stared down at her.

Finally, the corner of her mouth curled up. "Just another day at the office."

He set her on her feet and hugged her against his chest. "Thank you for being kick-ass at your job."

She squeezed him back. But added, "And yours, I guess. You gotta admit that gunshot wound looked good."

He shrugged. "Well, I'm not the only doctor here."

"But I'm on your turf," she said, also repeating words from two weeks ago at the scene of Sarah's delivery.

"Damn right you are," he said. He ran a thumb over her cheek. "And I never want you anywhere else."

"Right beside you, giving you a hard time and challenging you at every turn?" she asked.

"And making my heart nearly pound out of my chest when you're taking risks and when I'm so damned proud of you I can't stand it and when I'm overcome by how much I love you."

Her eyes went soft. "I love you, too."

And it was official, she absolutely could be kick-ass and soft and sweet at the same time.

Two weeks later, Dillon walked into the board meeting for the free clinic just after it started again. But this time he was holding Kit's hand.

Everyone stopped talking and turned their attention to Chance's newest power couple.

"Morning, everyone," Dillon said.

Kit gave him a smile and a wink as she slid into the chair just to the left of where he was standing, but Dillon stayed on his feet.

"Morning, Dillon," Don greeted. "We're eager to hear the big news."

Dillon had sent out an e-mail to the entire board yesterday, asking for this meeting and promising something big.

"Then let's get right to it," Dillon said. He looked at Kit, his heart swelling. They could do anything together, and they'd decided that it was silly to not just *do* the clinic together. Any project they'd taken on as a team had surpassed all expectations. It was stupid, really, to not approach this the same way they had the project at the park when they'd been in high school. They'd both focus on the things they were most passionate about, they'd push and argue with each other, and in the end, it would turn out perfectly. "Kit and I are taking over the development of the free clinic for Chance, separate from the hospital," he told everyone. "We've realized that we've gotten too bogged down in details and red tape. This community and its people need the services, Kit and

I are willing and able to offer those services, and we can worry about everything else as we go."

Don frowned as everyone around the table began shifting in their chairs and murmuring.

"Dillon," Don started, clearly choosing his words carefully, "we don't want you to think that the board and the town aren't supportive of the clinic."

Dillon looked at Frank Harvey and noticed he was simply sitting back in his chair, smiling.

"It has nothing to do with support," Dillon said. "We know you're all just doing your due diligence. But the truth is, Kit and I don't need the support. We can do this together, and we're tired of waiting around. That is not a shot at anyone," he added quickly. "We just realized that with our skills and passion, we can get this going now rather than waiting, and so that's what we're going to do."

Kit picked up the explanation. "So we're opening the clinic tomorrow. We've talked to the bank and to Tyler Morris," she said, referring to the real estate agent in town. "We'll be working out of the storefront on Main next to the hardware store. We'll have enough start-up money to get the basic supplies, but the main thing is we just need a place and . . ." She looked up at Dillon. "Us. This is our idea, our passion, and we have the licenses, skills, and desire to make it happen. We don't really need anything else."

Dillon really wanted to kiss her just then.

Don still looked concerned. "What about medications and lab and radiology?" he asked.

"Well, we're hoping that we can still get the grants in place and can get more staff to help out and that the hospital will want to work with us on those things," Dillon said. "But once we get it actually up and running, we know that everyone will see how great it is and will *want* to be a part of it."

"You're going to staff it with just the two of you?" Karen asked. "That's a lot to take on."

Kit nodded. "It is. Which makes it right up our alley."

Yep, he really needed to kiss her. Soon.

"So you're both on the same page on everything now?" Karen asked. "I know you had some opposing views."

Kit laughed. "We still do. We always will. That's what ensures this clinic will be the very best that it can possibly be."

She gave him a grin that made Dillon's heart completely full. They basically had a card table, a couple of chairs, some basic supplies, and a lot of educational brochures. But they were going to open the clinic tomorrow. Together. And it was going to be amazing.

Frank sat forward in his chair and said, "Kit. Dillon. I know I speak for everyone here when I say I have every faith that this will turn out wonderfully. And we'll all do what you really need us to do—stay out of your way."

Dillon grinned at that, and Kit smiled and rose from her seat. "Thank you, Frank."

Dillon took Kit's hand, and they started for the door.

"That's it?" Don asked. "That's all the discussion this needs?"

"It is," Kit said with a nod. "But you're all welcome to our grand opening tomorrow. There will be balloons and cookies."

Dillon chuckled as he held the door open for her. She didn't know it, but there would also be a big-ass diamond ring on top of a s'more for her as soon as the last person left the building.

He was pretty sure she'd say yes. But he wasn't sure he'd mind if she needed a little convincing.

And yes, he did realize that he was going to beat both Max and Jake to proposing.

Six months later

"Hell yeah!" Dillon's arm shot into the air, and he swung to face Kit with a huge grin. "I won!"

She laughed. "Yep, number one in the rooster races. Way to go."

But he grabbed the trophy from her and picked her up with one arm around her, giving her a big, long kiss in front of everyone. Then he set her back on her feet. "And tell Jake that you did not fix this race so I would win."

"How would I fix a rooster race?" she asked with a laugh. "Your cock was definitely the fastest."

Jake and Max laughed. "Fastest," Max said. "Not sure that's *really* a compliment when we're talking cocks."

"Yeah, she didn't say biggest or best," Jake pointed out.

But Dillon gave her a wink and swatted her on the ass. "My cock and I are number one, and I have a trophy to prove it. That's all I need."

She rolled her eyes but laughed.

The guys moved off toward the frozen-lemonade stand, and Kit felt Bree and Avery move up next to her.

"You totally fixed the race, didn't you?" Avery asked, tucking her hair behind her ear, the diamond in her engagement ring winking in the sunlight.

Kit just grinned.

"*How* did you fix a rooster race?" Bree wanted to know.

"I can't give away my secrets," she said.

"Okay, maybe more important, *why* did you fix it?" Avery asked. "Does Dillon really need to win *everything*?"

Kit shook her head. "Nah, but it does soften him up, and that makes it easier to beat him later."

"What are you playing later?" Bree asked.

"Chutes and Ladders."

Bree rolled her eyes. "That's so weird. You guys play that game all the time. I don't get it."

"You're both weird," Avery said. "You should just call your ice-cream sundaes and board games what they are—hot, rocking sex."

Bree turned to Kit with her eyes wide. "*Oh*. Chutes and Ladders is a code for sex?"

Kit laughed and put an arm around each of her girlfriends. "No. We actually play. You and Max don't actually eat ice cream?"

Bree laughed. "Oh, we do. But it's definitely a code. We eat ice cream while we—"

"Okay," Kit interrupted. "Got it."

A second later, Bree frowned. "You might have to explain how the Chutes and Ladders thing goes."

"Strip Chutes and Ladders," Kit said simply. She wouldn't ruin their assumptions by telling them that she and Dillon had had some really amazing *talks* because of Chutes and Ladders.

"But why that game?"

Kit laughed. "It's kind of a long story."

"Well, whatever," Bree said. "I'm glad you're happy." She grinned at both of them. "I'm glad we're *all* happy. It's awesome."

Kit pulled in a deep breath. "It is. Completely." She squeezed her friends.

"Oh, and I can't wait to show you the flowers for the wedding!" Bree suddenly exclaimed as Amelia, the town florist, started toward them. "Amelia did a great job."

Bree was as surprised as anyone by how much she was enjoying wedding planning, but she really was. Avery and Jake would be married first, but only by one day. They would say "I do" on the anniversary of last year's tornado. Bree and Max would be the next day. And then Kit and Dillon would be in December. On the date of the big blizzard. Sarah, Tim, and Caleb would even be there, celebrating the wedding . . . and Caleb's first birthday.

Kit knew that Dillon really did like to be first at things, but he hadn't even blinked when Jake told him the date of his and Avery's wedding. It was perfect for them, and Dillon knew it. And Kit thought that maybe Jake was even hoping for a tornado warning that night. Not a total storm, of course, but some storm clouds would be very appropriate.

Avery nodded. "Yeah, the weather here might really suck sometimes, but it sure does stir up some fun."

It really did. She and Dillon might actually play Chutes and Ladders and talk. But the blanket tents and s'mores were a whole other thing.

ABOUT THE AUTHOR

 *New York Times* and *USA Today* bestselling author Erin Nicholas has written more than thirty sexy, fun contemporary romances, described as "toe-curling," "steamy," and "enchanting." She loves reluctant heroes, imperfect heroines, and happily ever afters.

Erin lives in the Midwest with her husband (who only wants to read the sex scenes in her books), her kids (who will *never* read the sex scenes in her books), and her family and friends (who claim to be "shocked" by the sex scenes in her books).

Sign up for Erin's newsletter at www.erinnicholas.com/newsletter.html and never miss any news!

You can find Erin on the Web at www.ErinNicholas.com, and also on Twitter (@ErinNicholas) and Facebook (www.facebook.com/ErinNicholasBooks).

And join her SUPER FAN page on Facebook for insider peeks, exclusive giveaways, chats, and more! Visit www.facebook.com/groups/ErinNicholasSuperFans.

Made in the USA
Middletown, DE
07 July 2023

34676219R00151

They've competed since childhood, but now love might win.

Dillon Alexander has been Kit Derby's nemesis since third grade, when he beat her in the school spelling bee. They've been competing ever since, driving each other to be the best at everything from science fairs to bake sales. While working together one night during their senior year, they stopped bickering long enough to share an emotionally charged kiss. But a tragedy that same night left them both racked with guilt, driving Dillon out of town and leaving Kit determined to keep her distance.

Now an emergency room physician, Dillon has returned to their hometown of Chance, Nebraska. Soon he and Kit fall back into old habits, sparring in public while trying to stay out of each other's arms. But when a blizzard traps them overnight at Kit's grandmother's farmhouse, the real competition begins: Who will be the first to give in to the feelings they've denied for a decade?

ISBN 978-1542047289

51295

9 781542 047289